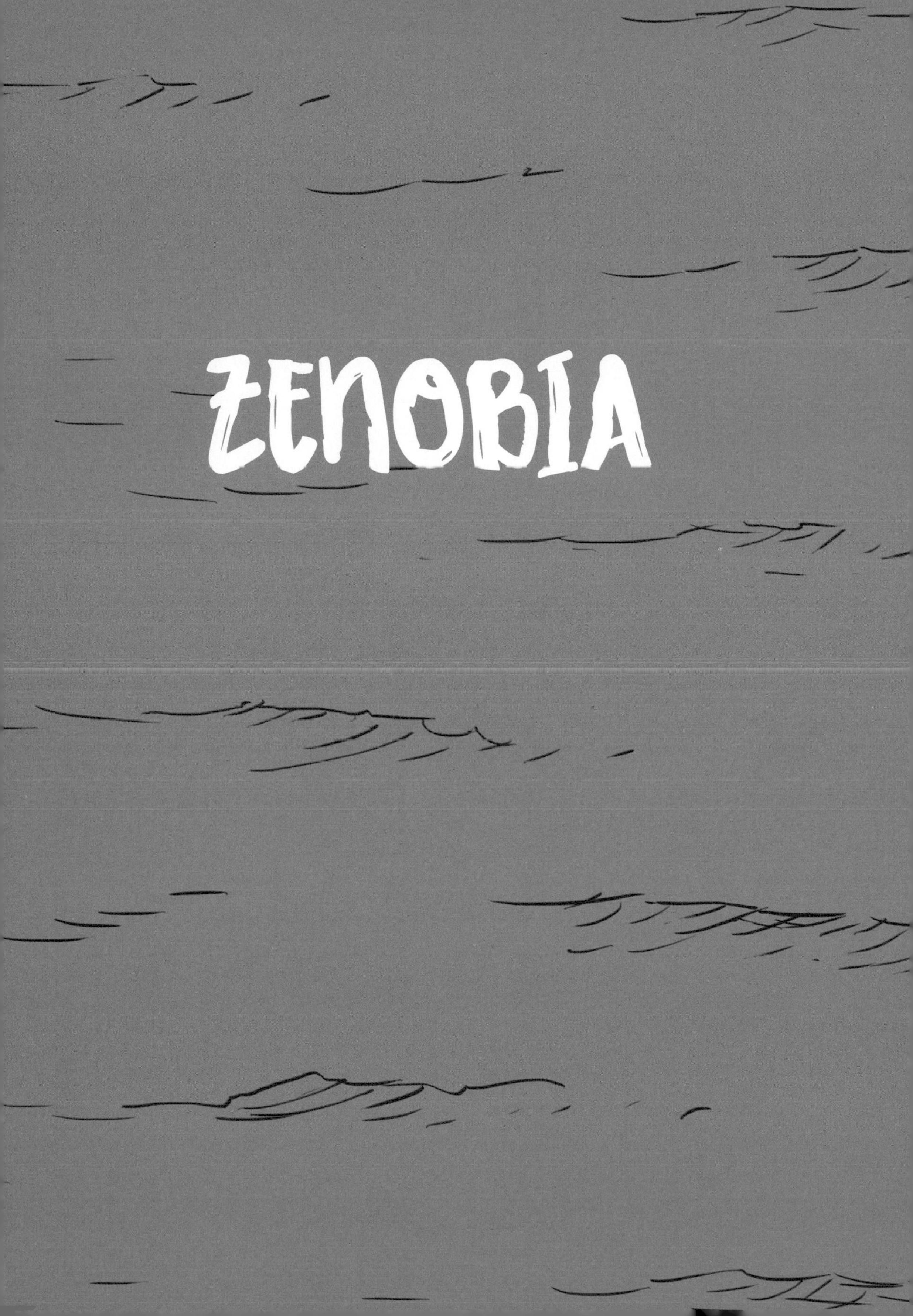
ZENOBIA

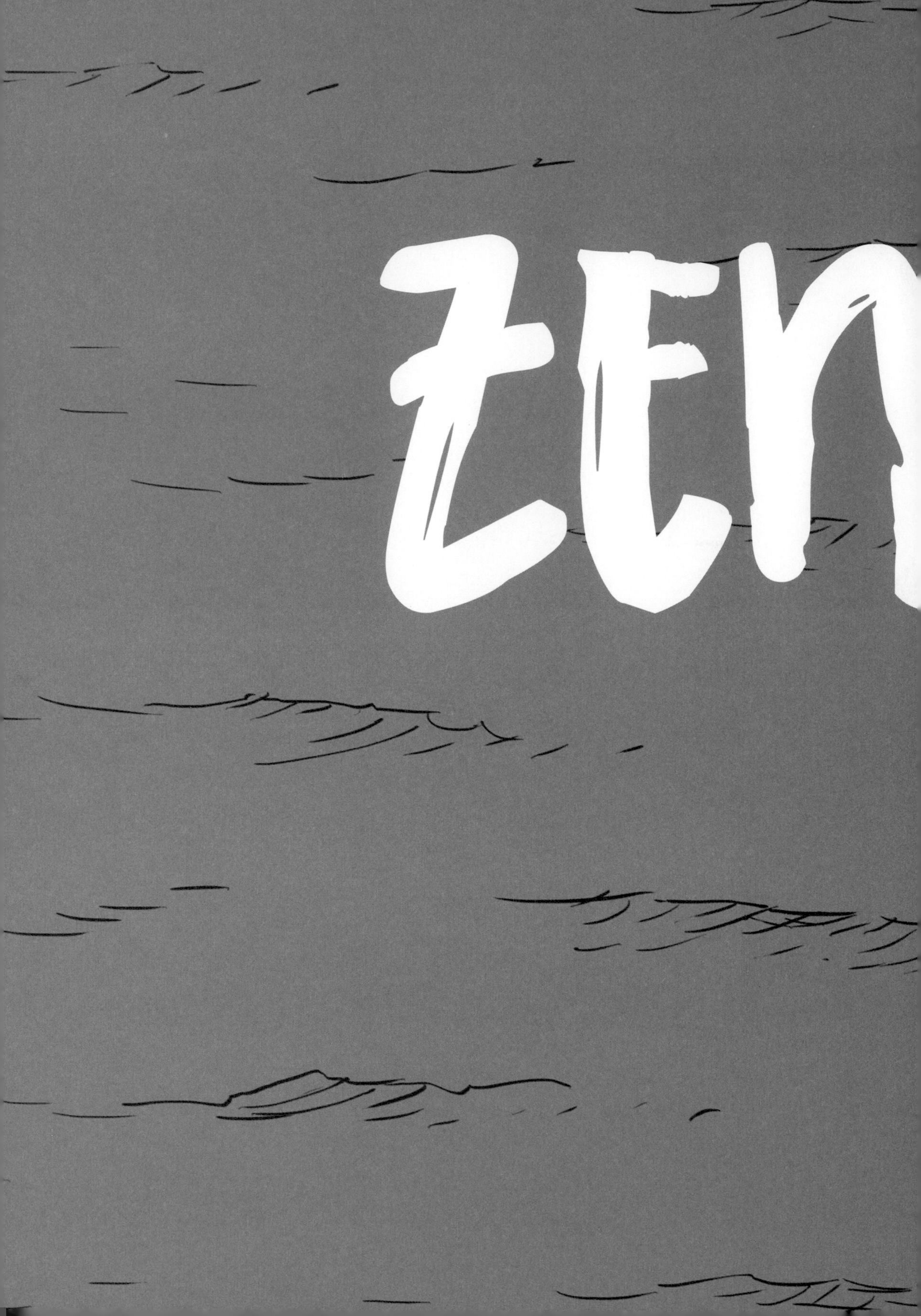
zen

OBIA

MORTEN DÜRR

AND LARS HORNEMAN

SEVEN STORIES PRESS
New York • Oakland • London

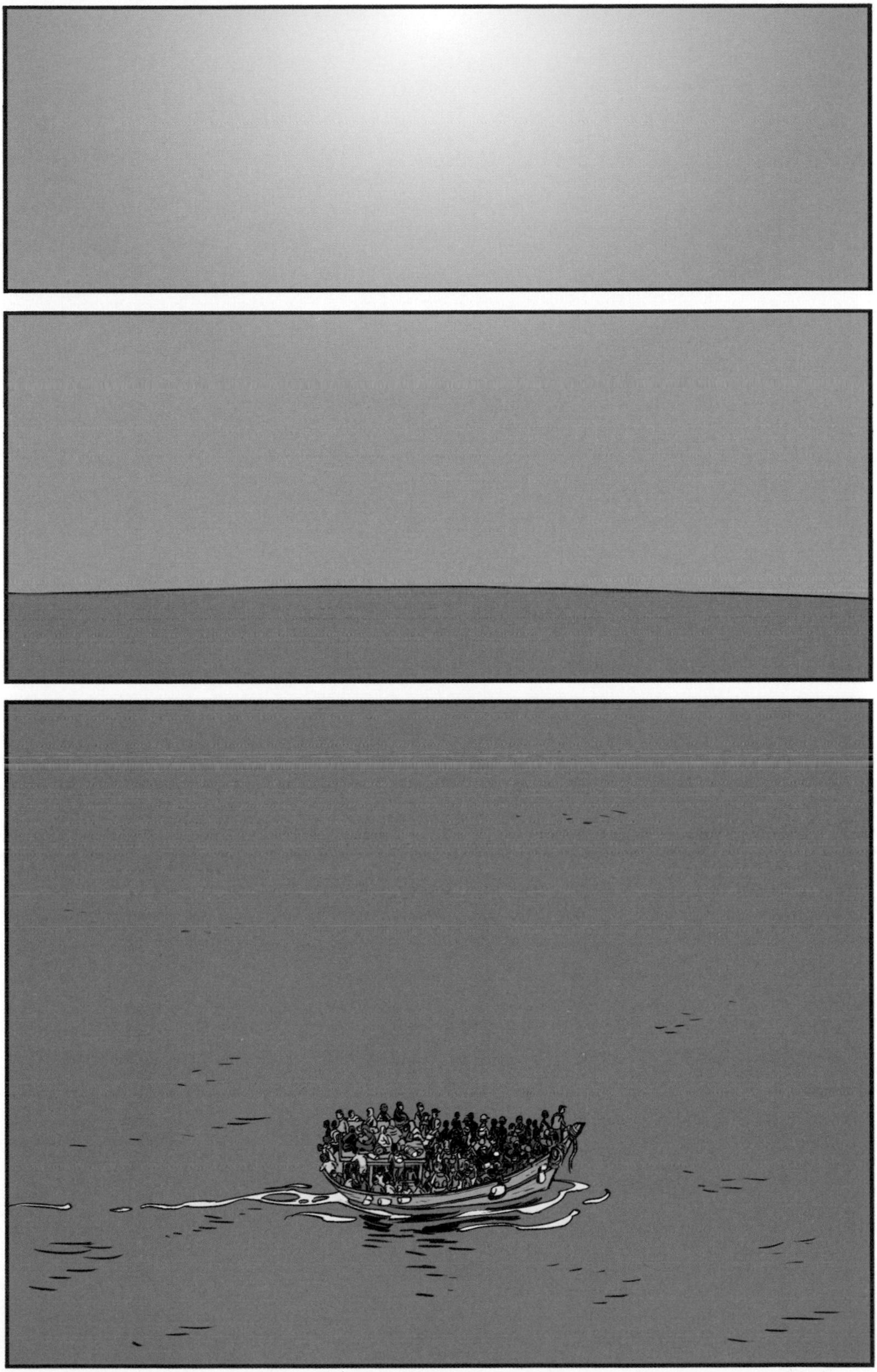

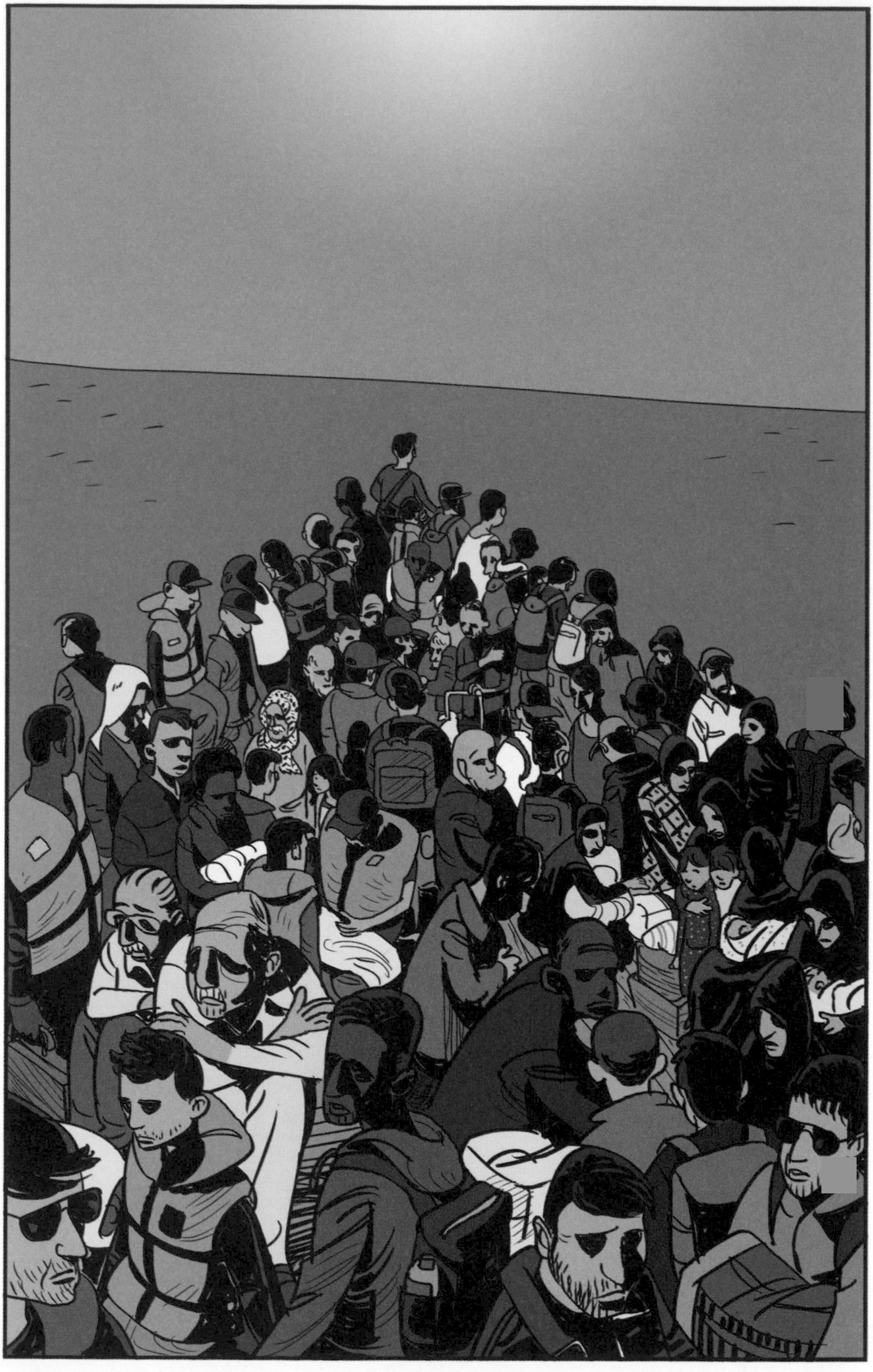

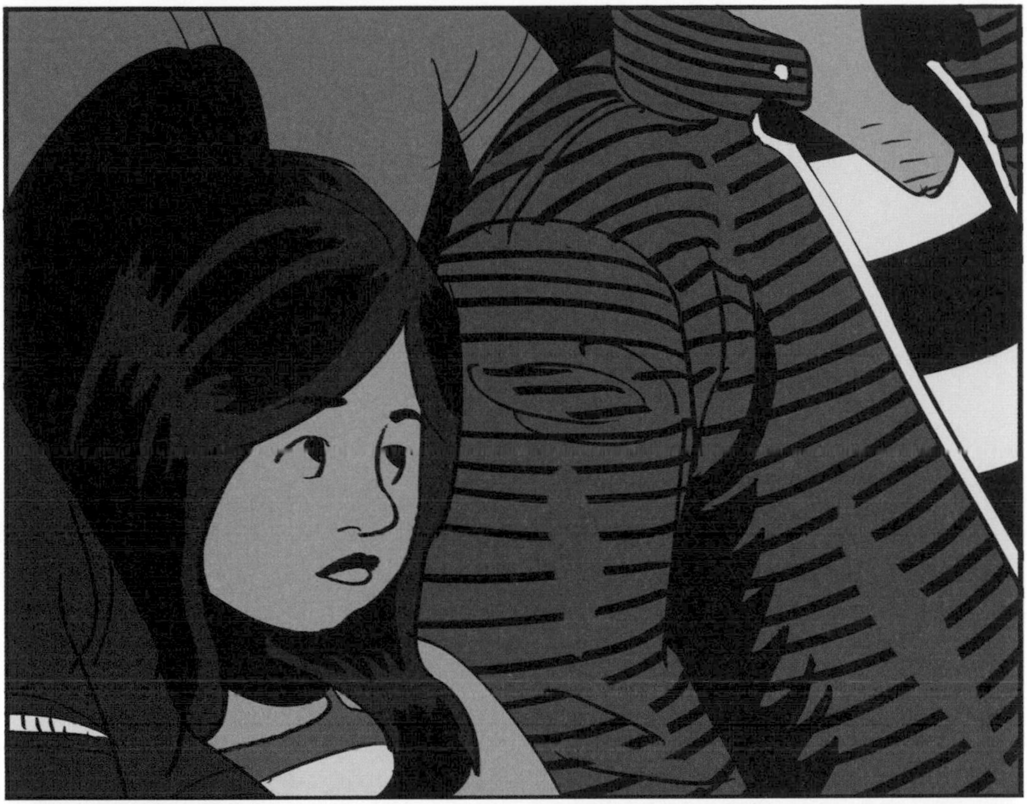

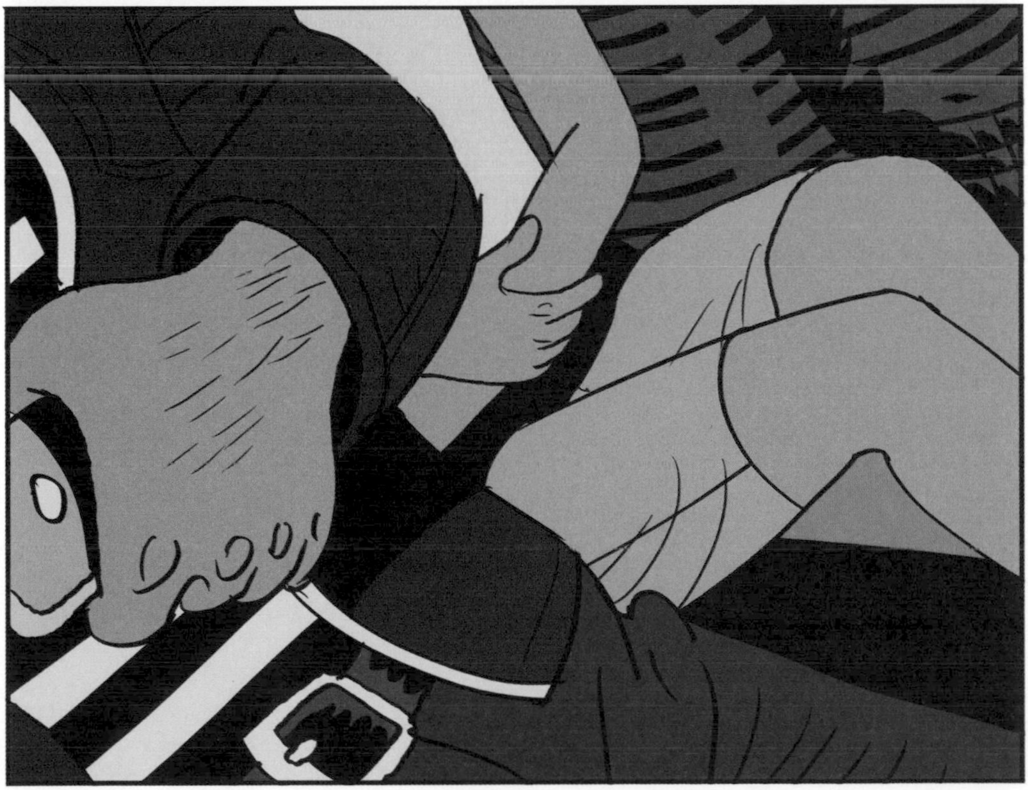

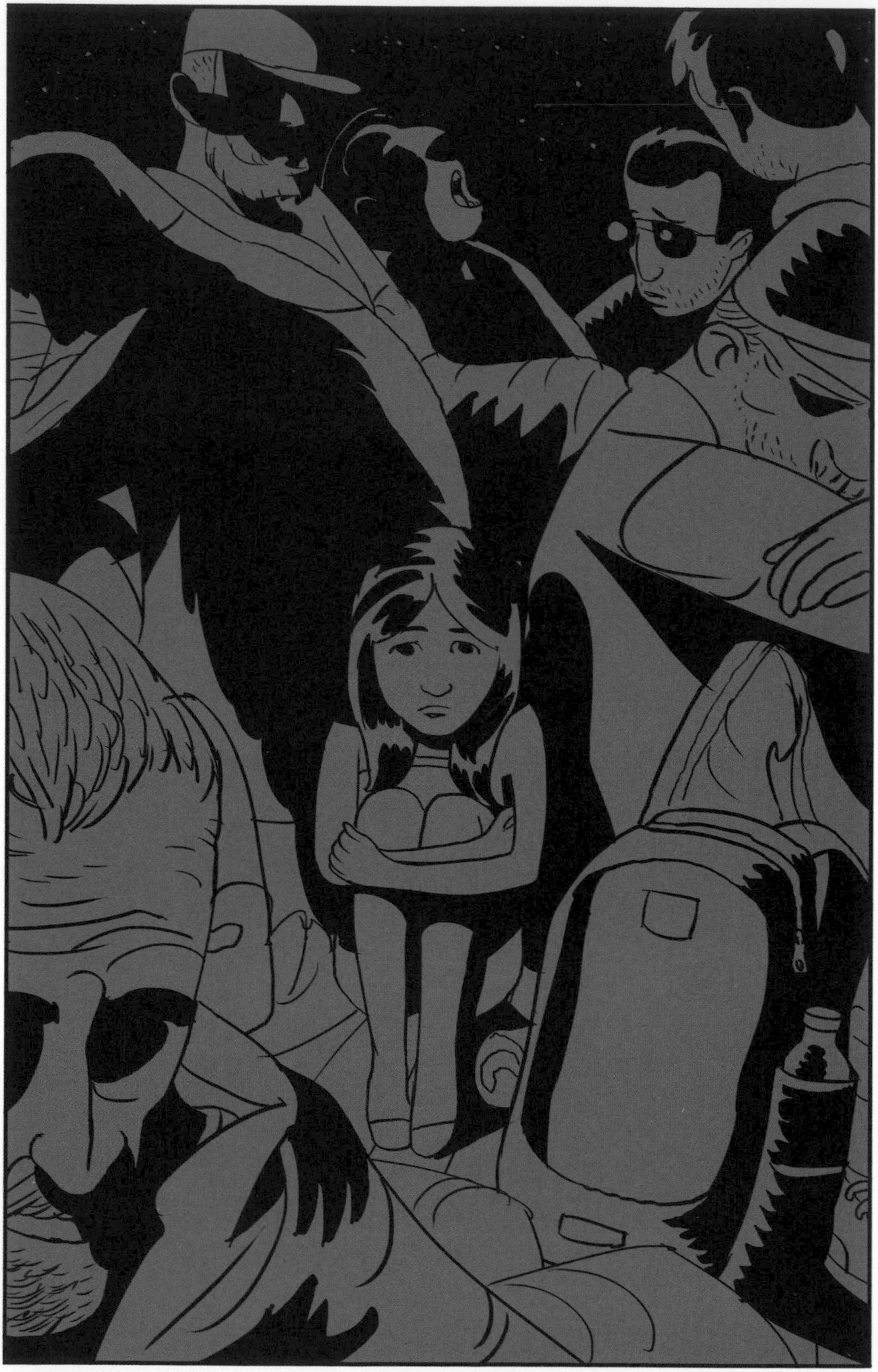

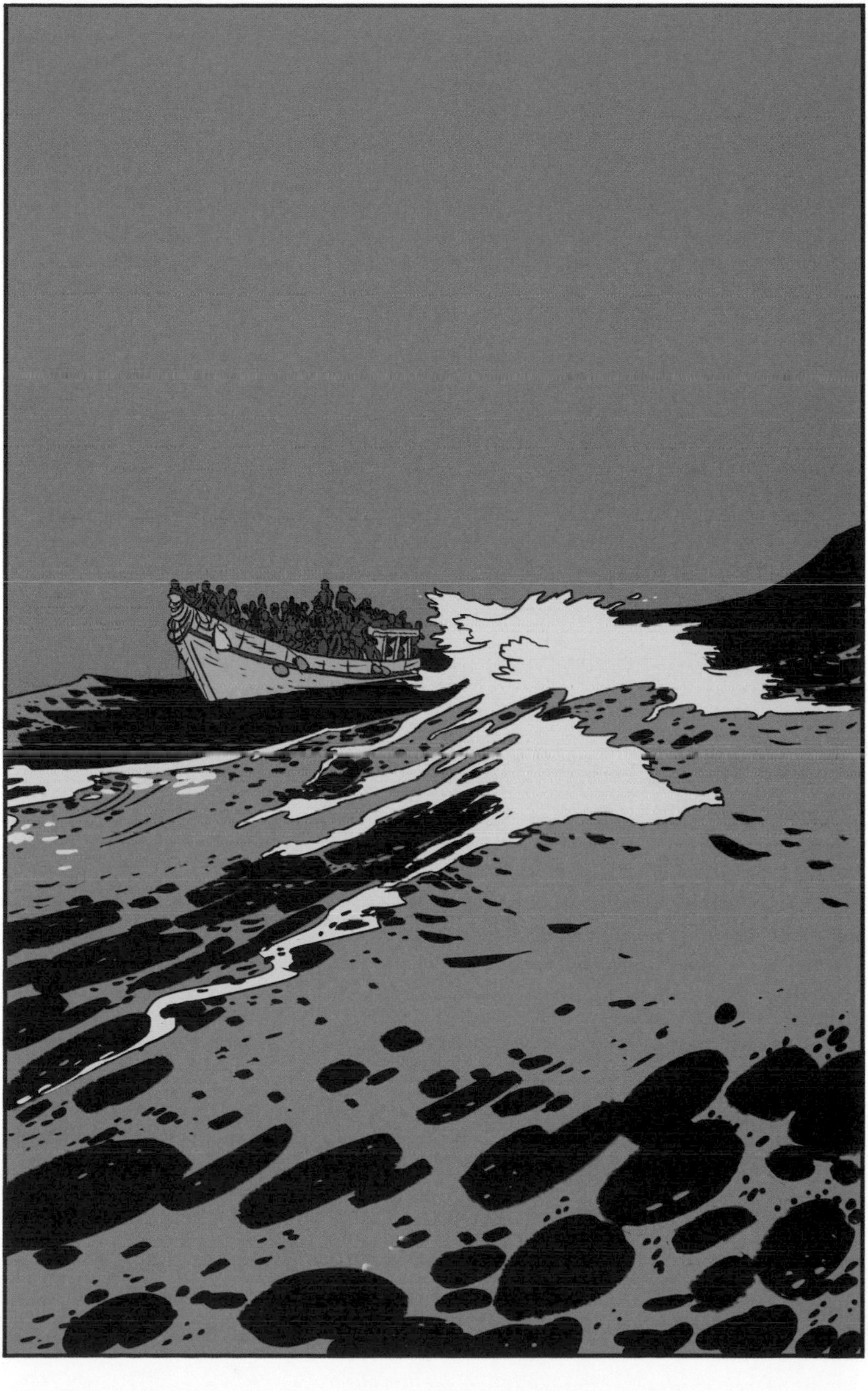

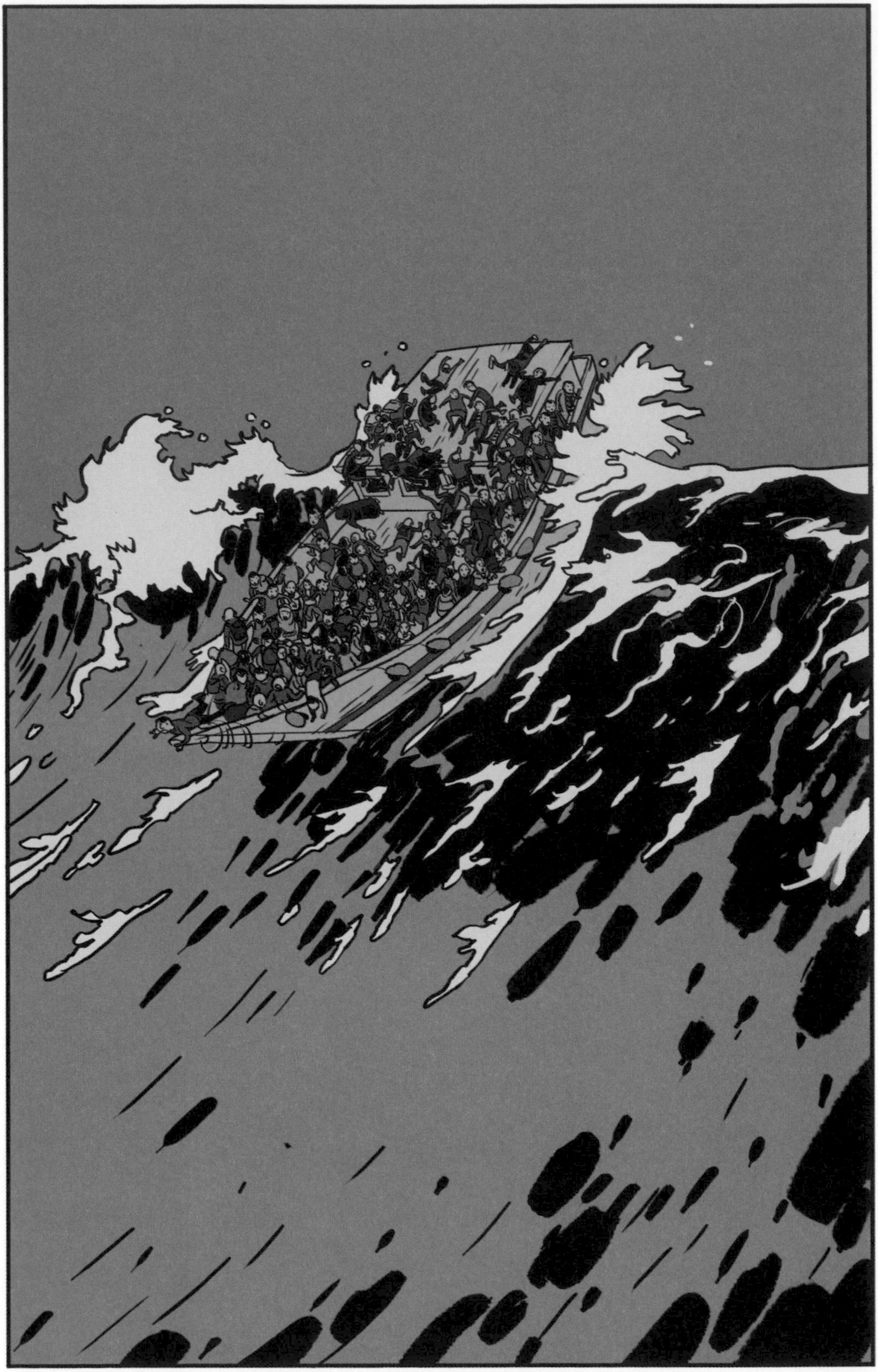

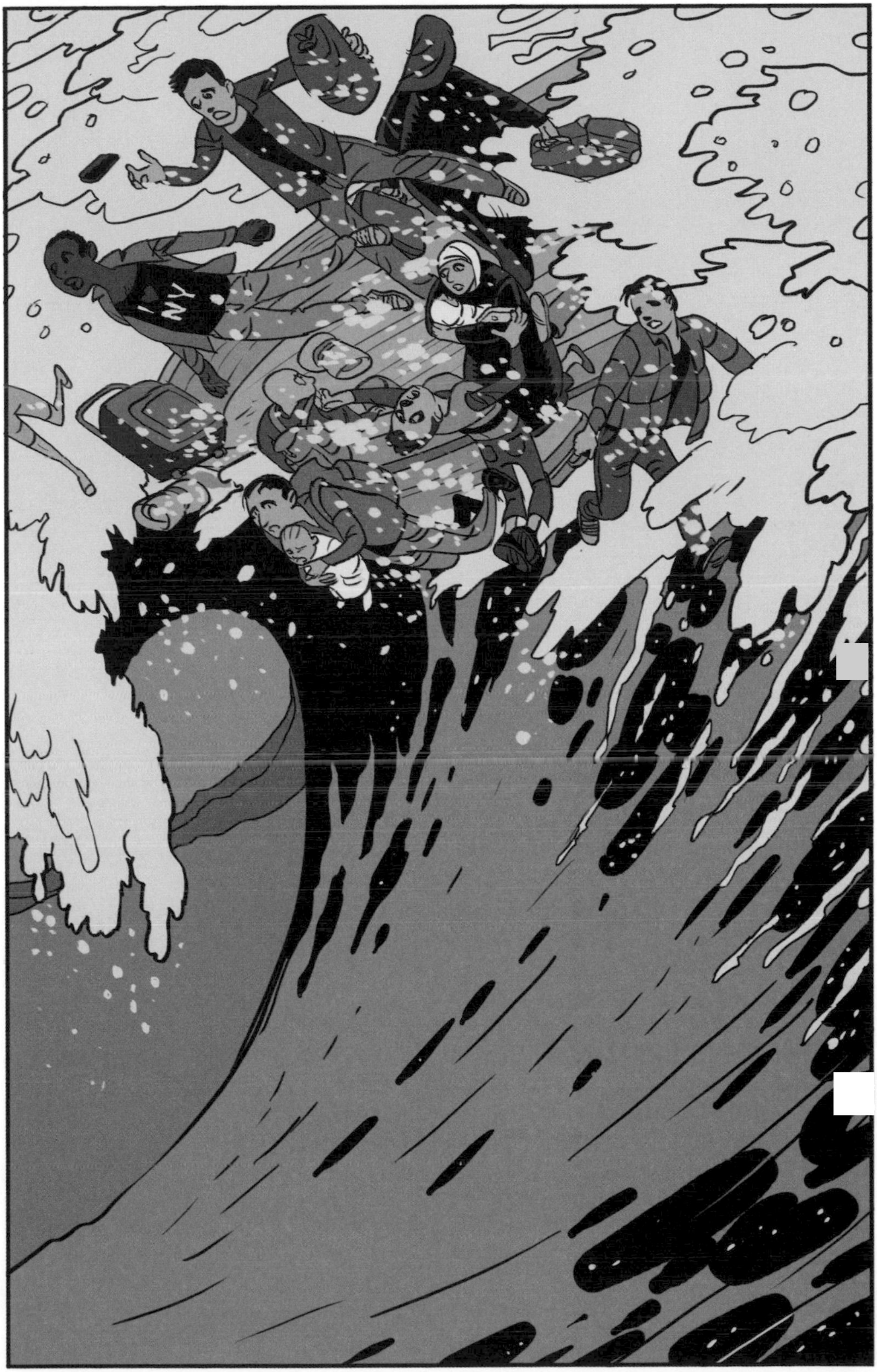
I ♥ NY

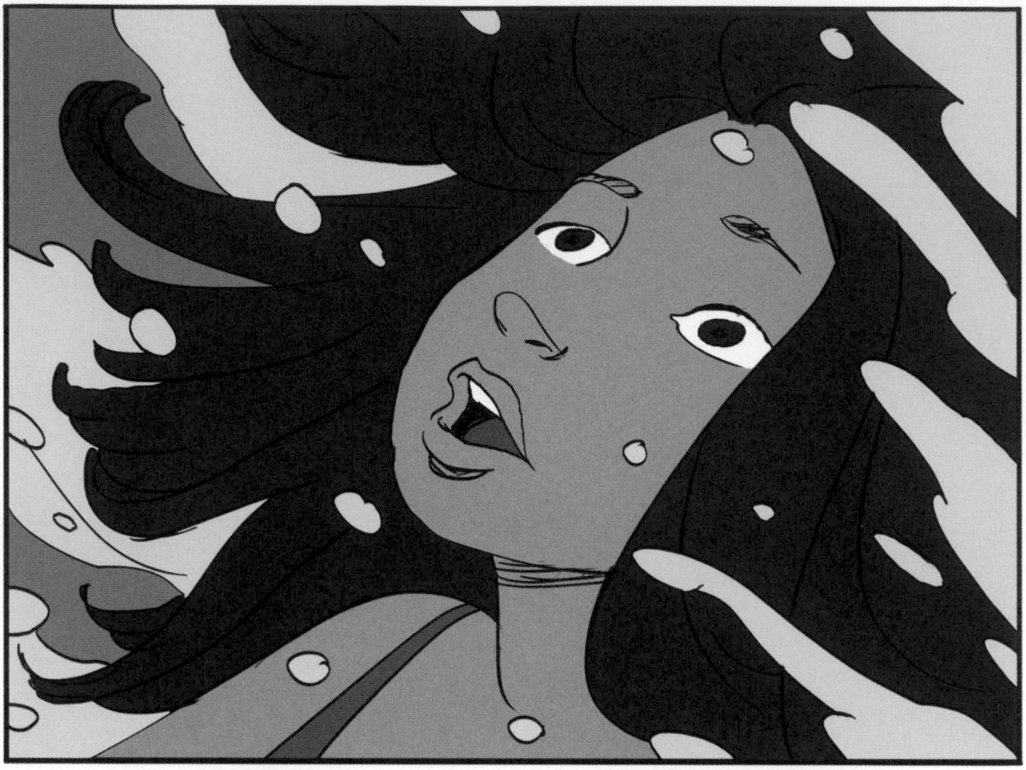

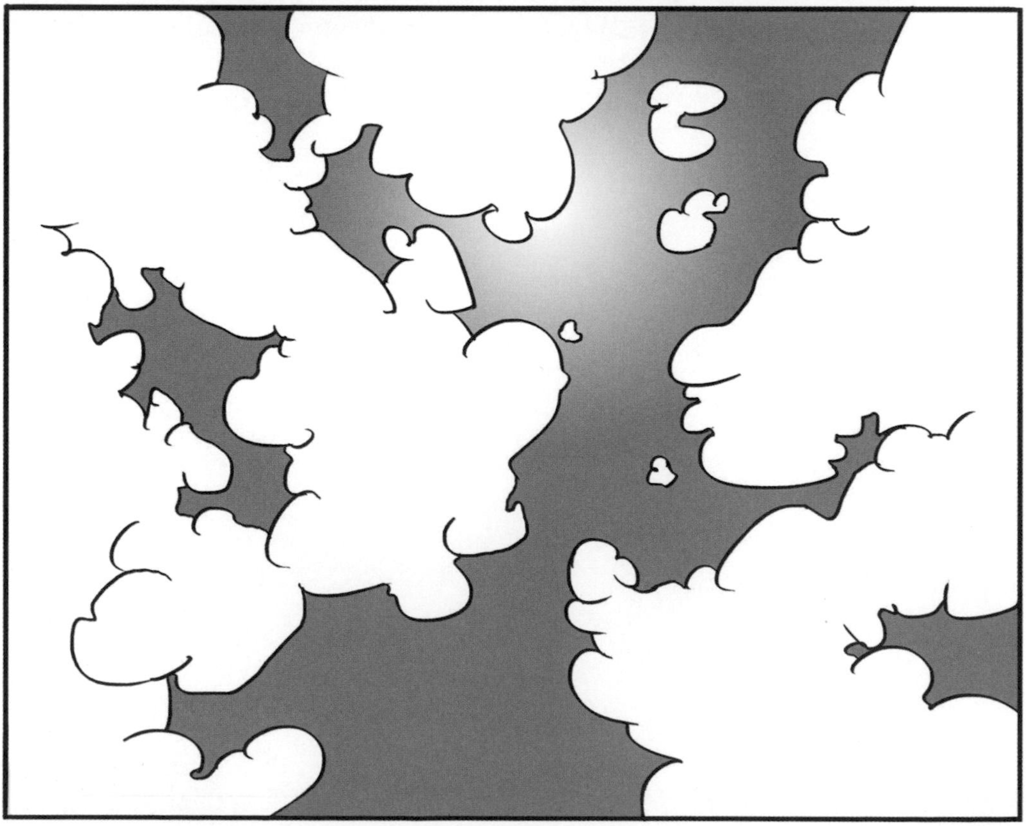

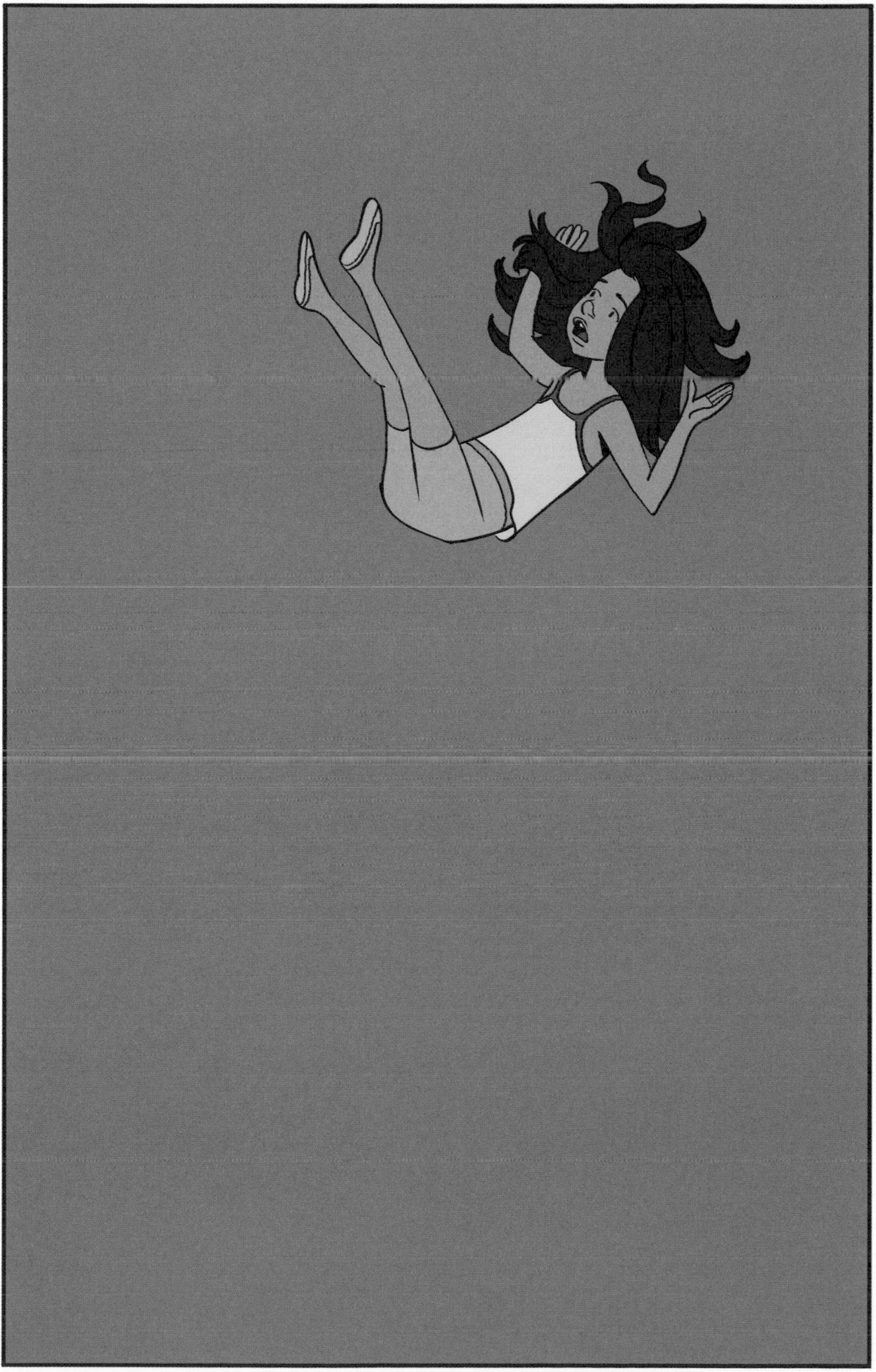

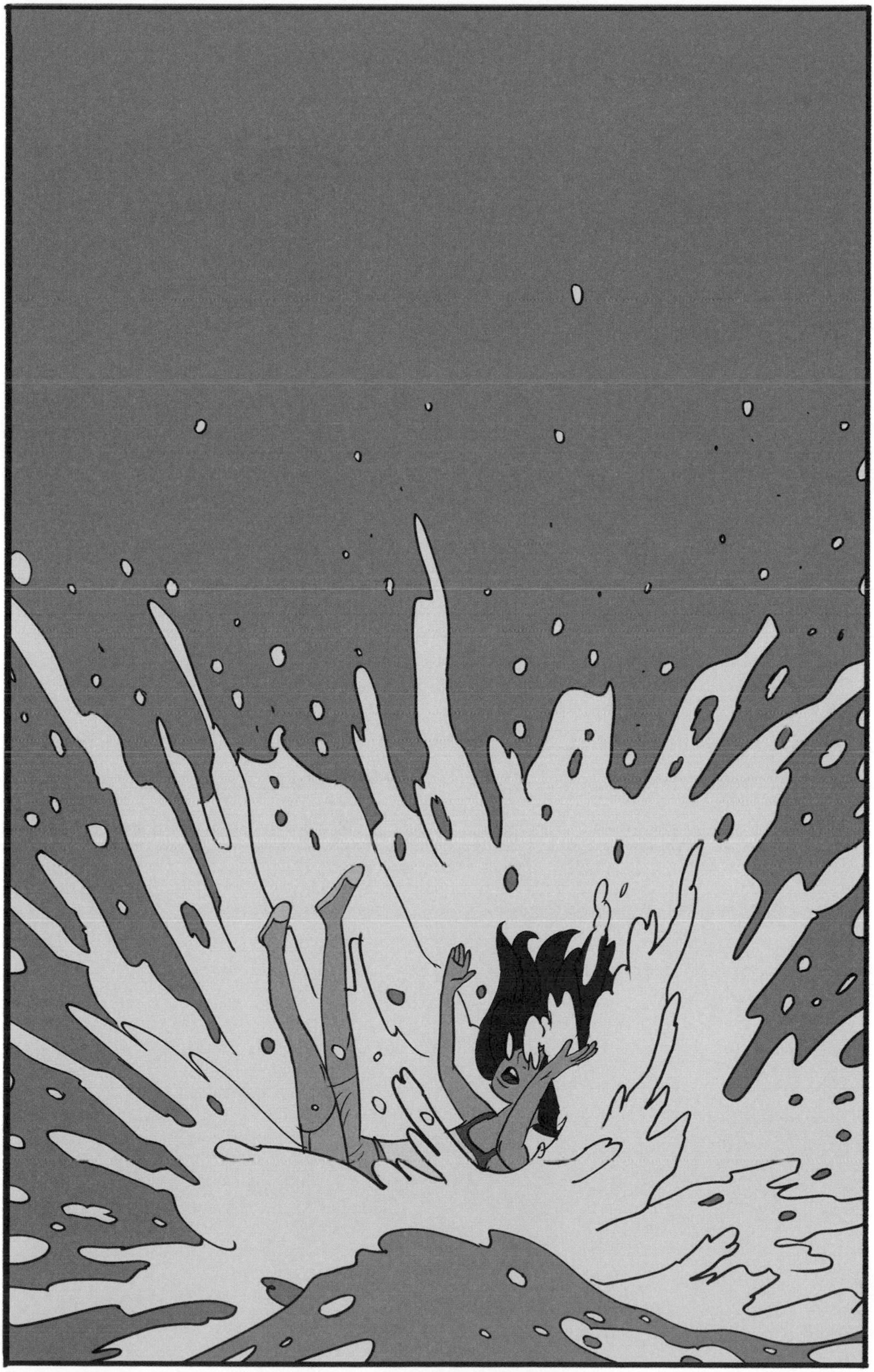

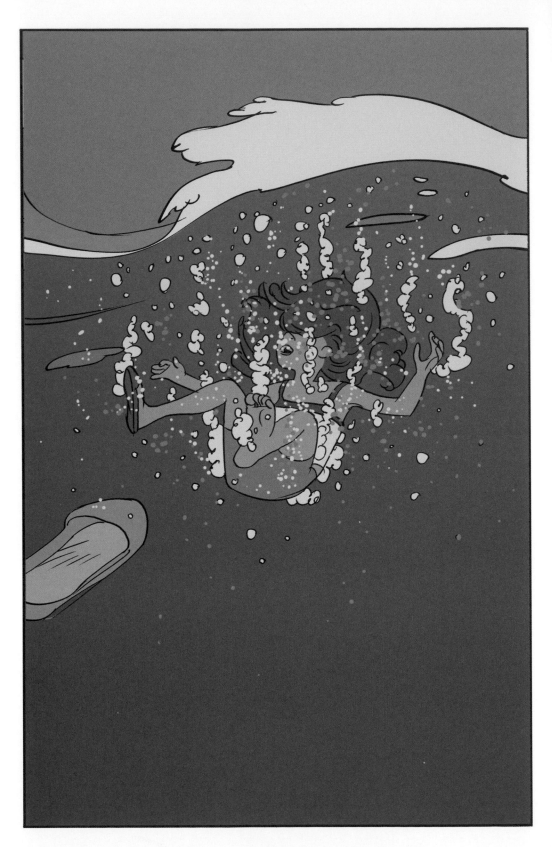

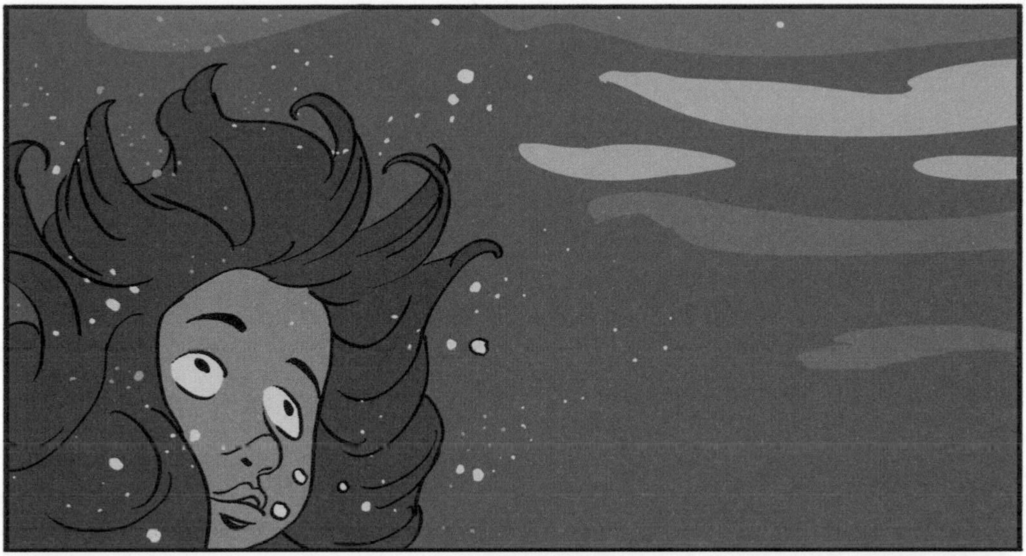

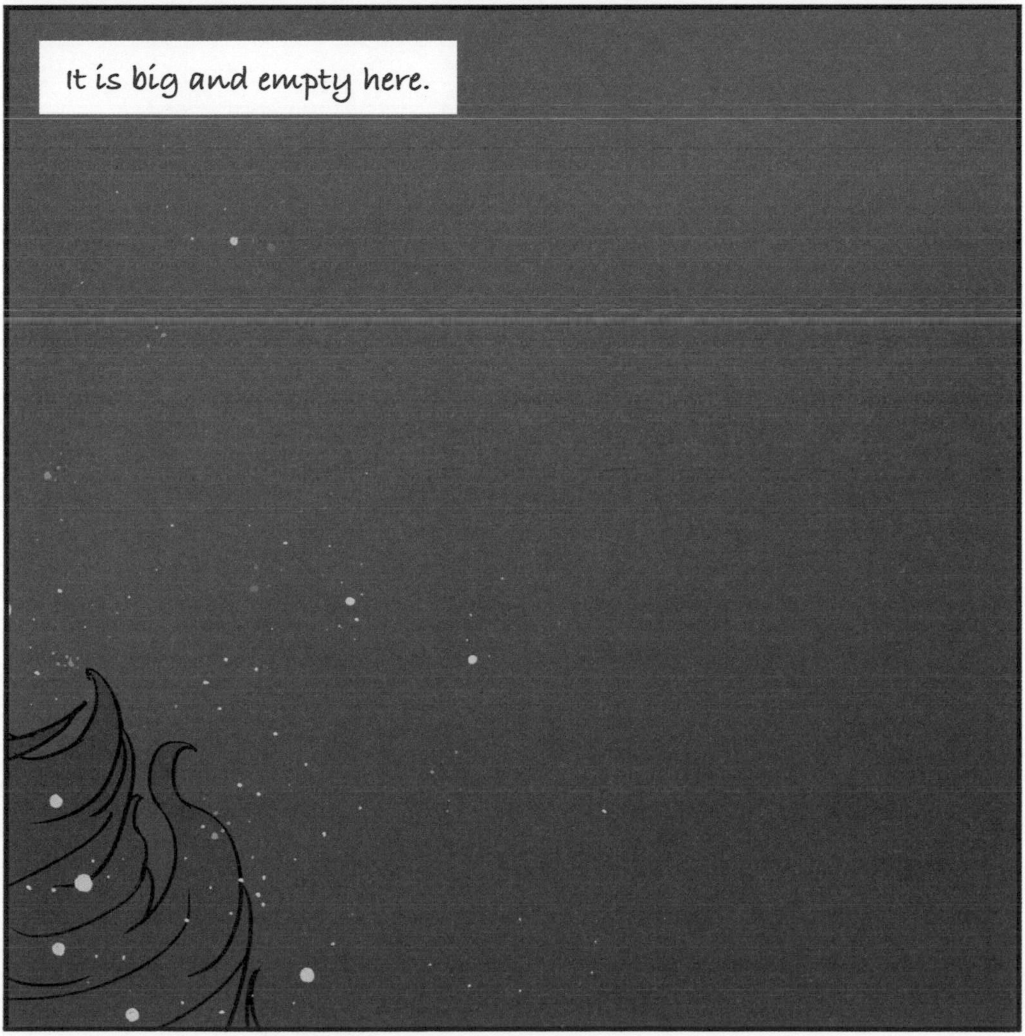
It is big and empty here.

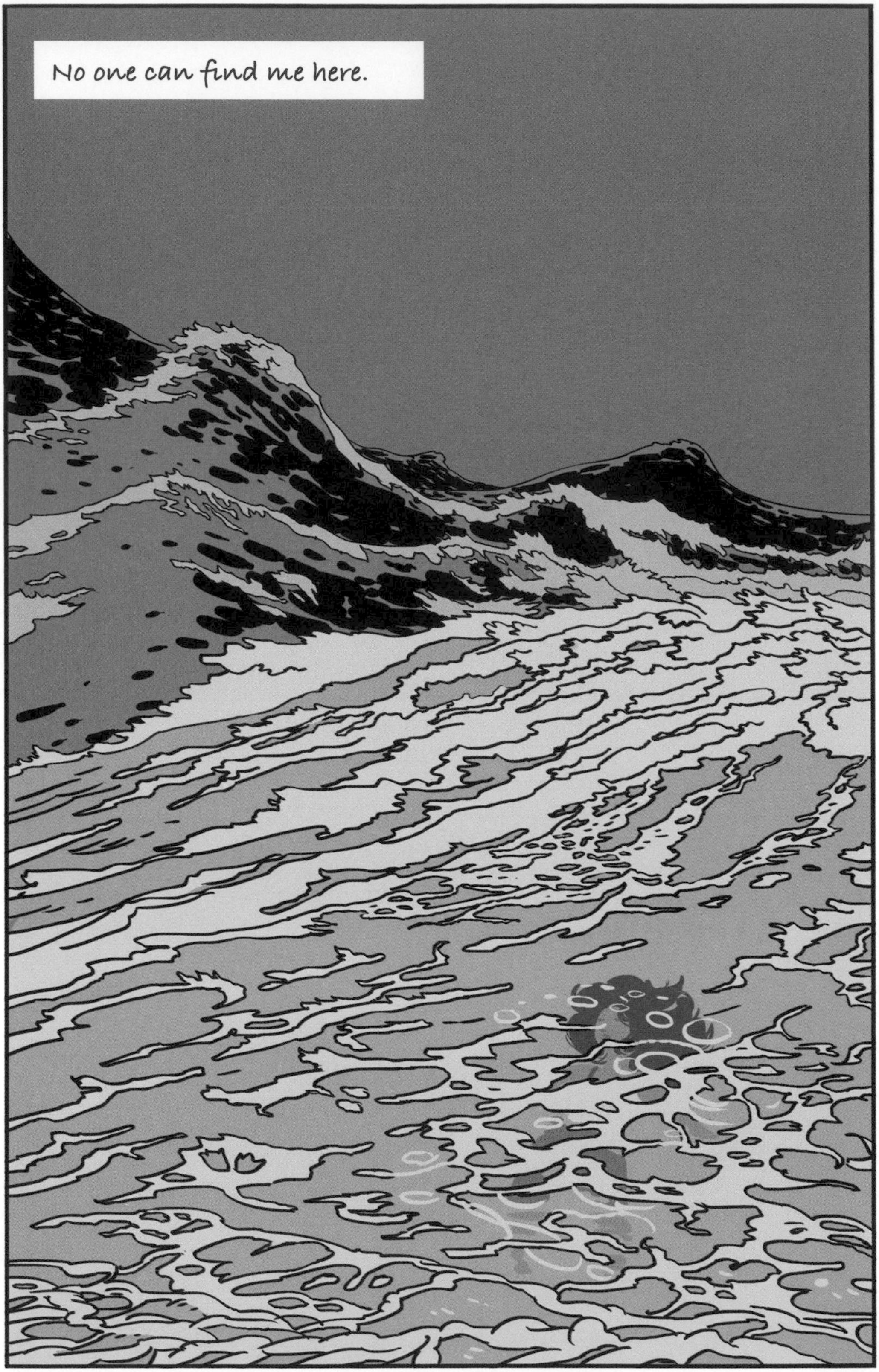
No one can find me here.

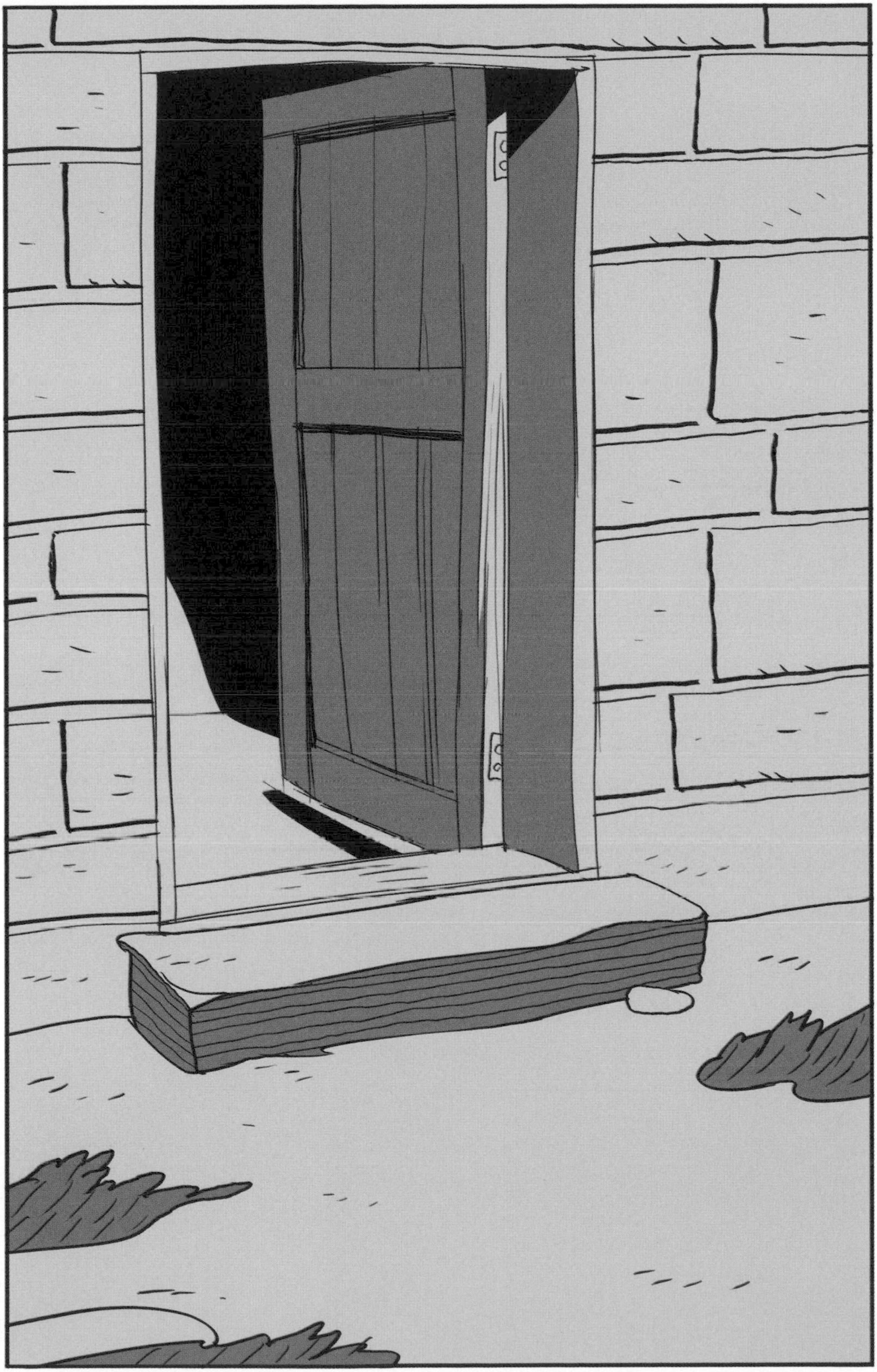

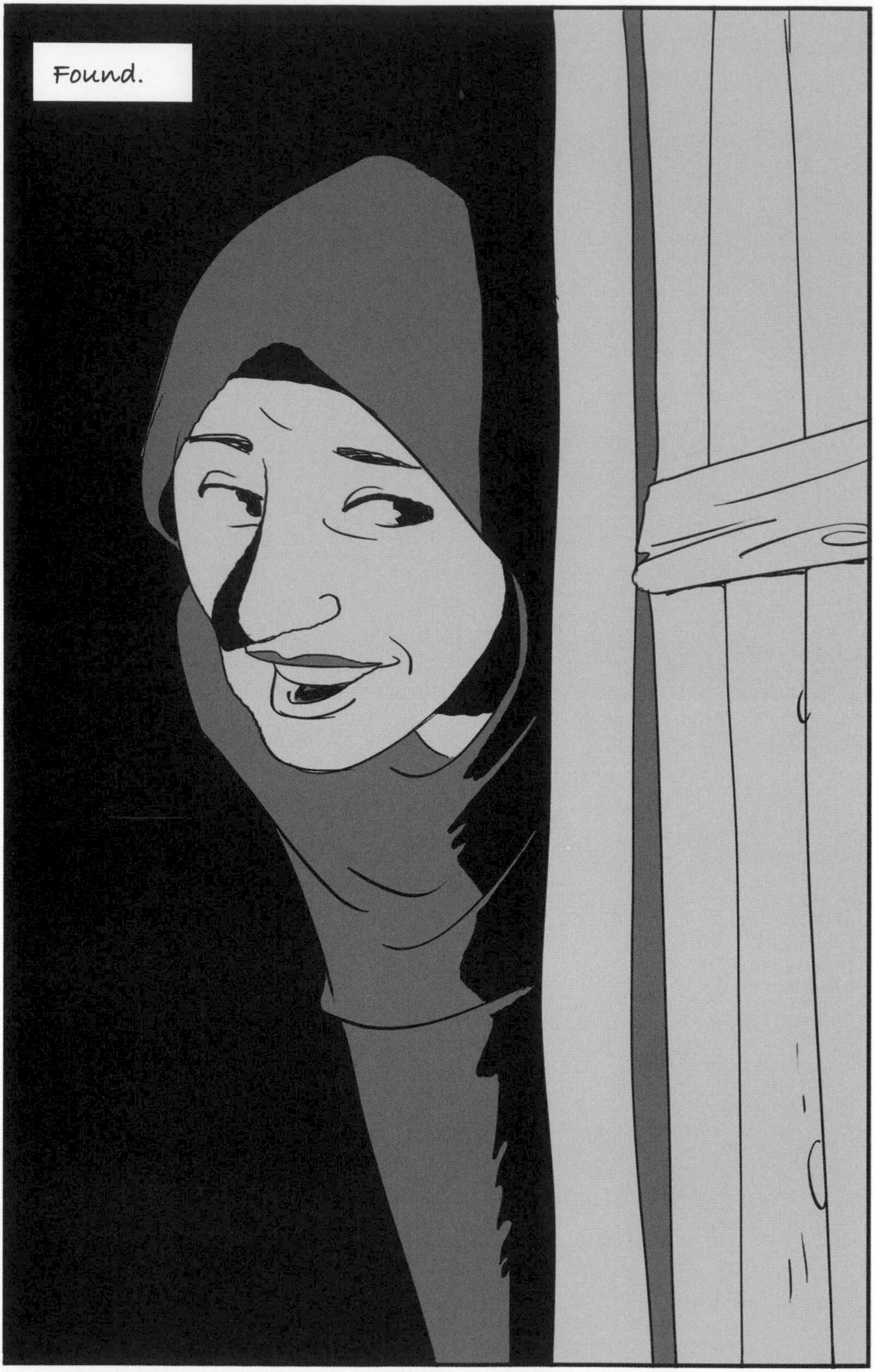
Found.

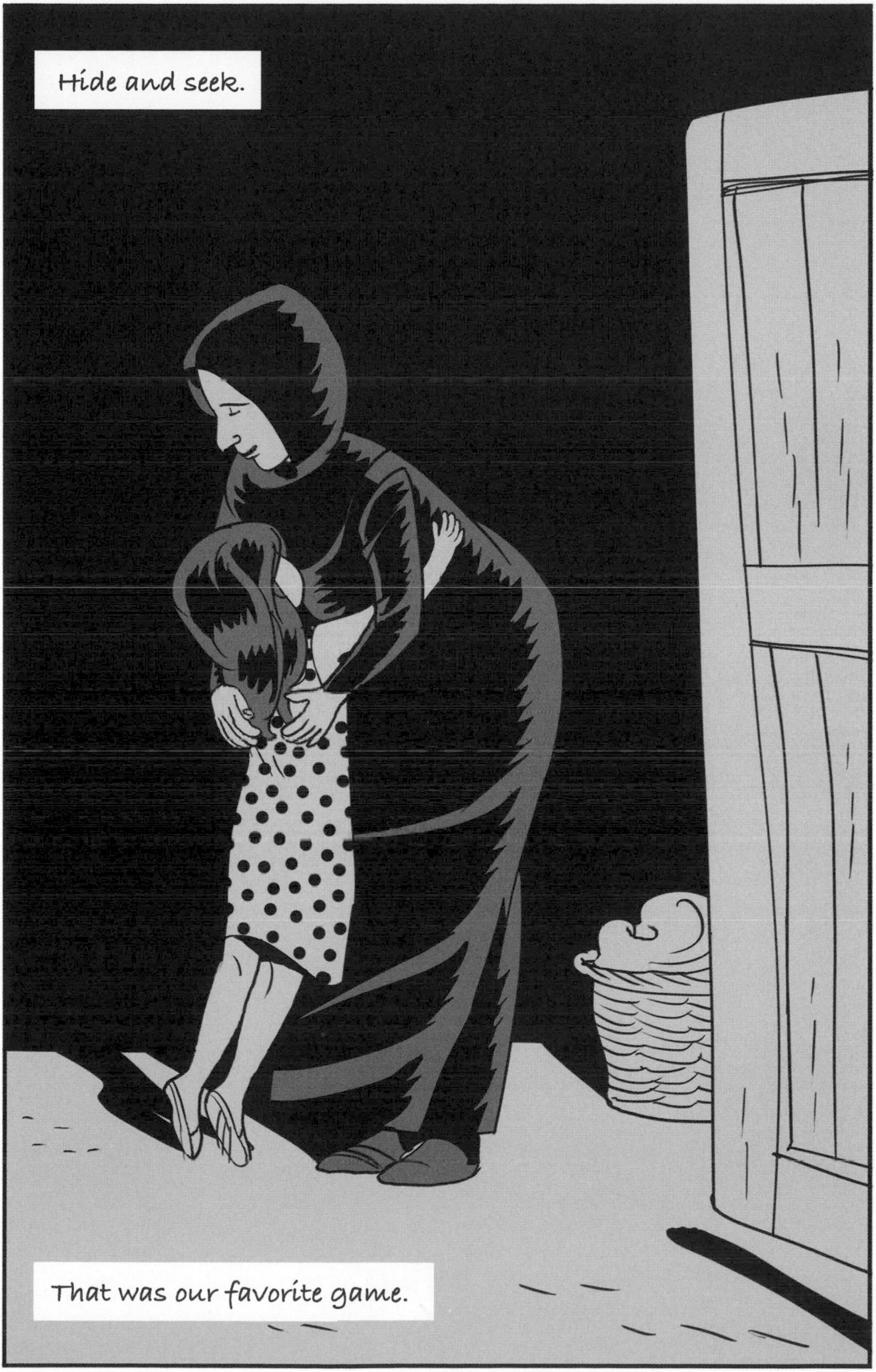
Hide and seek.
That was our favorite game.

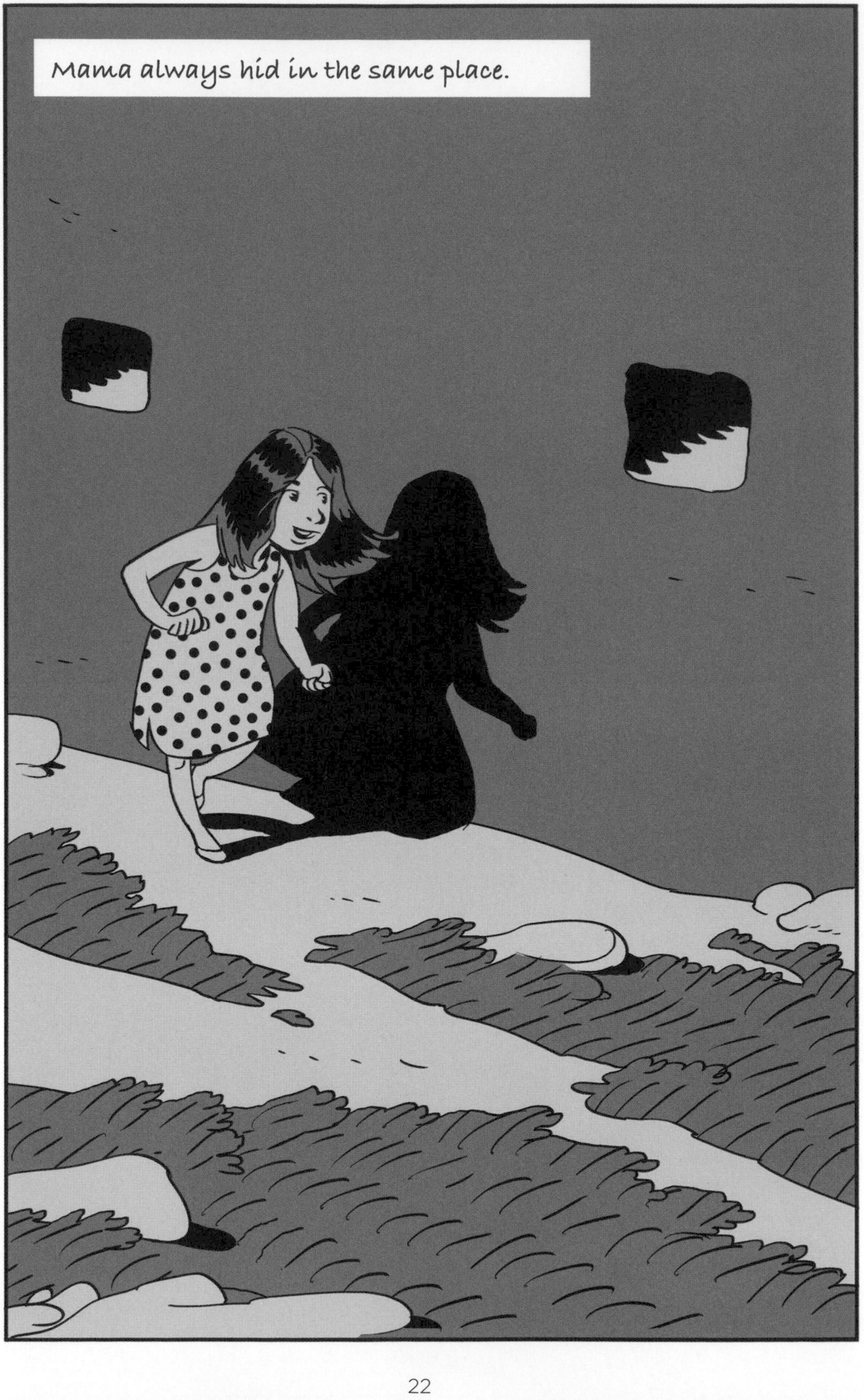
Mama always hid in the same place.

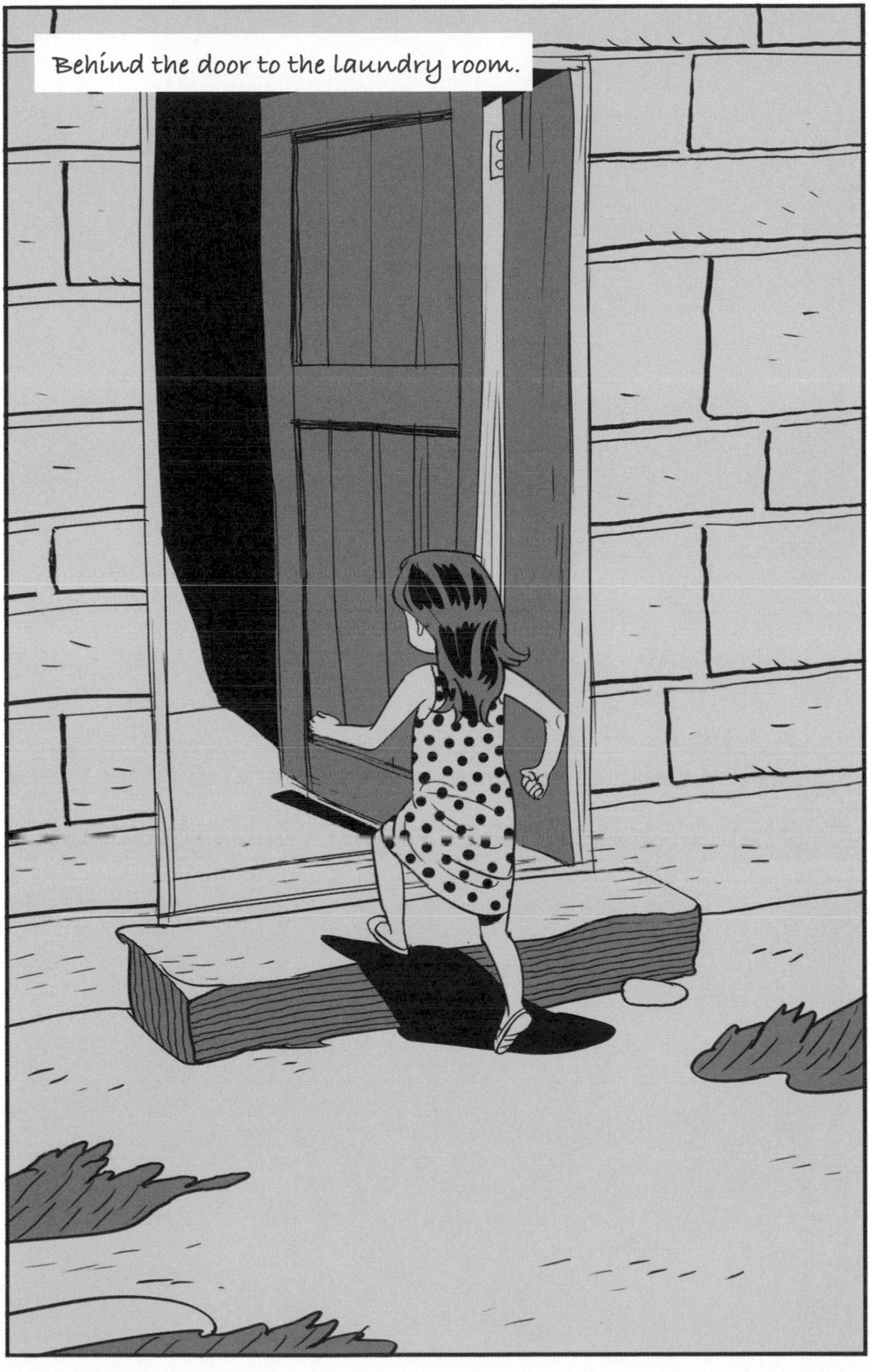
Behind the door to the laundry room.

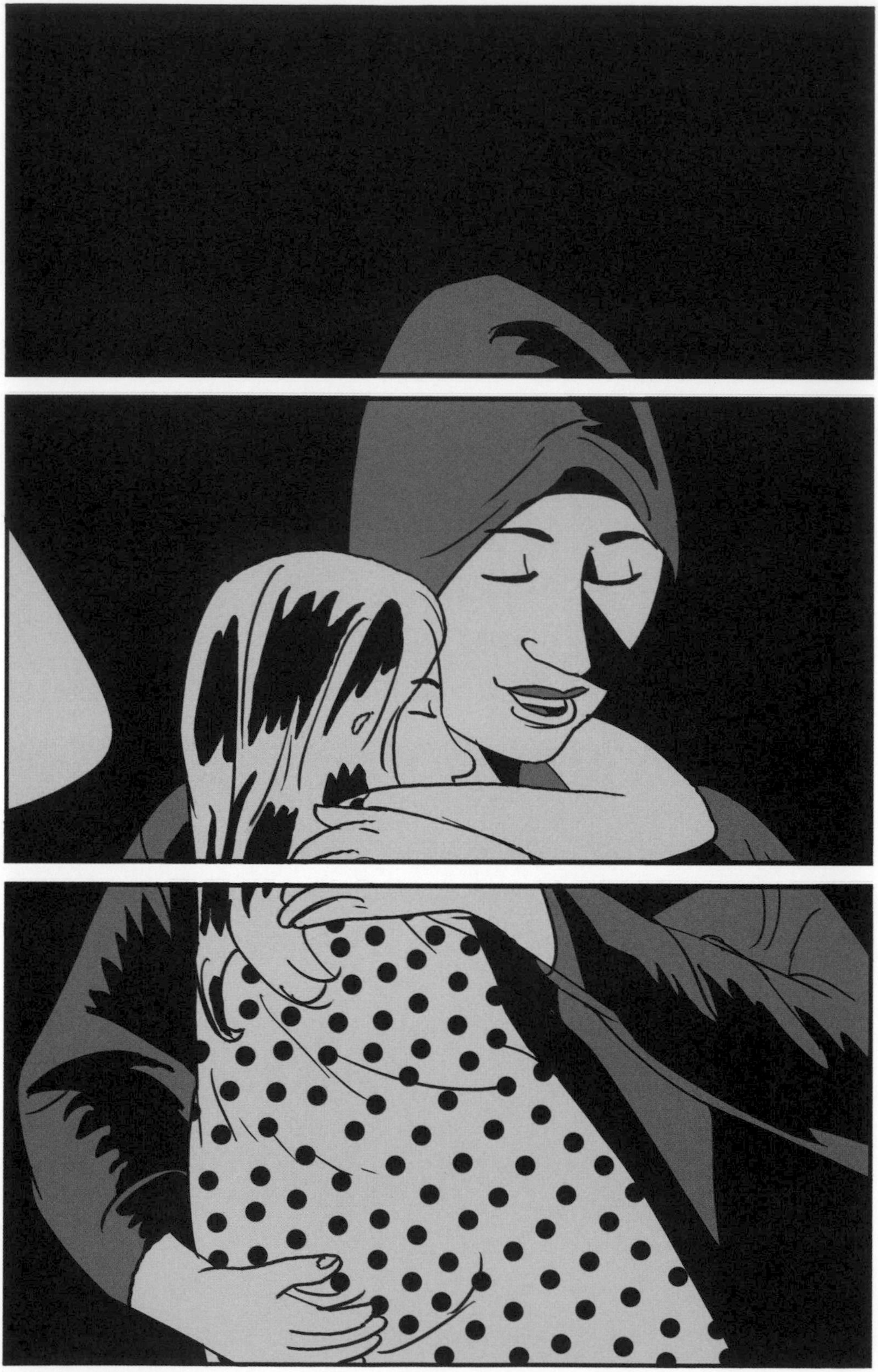

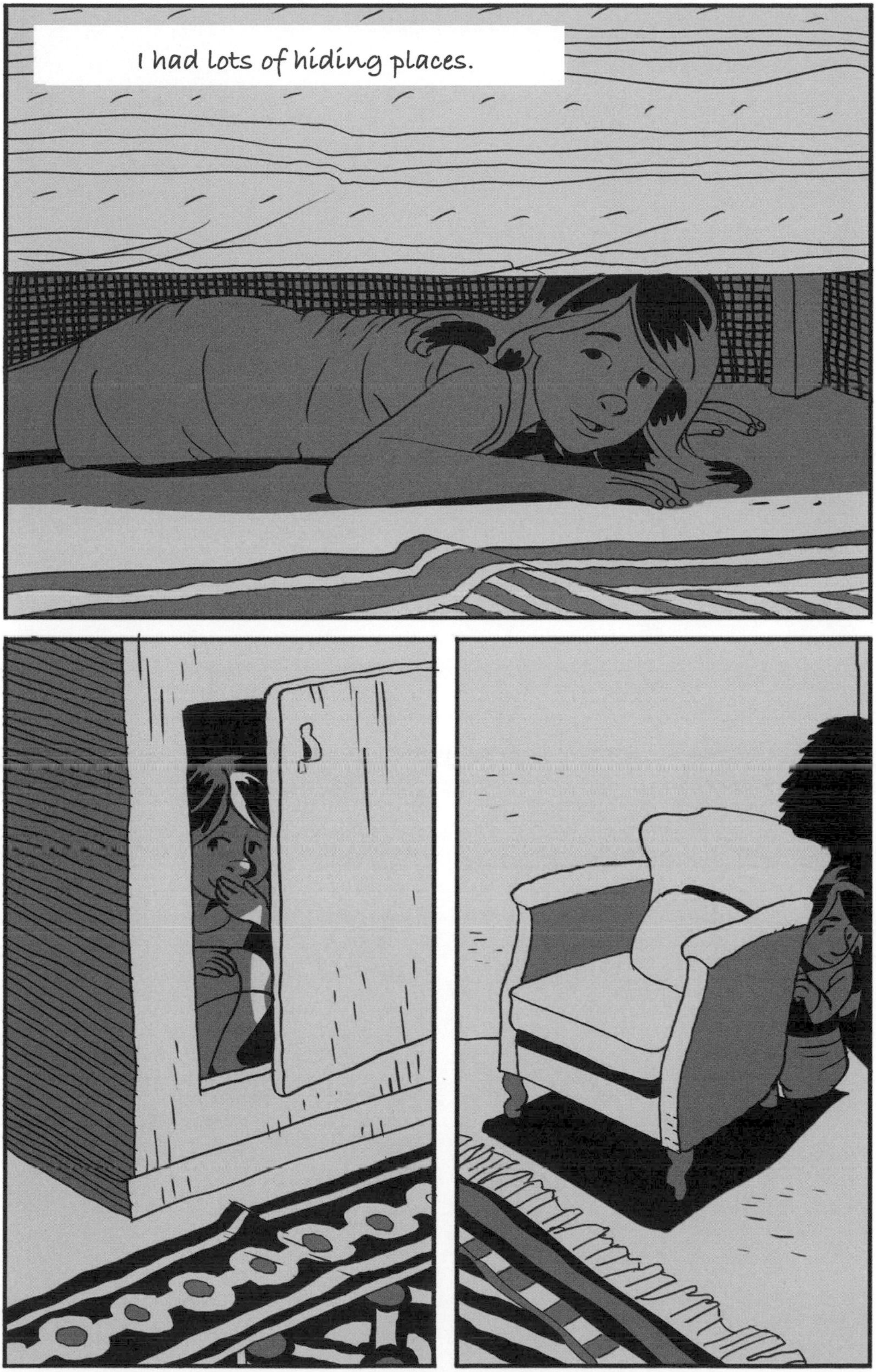
I had lots of hiding places.

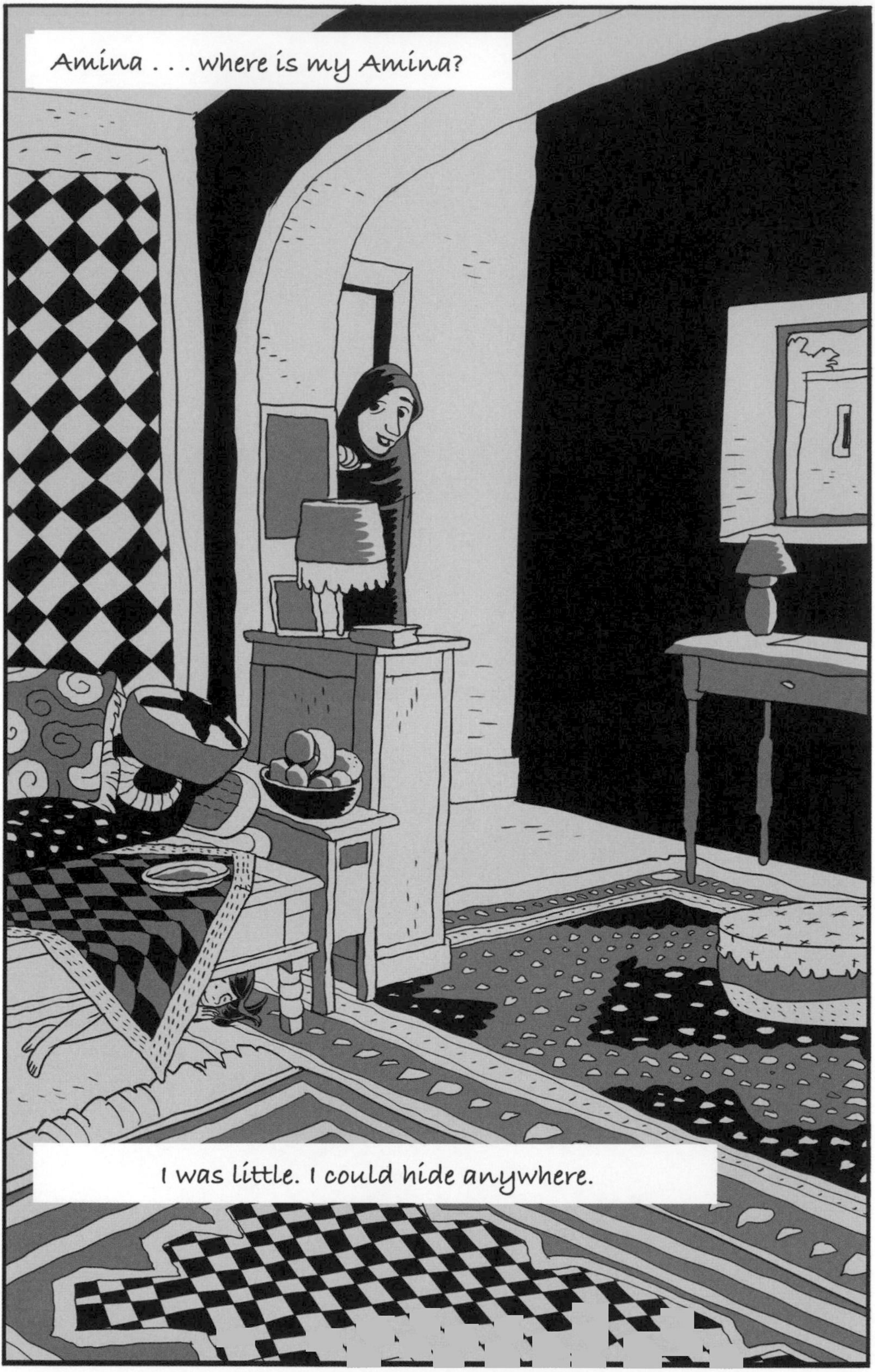
Amina . . . where is my Amina?
I was little. I could hide anywhere.

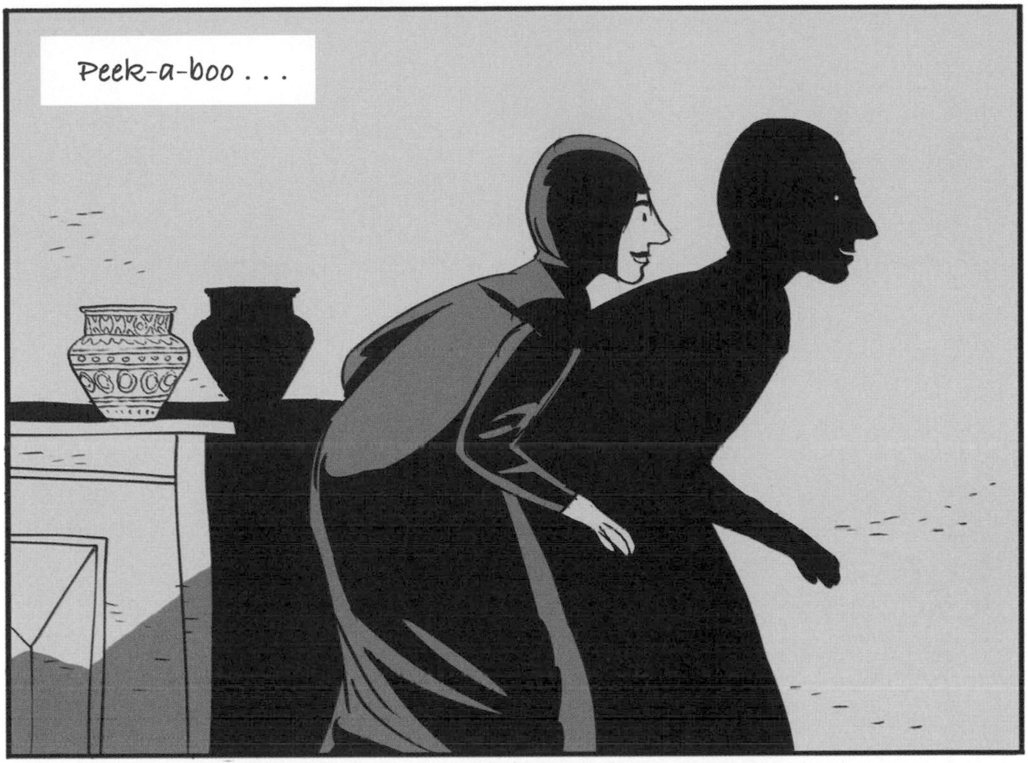
Peek-a-boo . . .

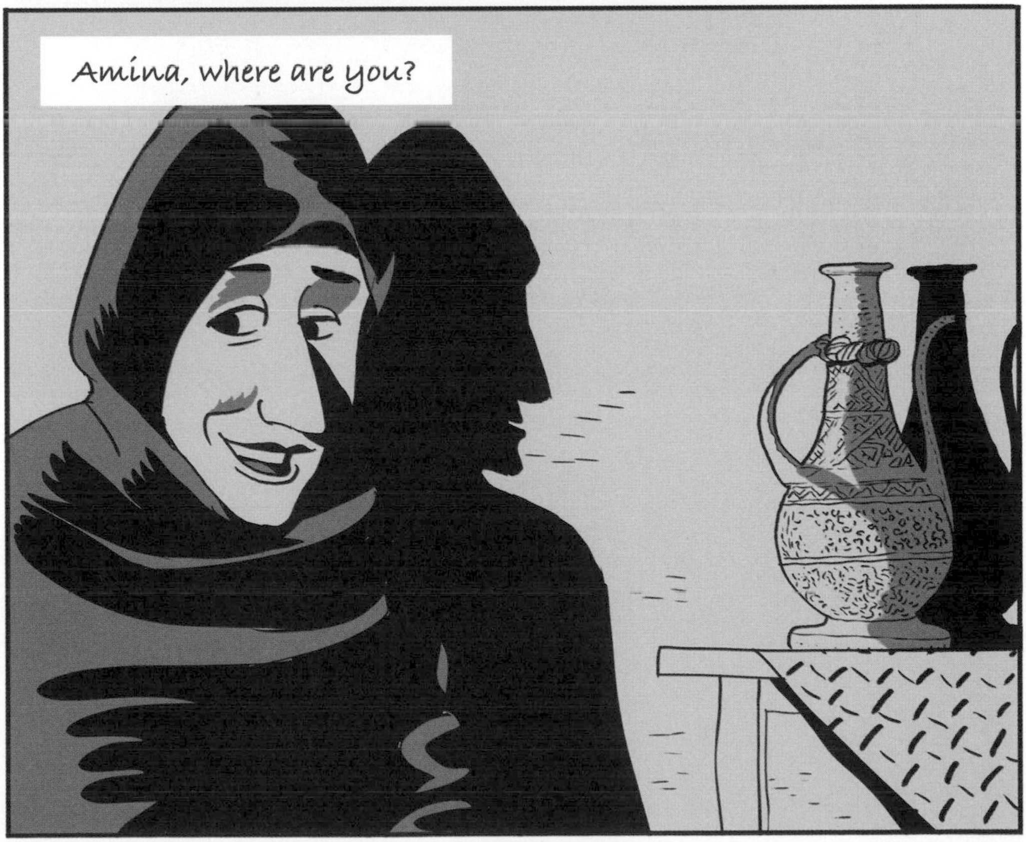
Amina, where are you?

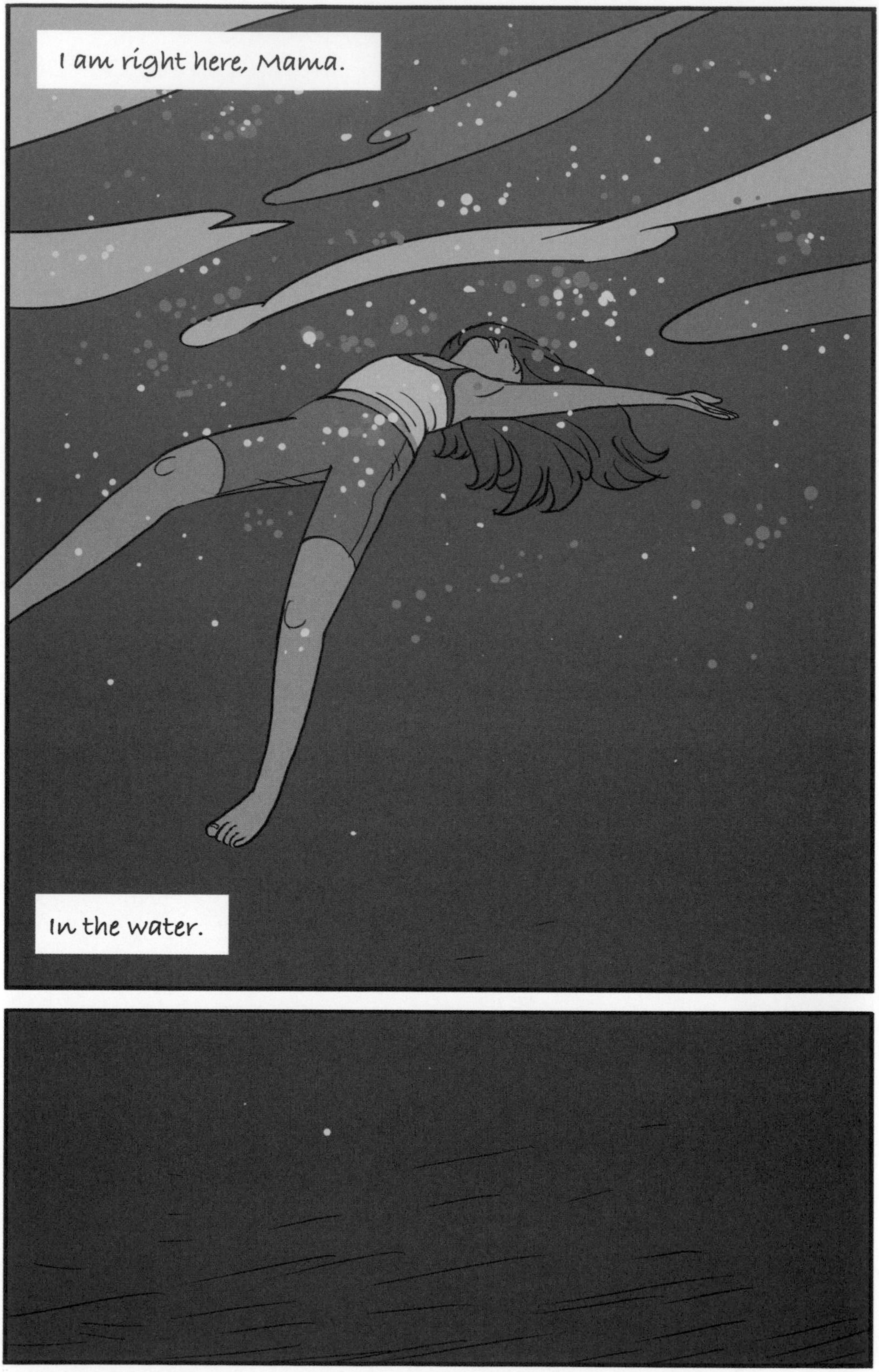
I am right here, Mama.
In the water.

Amina!

Let's cook!

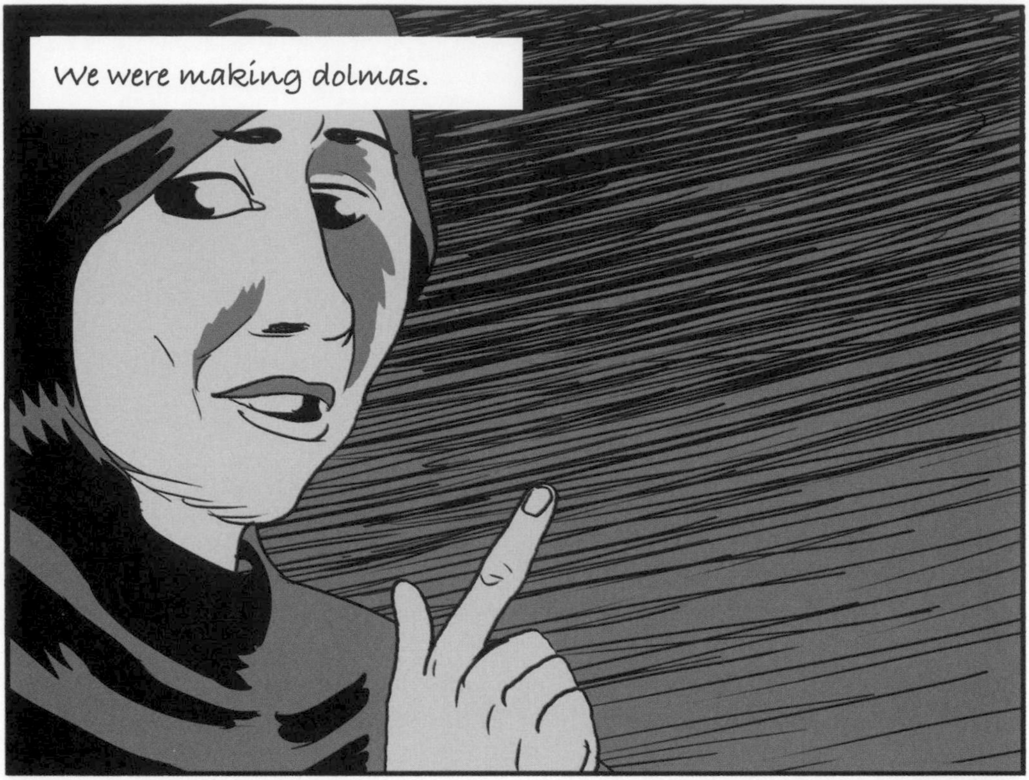
We were making dolmas.

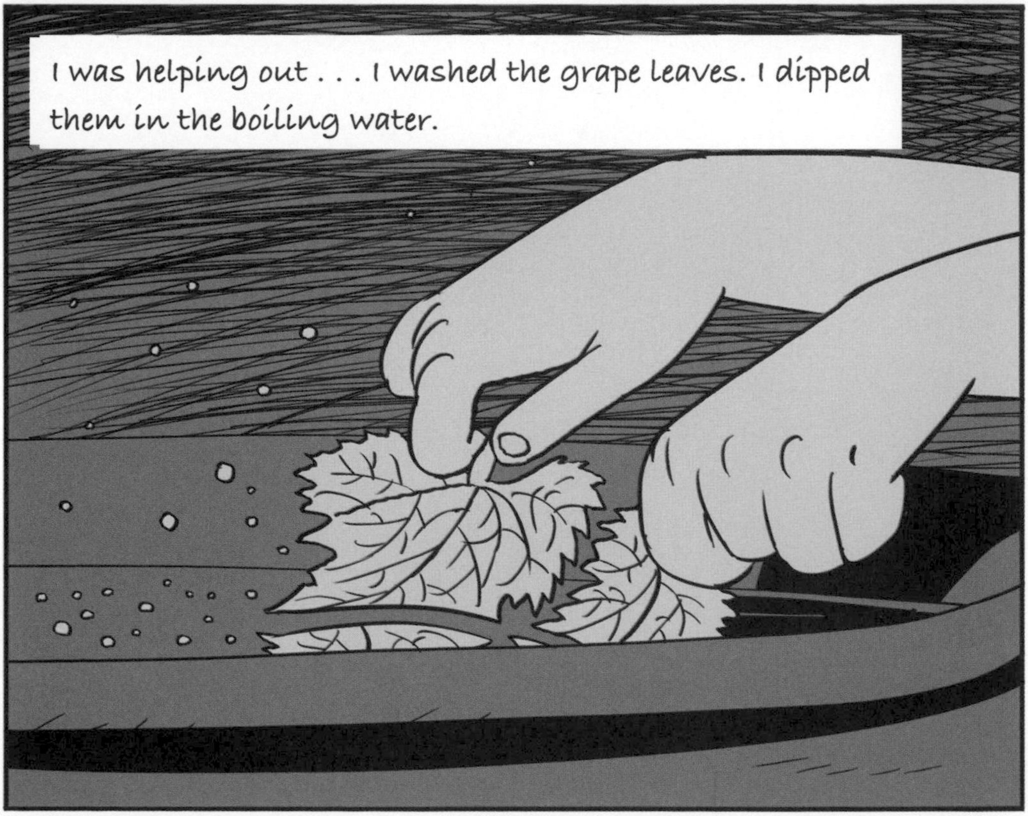
I was helping out . . . I washed the grape leaves. I dipped them in the boiling water.

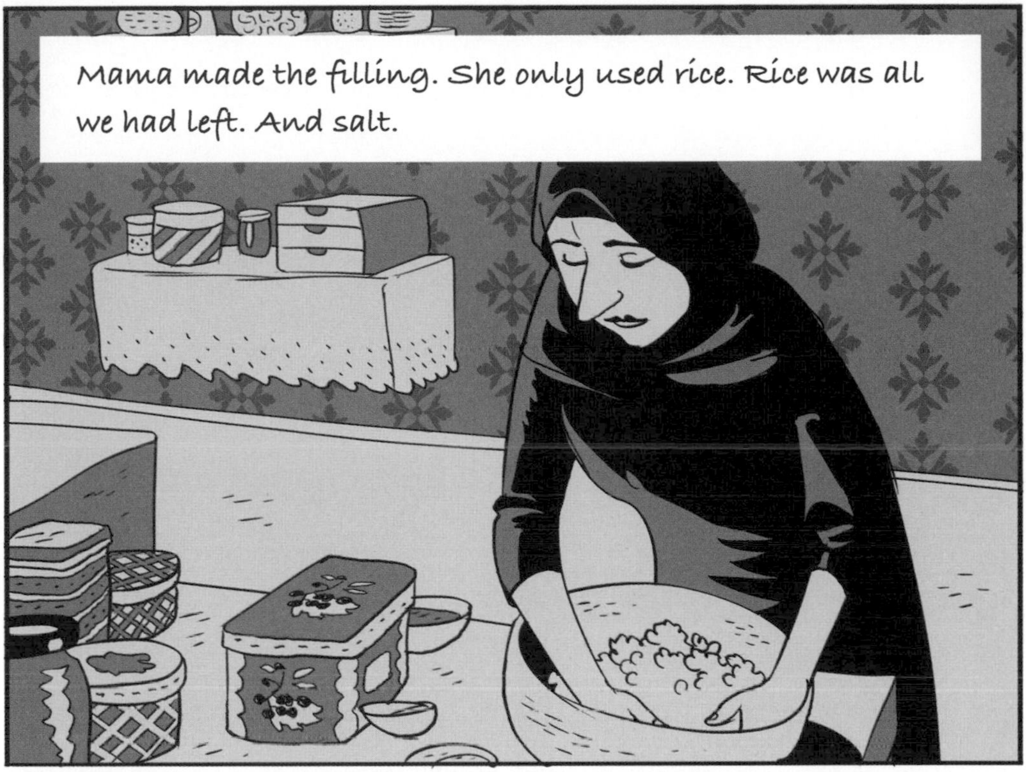
Mama made the filling. She only used rice. Rice was all we had left. And salt.

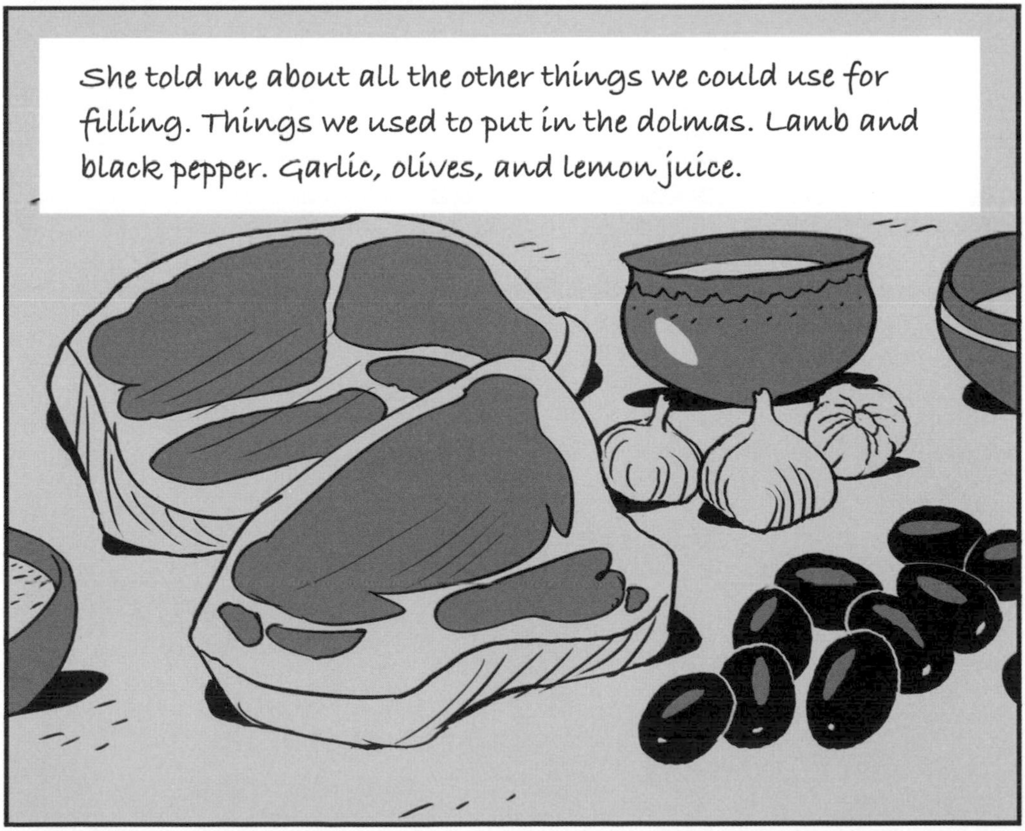
She told me about all the other things we could use for filling. Things we used to put in the dolmas. Lamb and black pepper. Garlic, olives, and lemon juice.

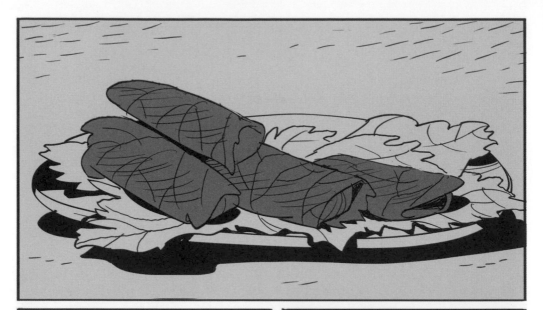

When Papa got back he tasted the dolmas.

It's good . . . but maybe a little too salty.

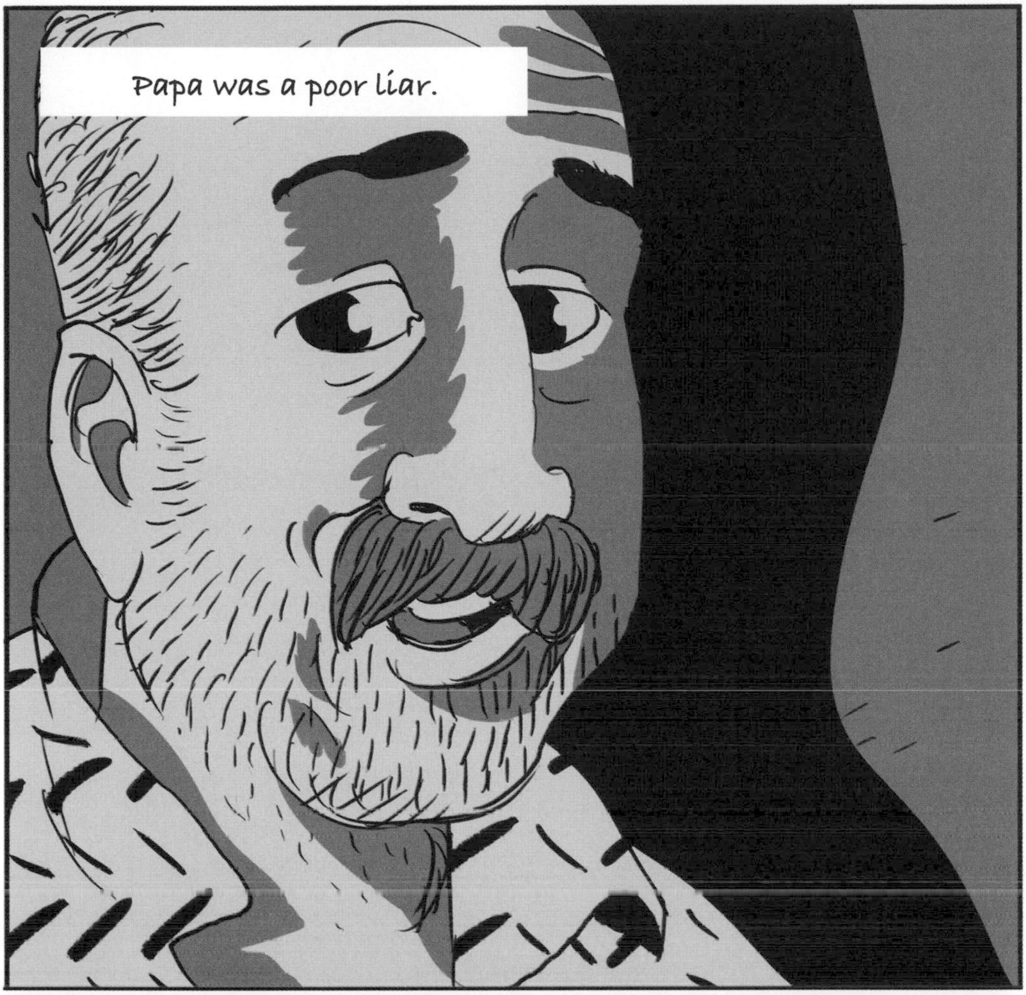
Papa was a poor liar.
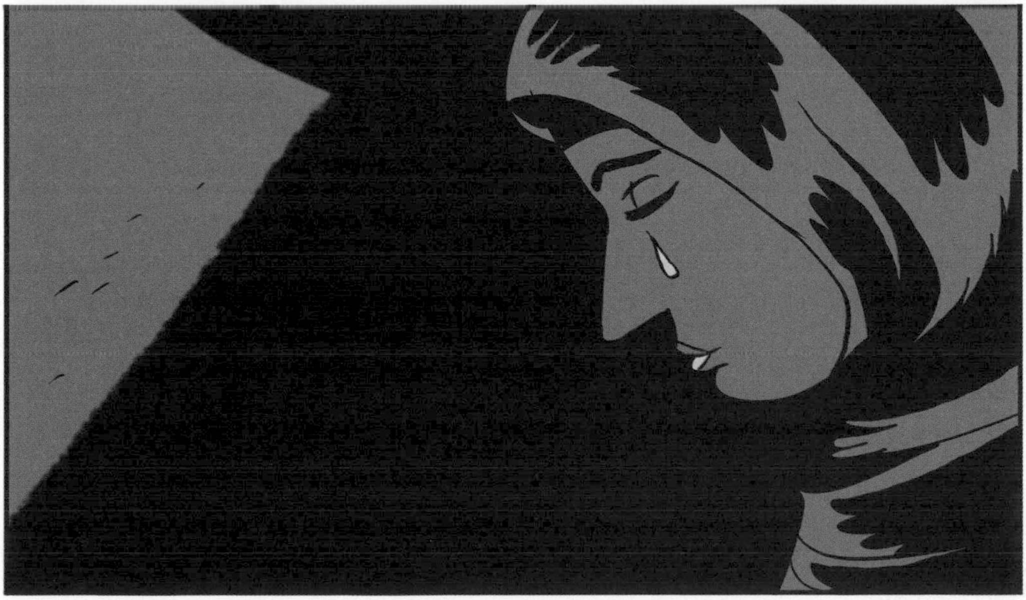

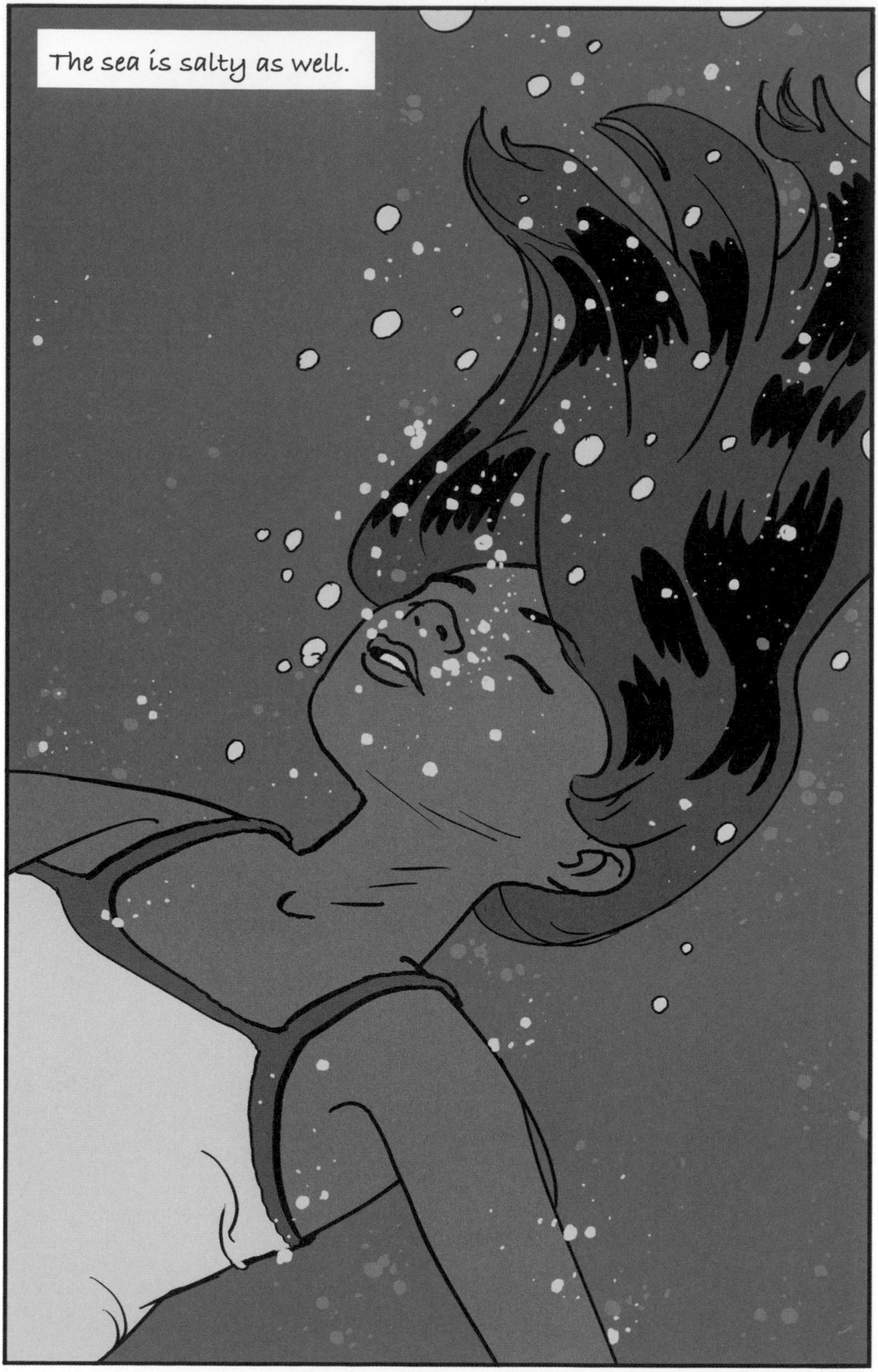
The sea is salty as well.

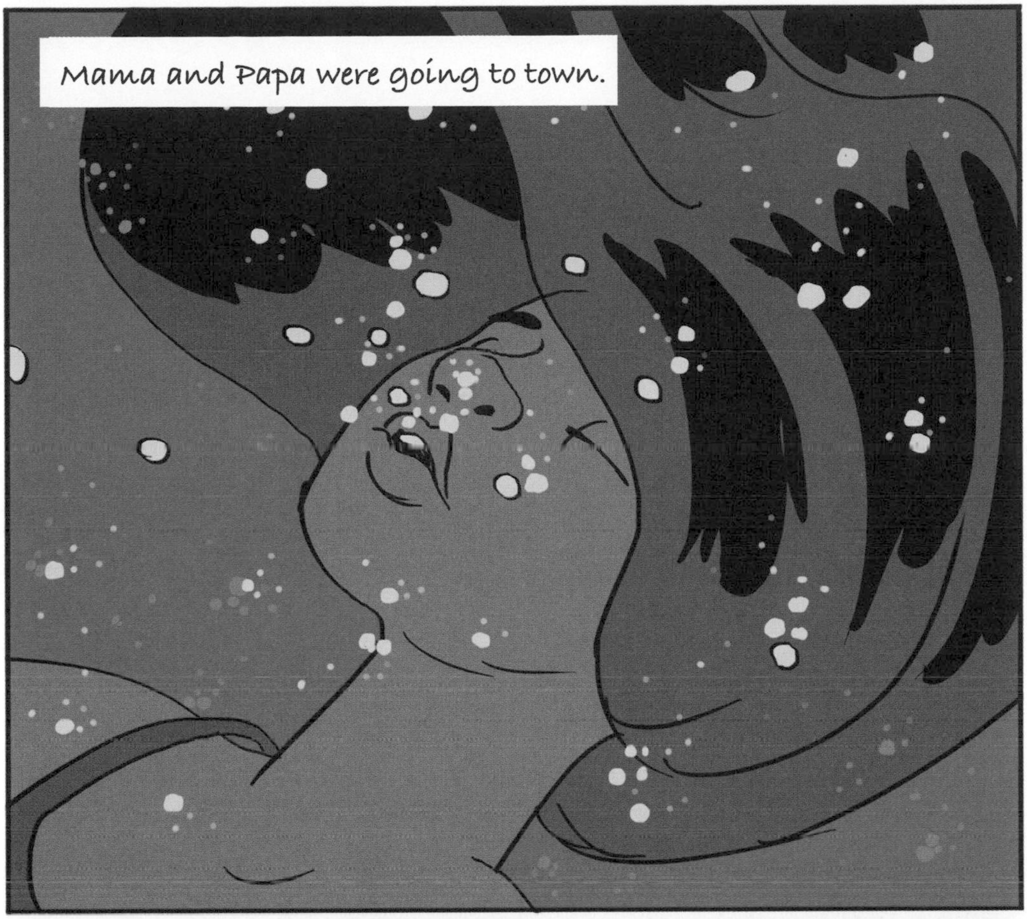
Mama and Papa were going to town.

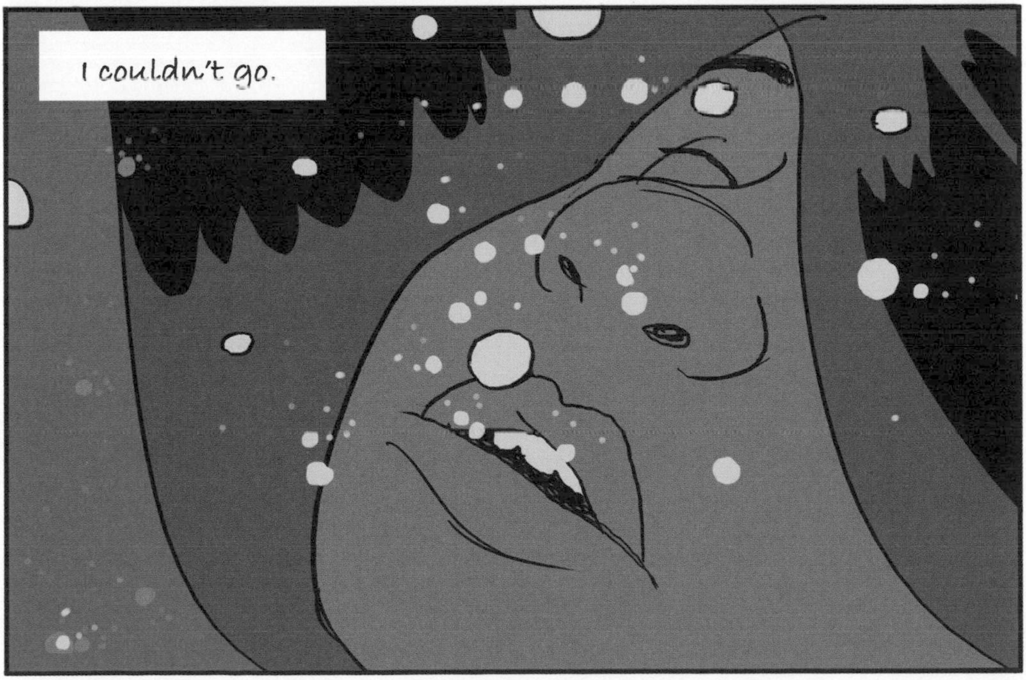
I couldn't go.

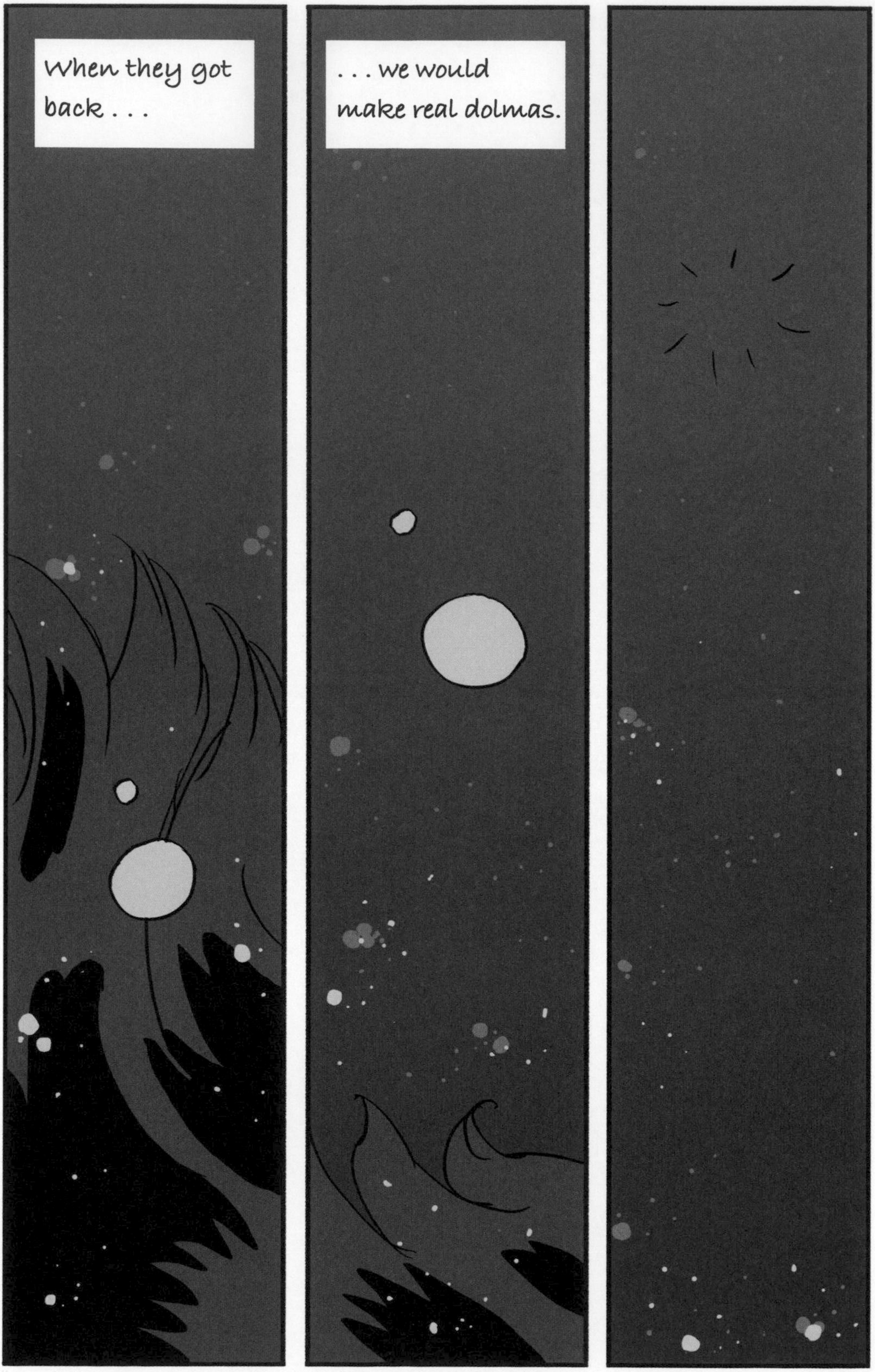
When they got back . . .
. . . we would make real dolmas.

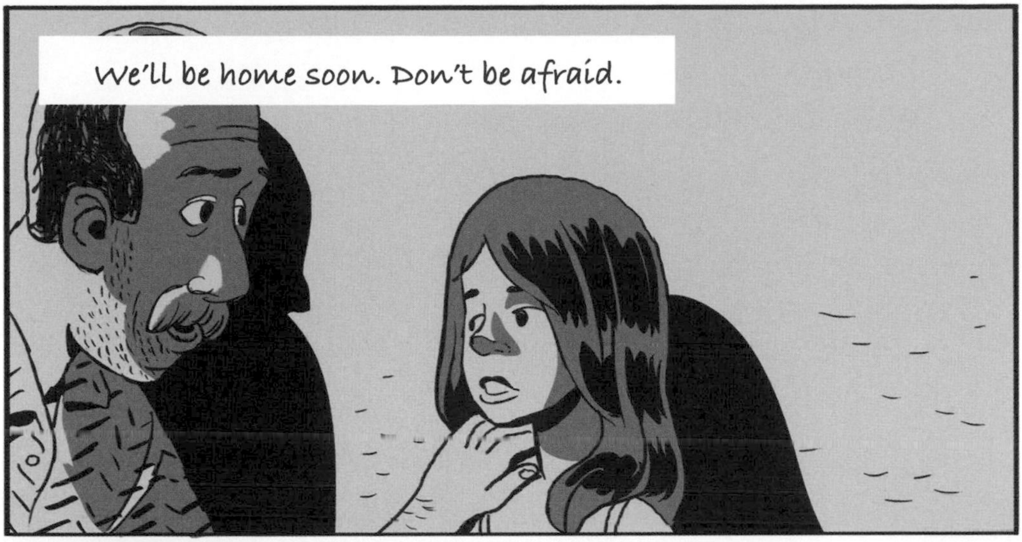
We'll be home soon. Don't be afraid.

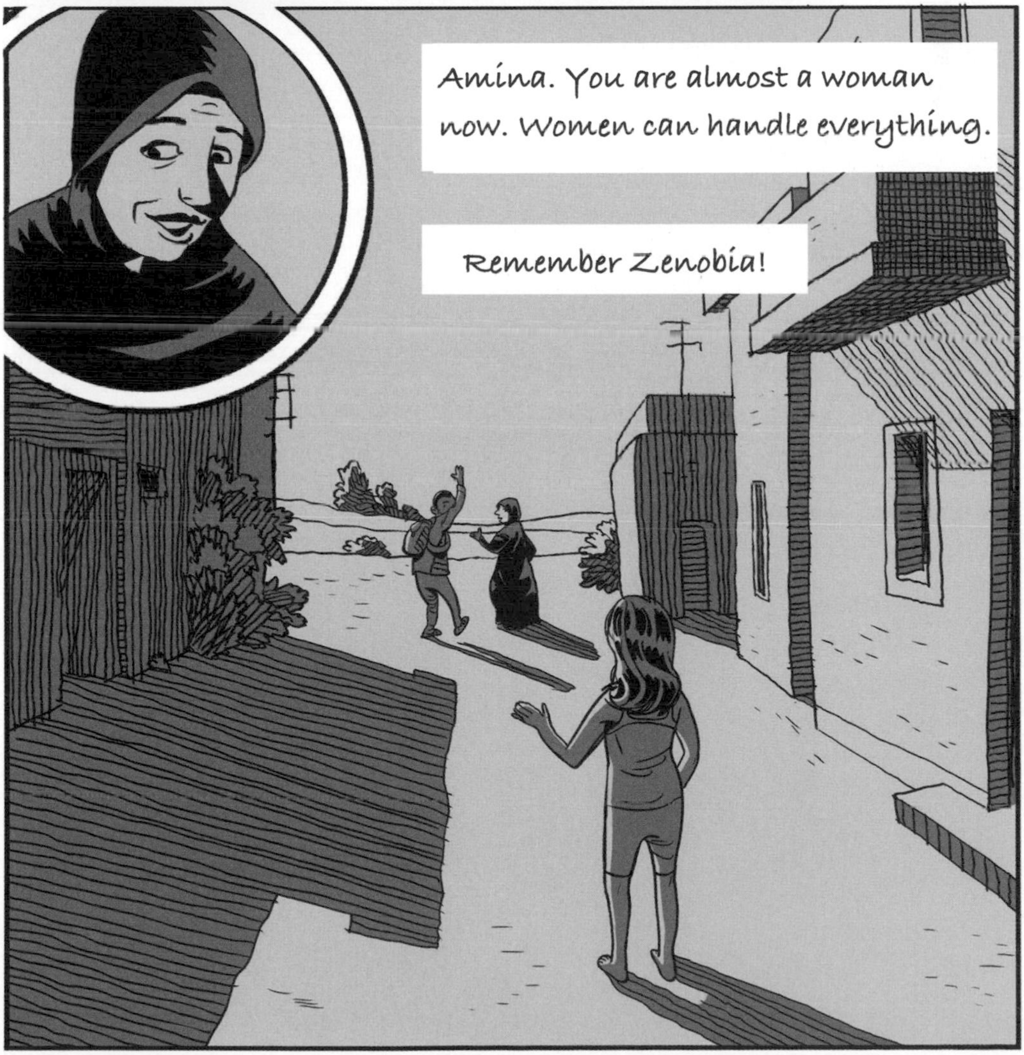
Amina. You are almost a woman now. Women can handle everything.
Remember Zenobia!

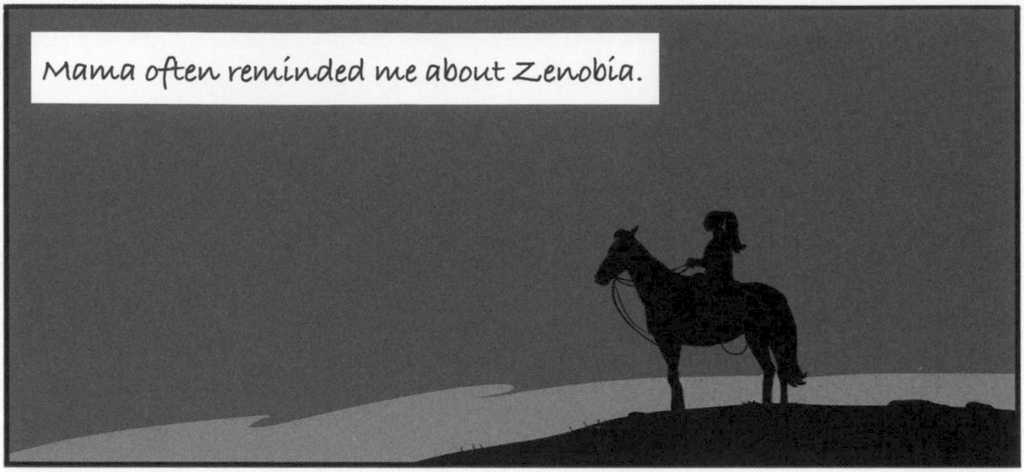
Mama often reminded me about Zenobia.

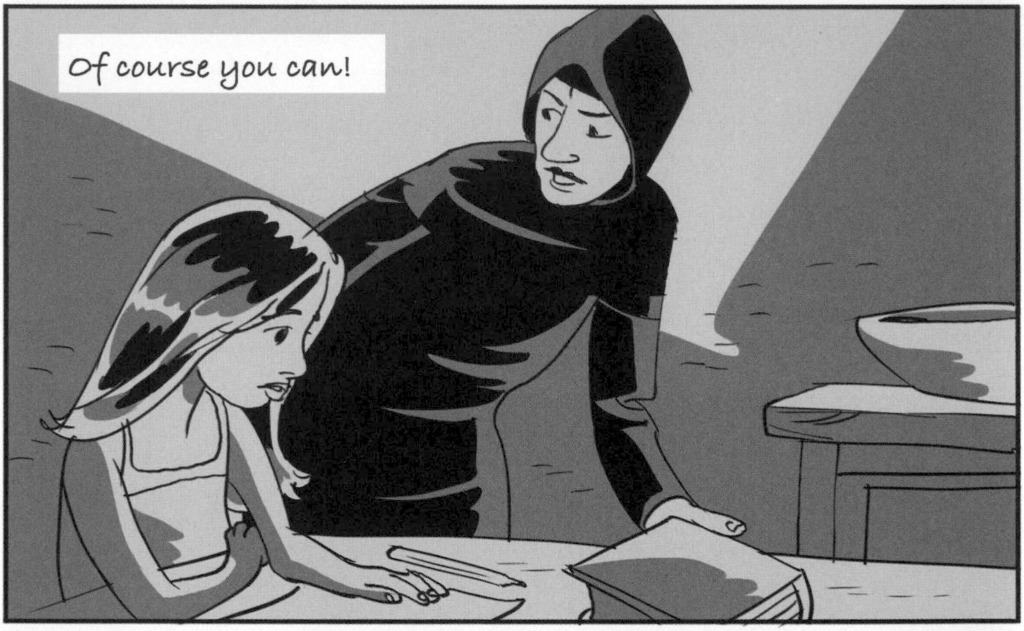
Of course you can!

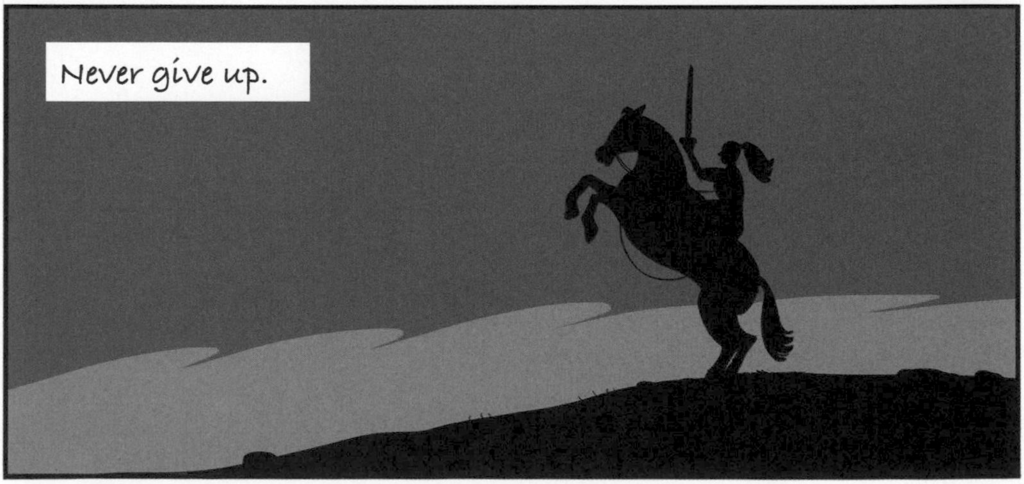
Never give up.

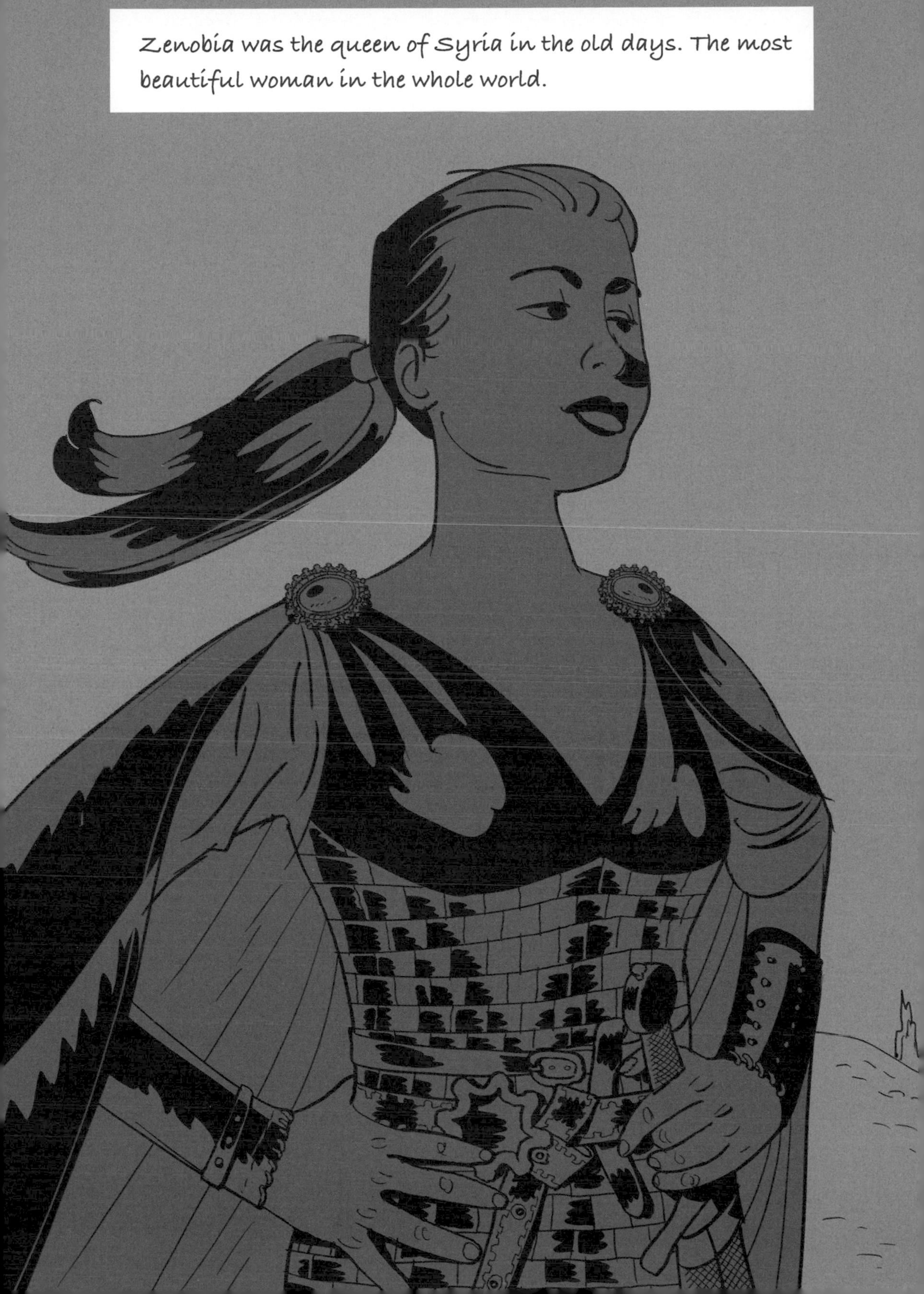
Zenobia was the queen of Syria in the old days. The most beautiful woman in the whole world.

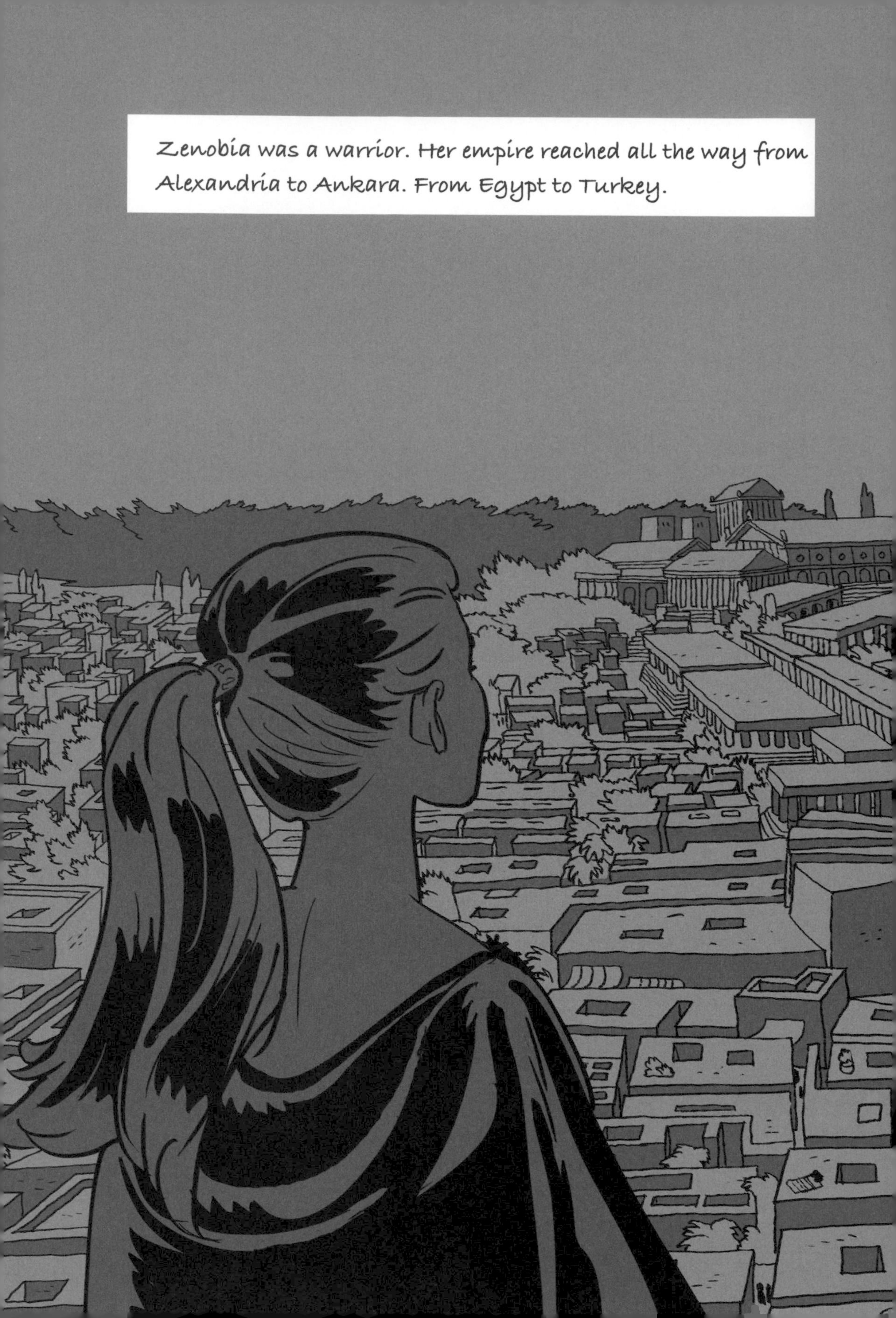
Zenobia was a warrior. Her empire reached all the way from Alexandria to Ankara. From Egypt to Turkey.

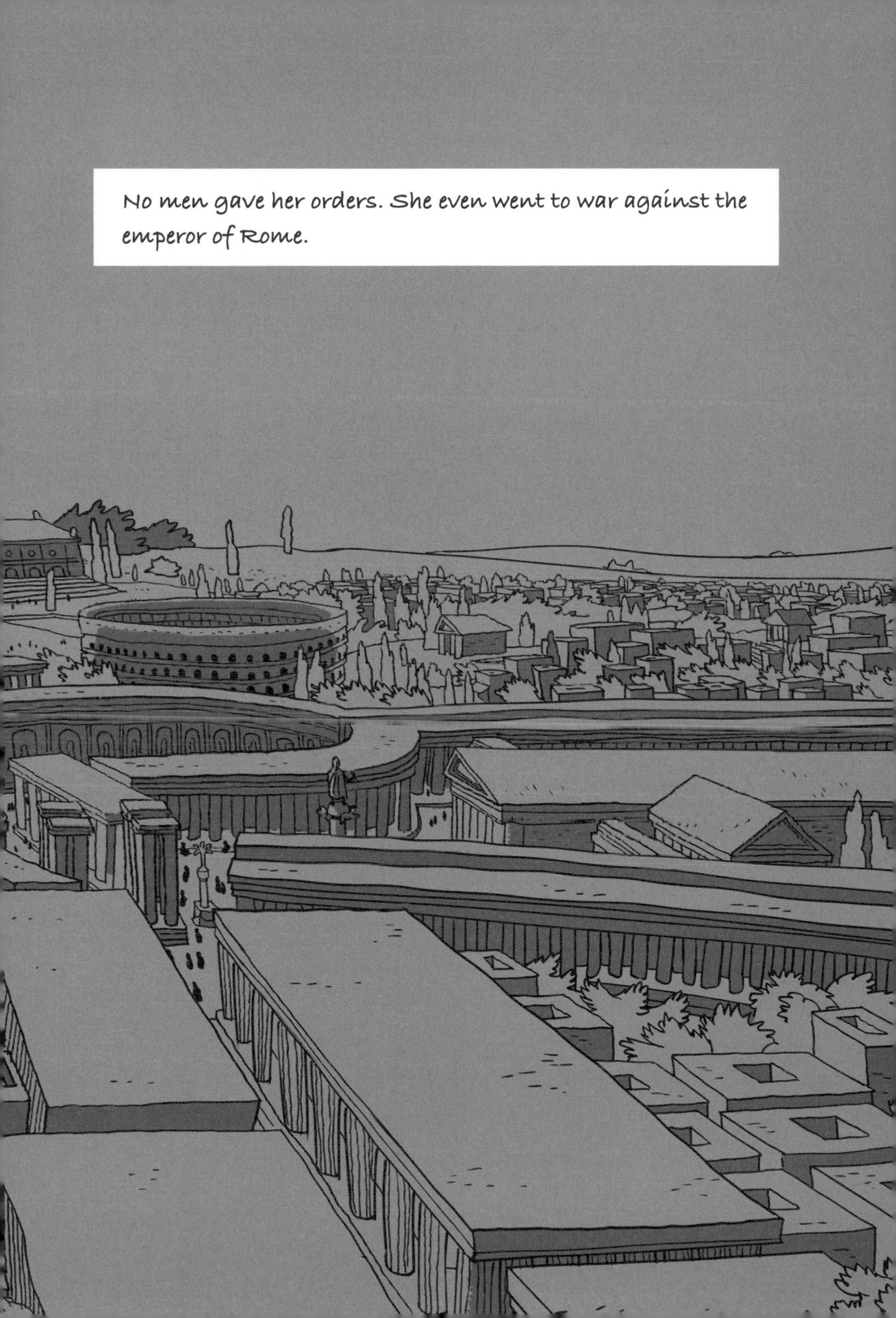
No men gave her orders. She even went to war against the emperor of Rome.

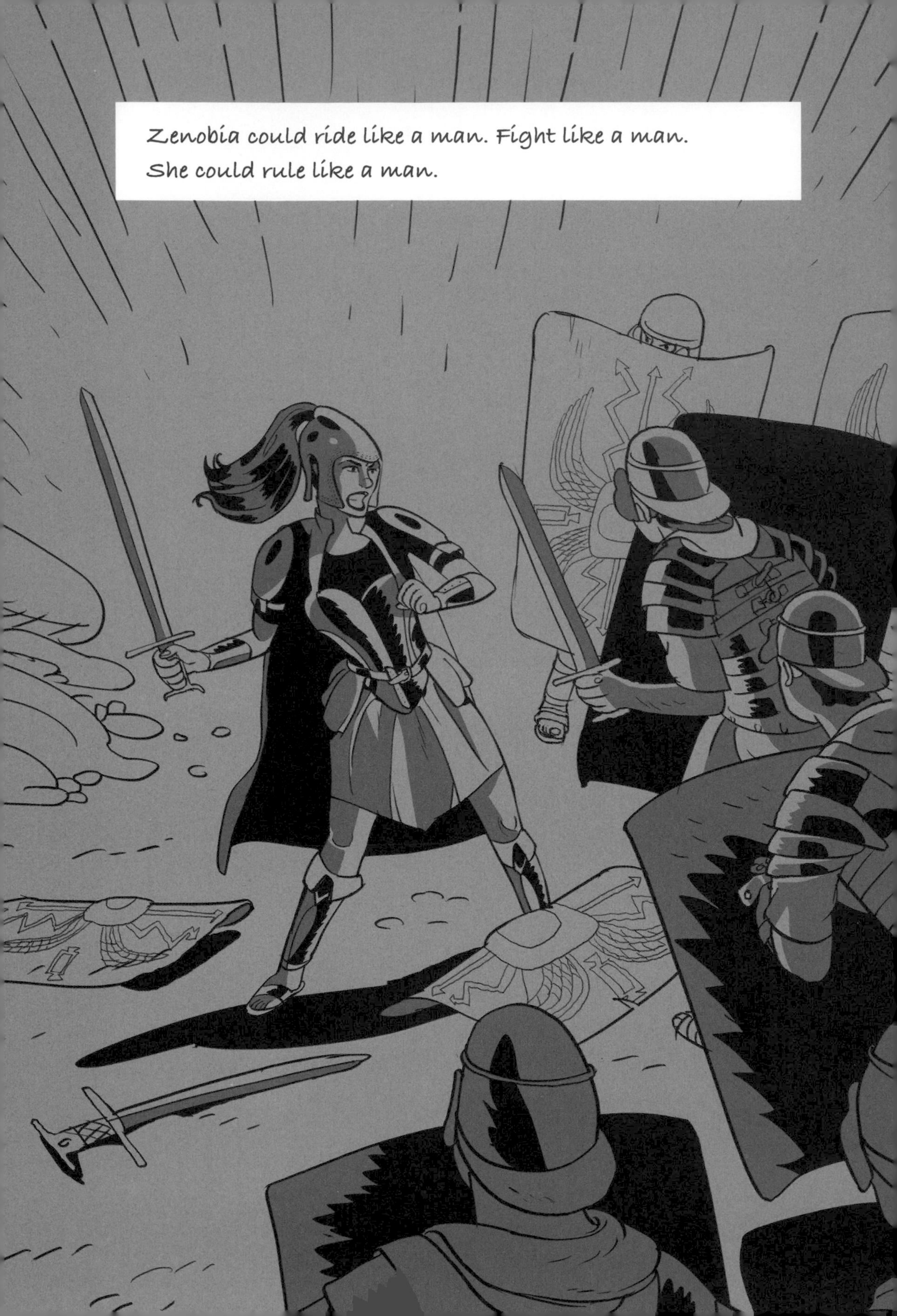
Zenobia could ride like a man. Fight like a man.
She could rule like a man.

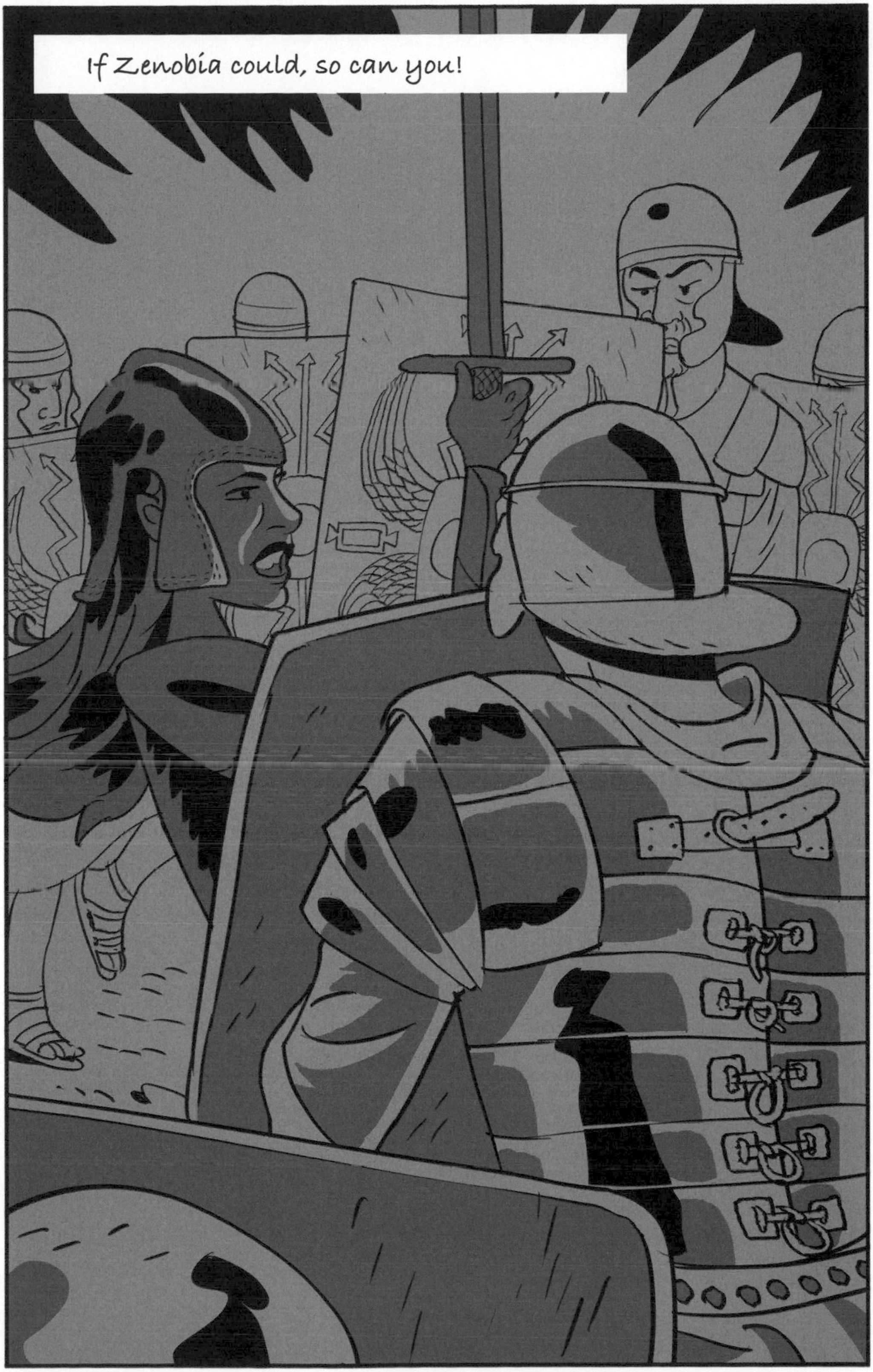
If Zenobia could, so can you!

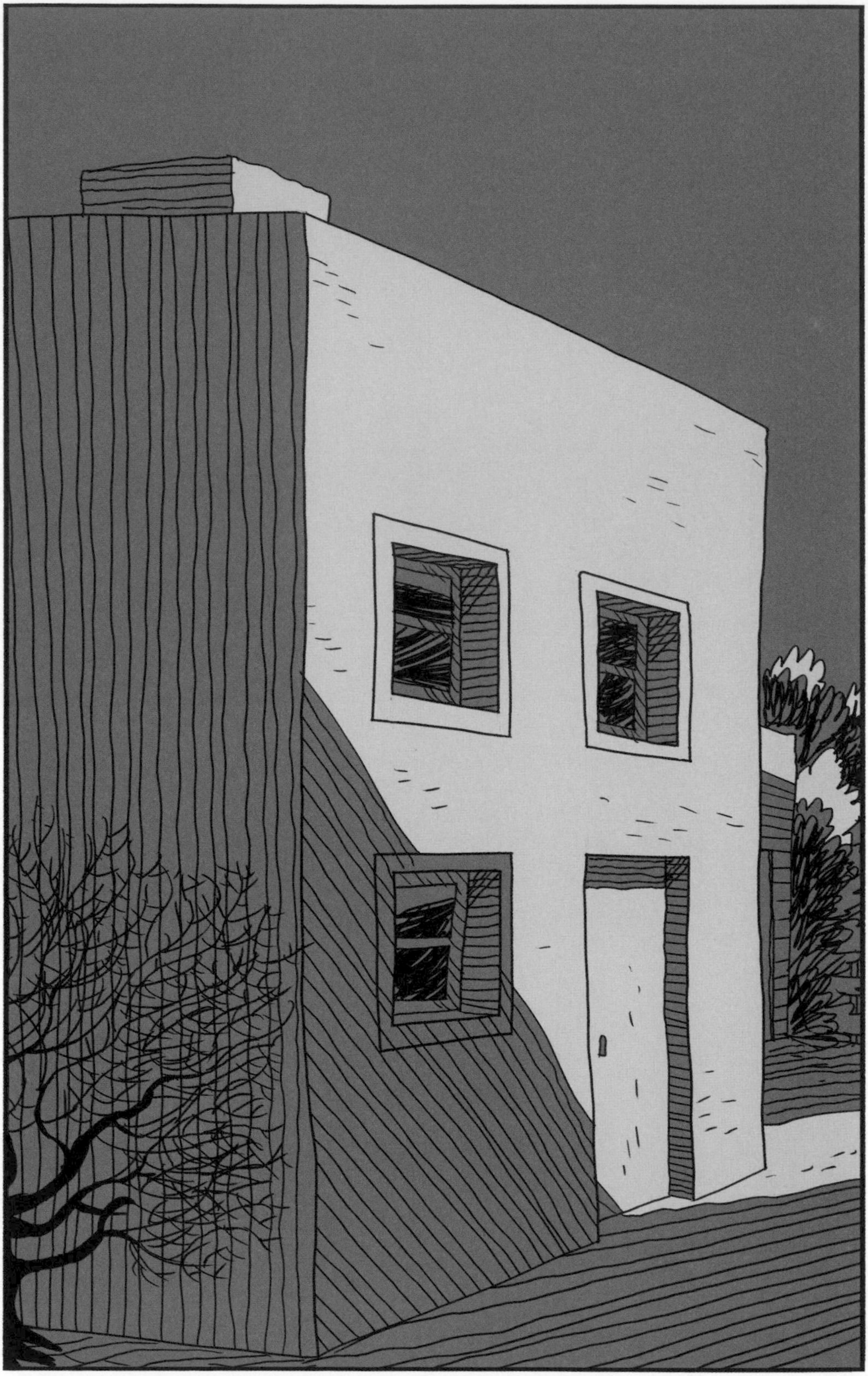

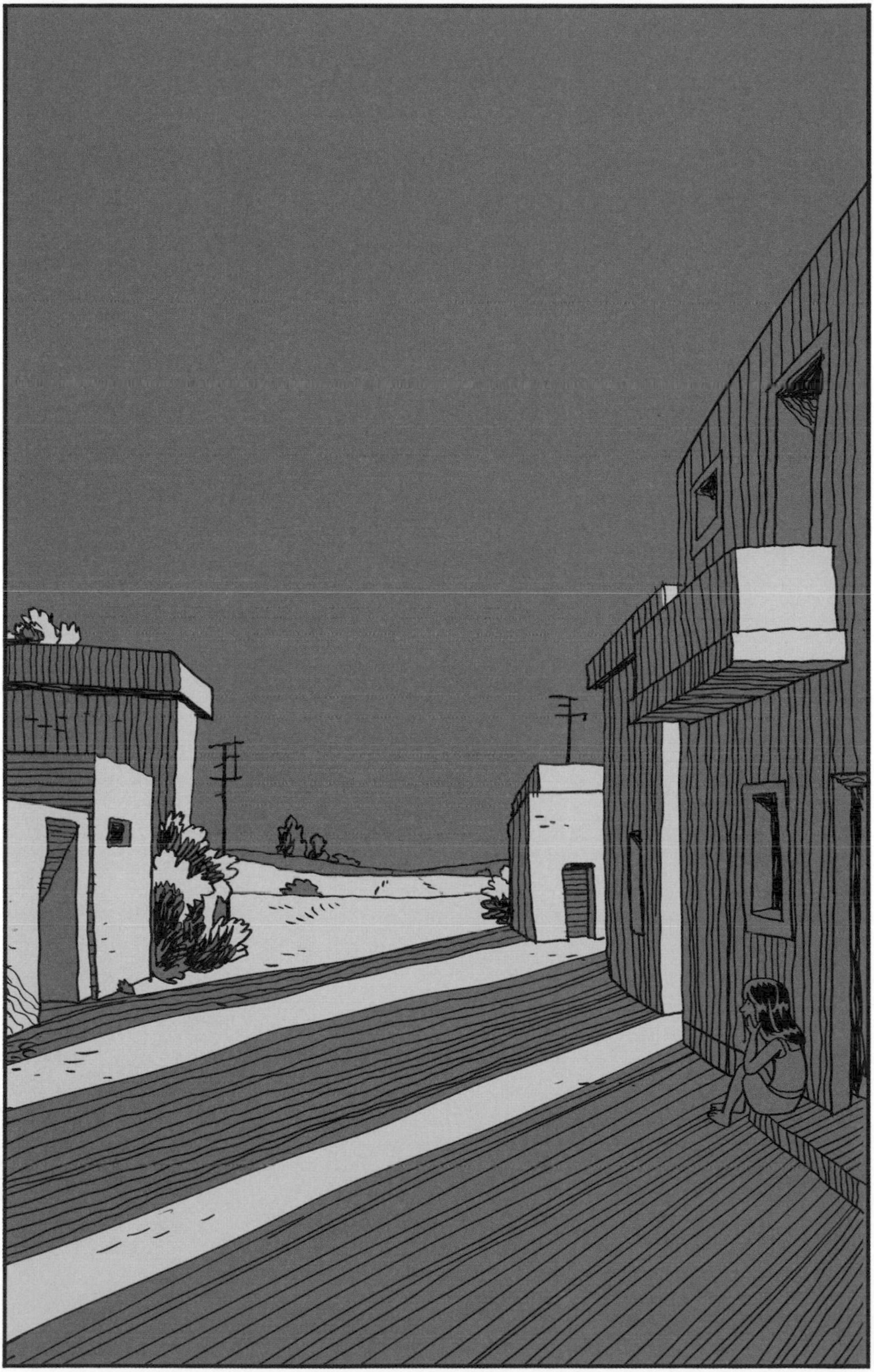

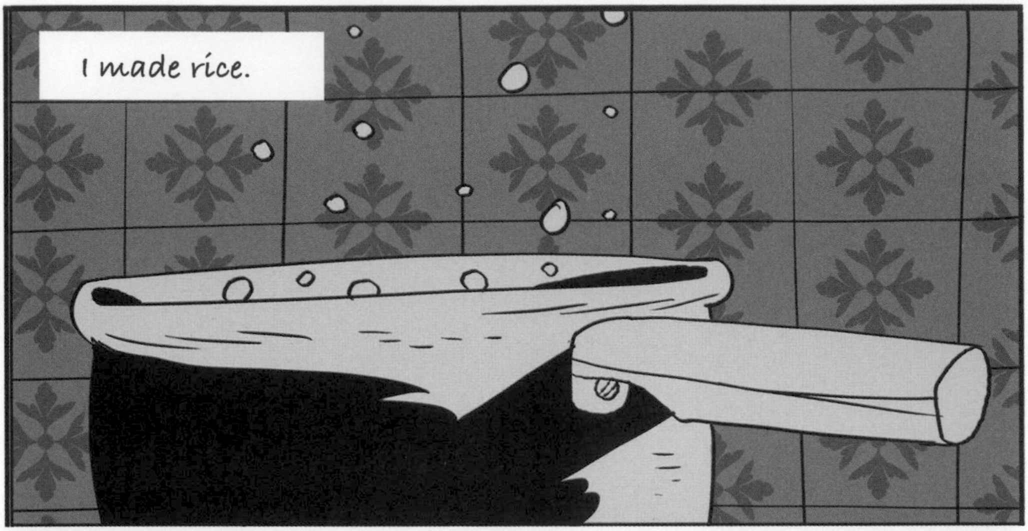
I made rice.

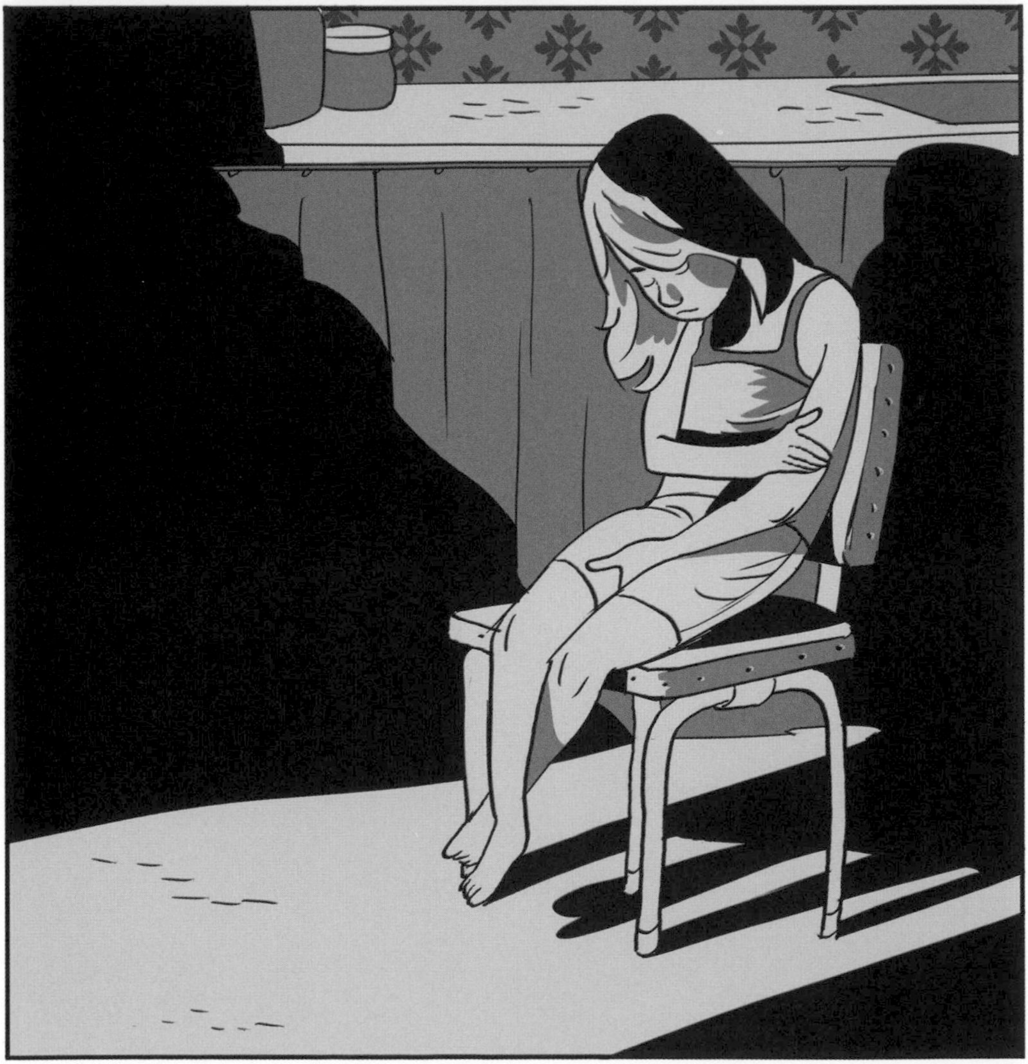

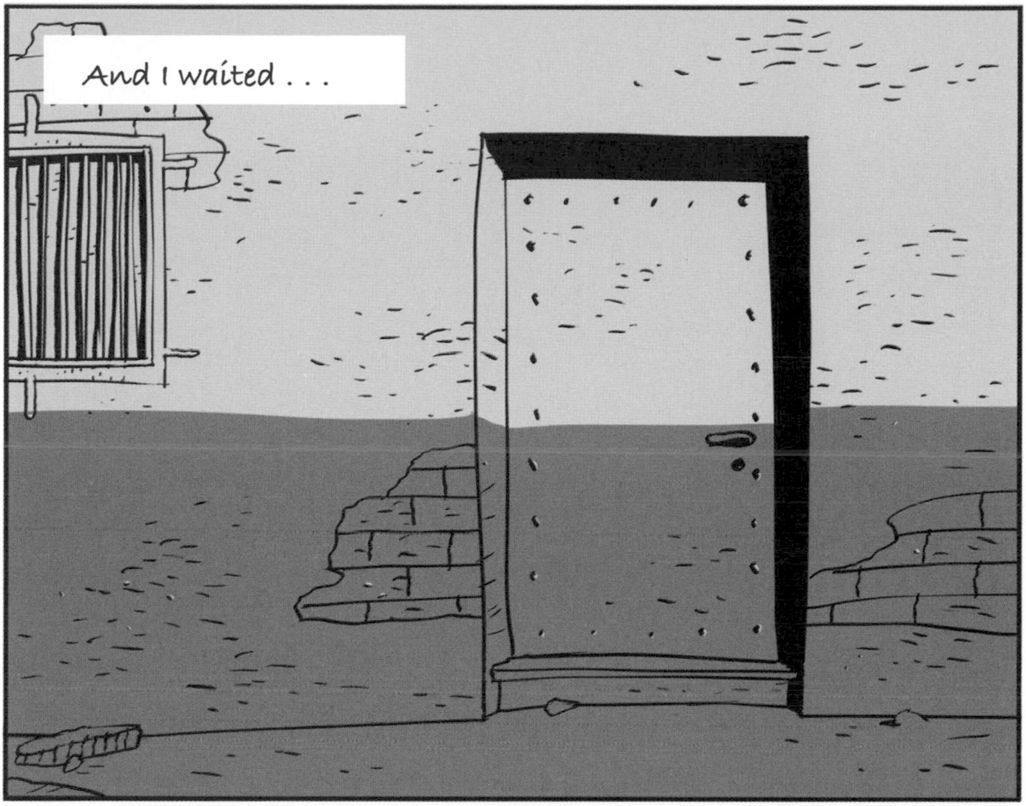
And I waited . . .

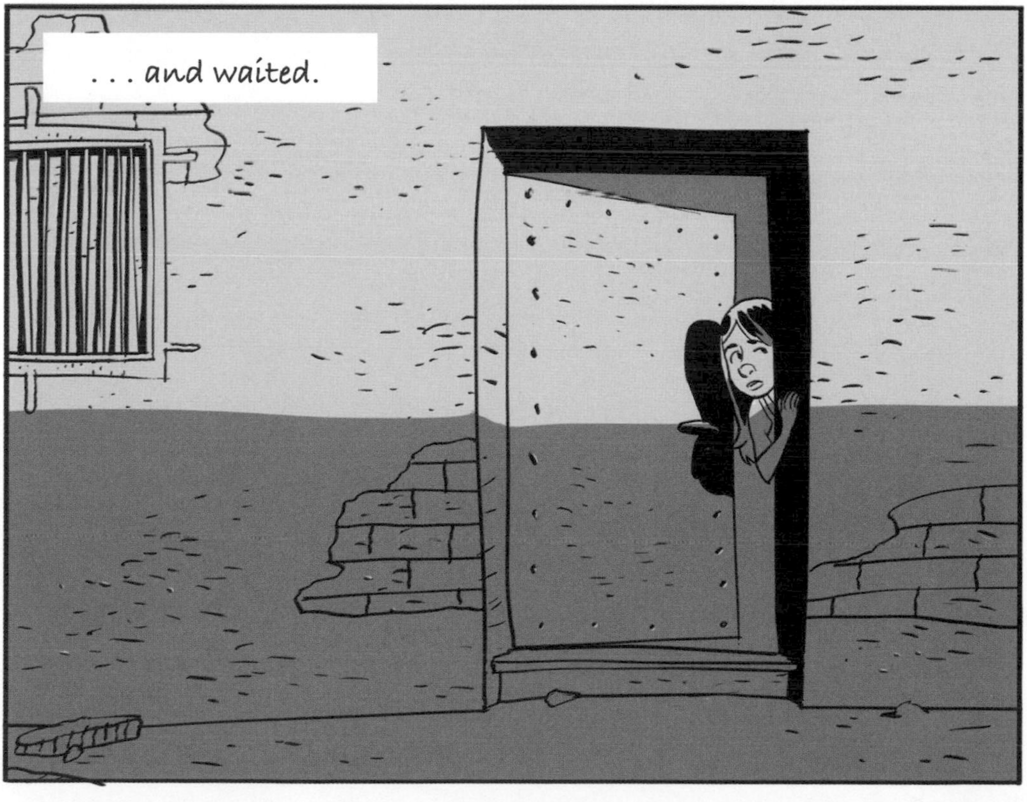
. . . and waited.

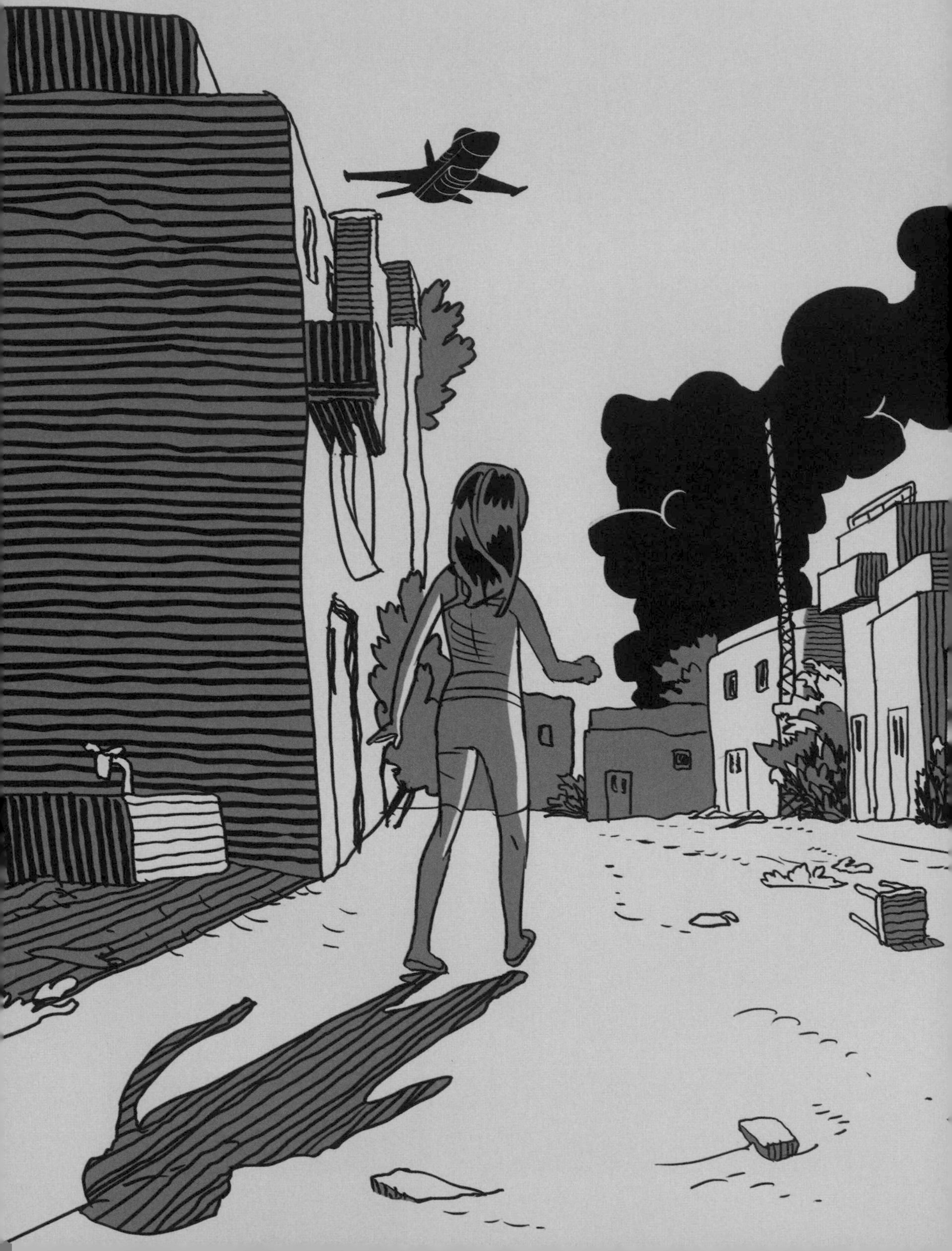

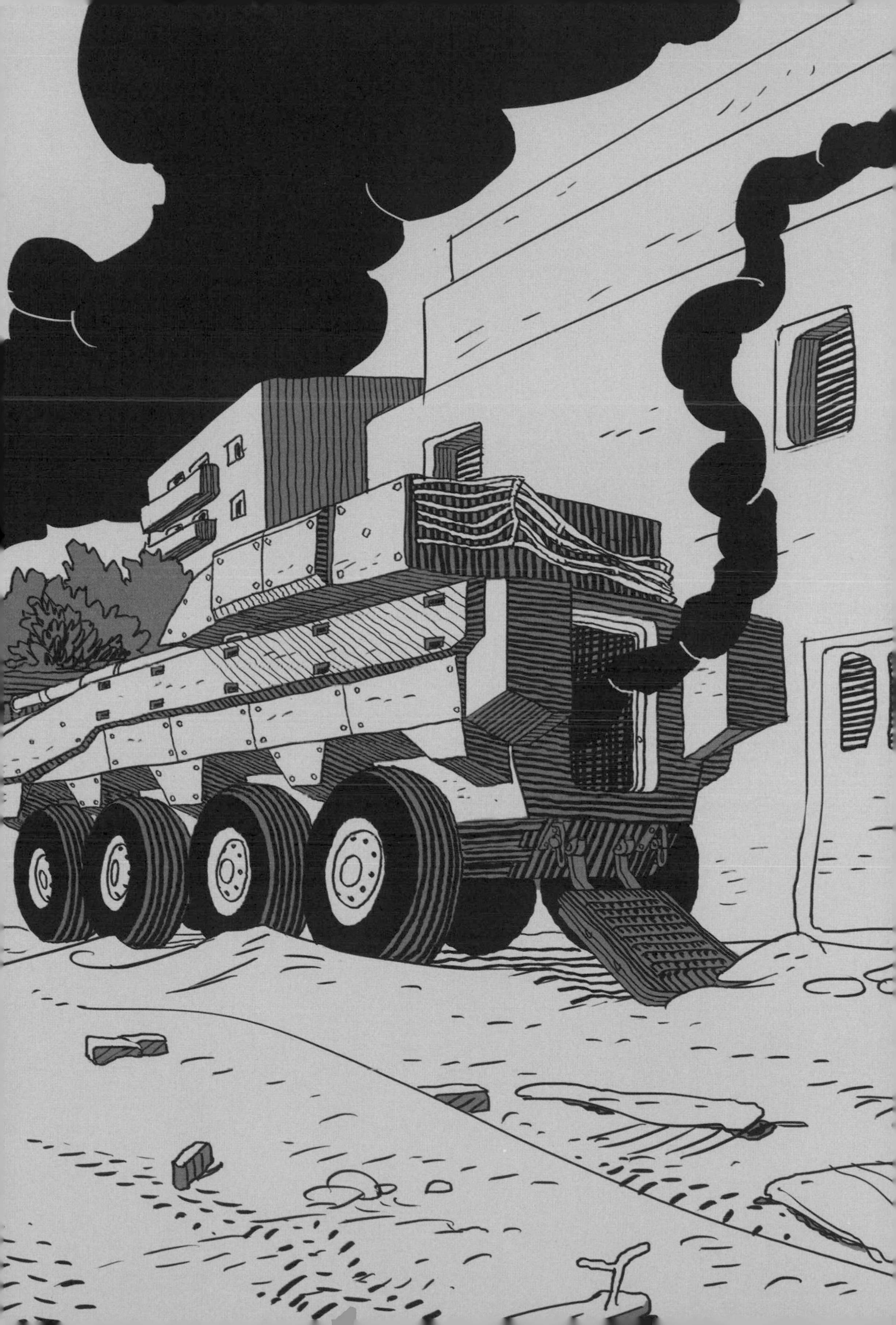

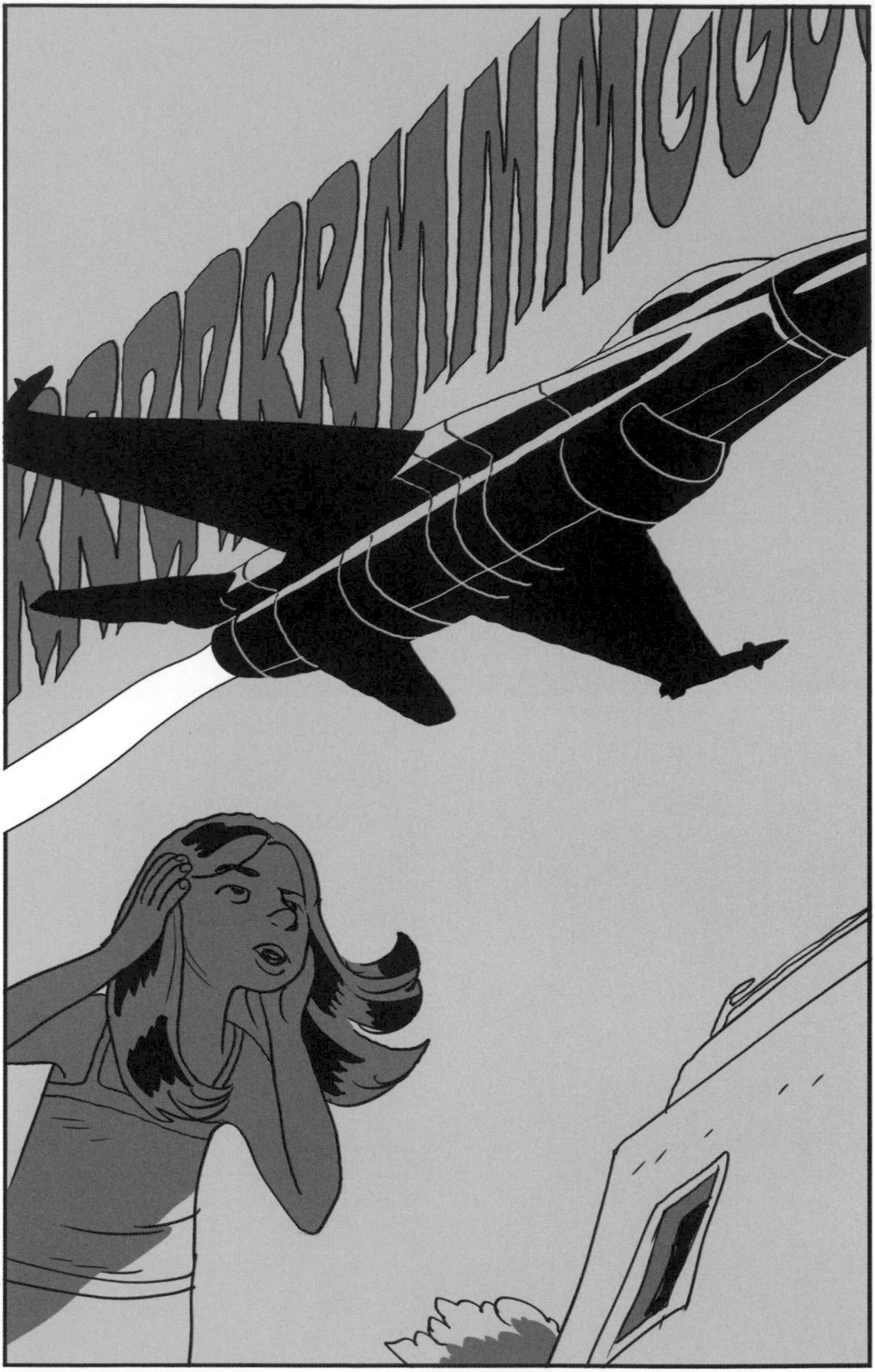

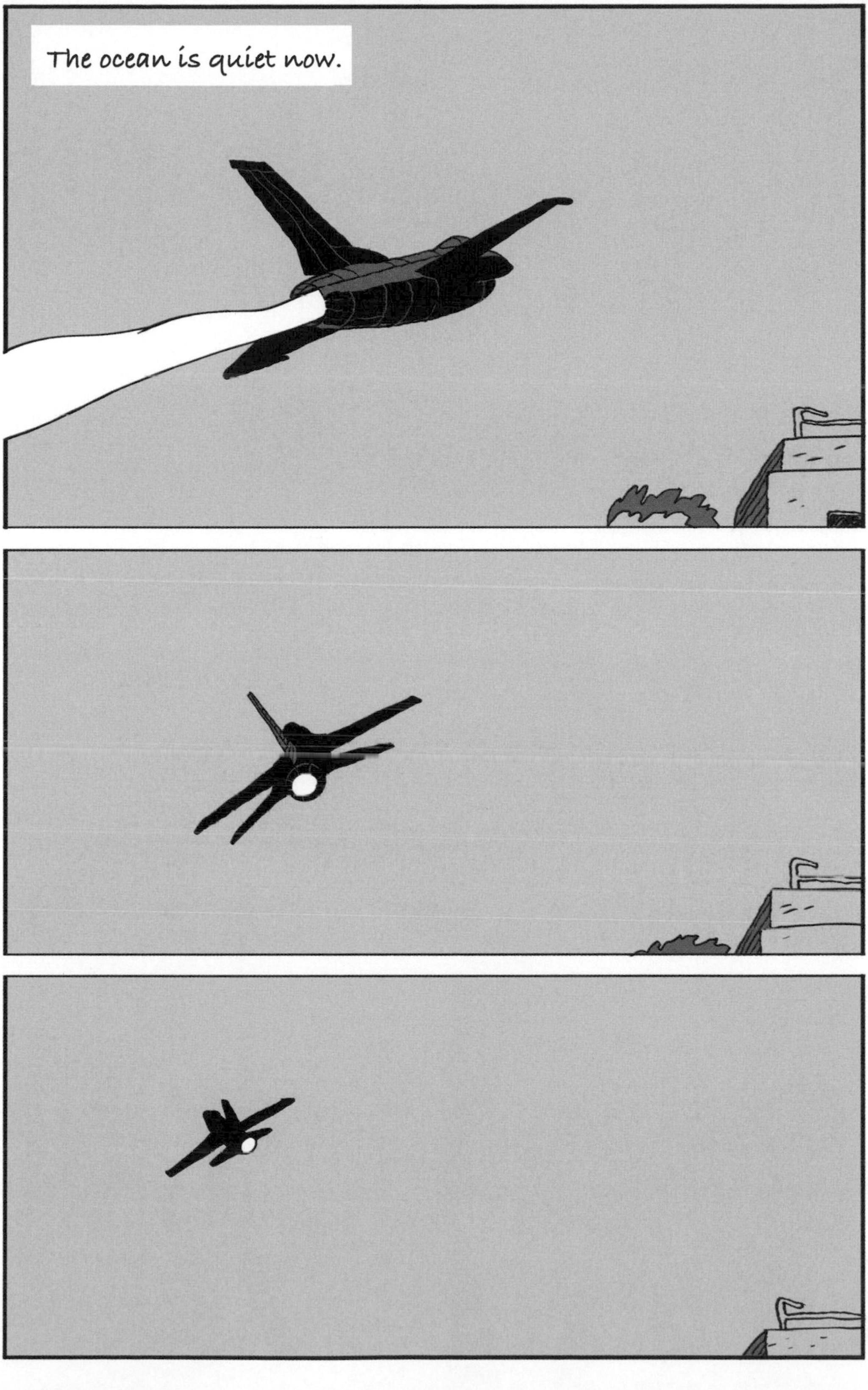
The ocean is quiet now.

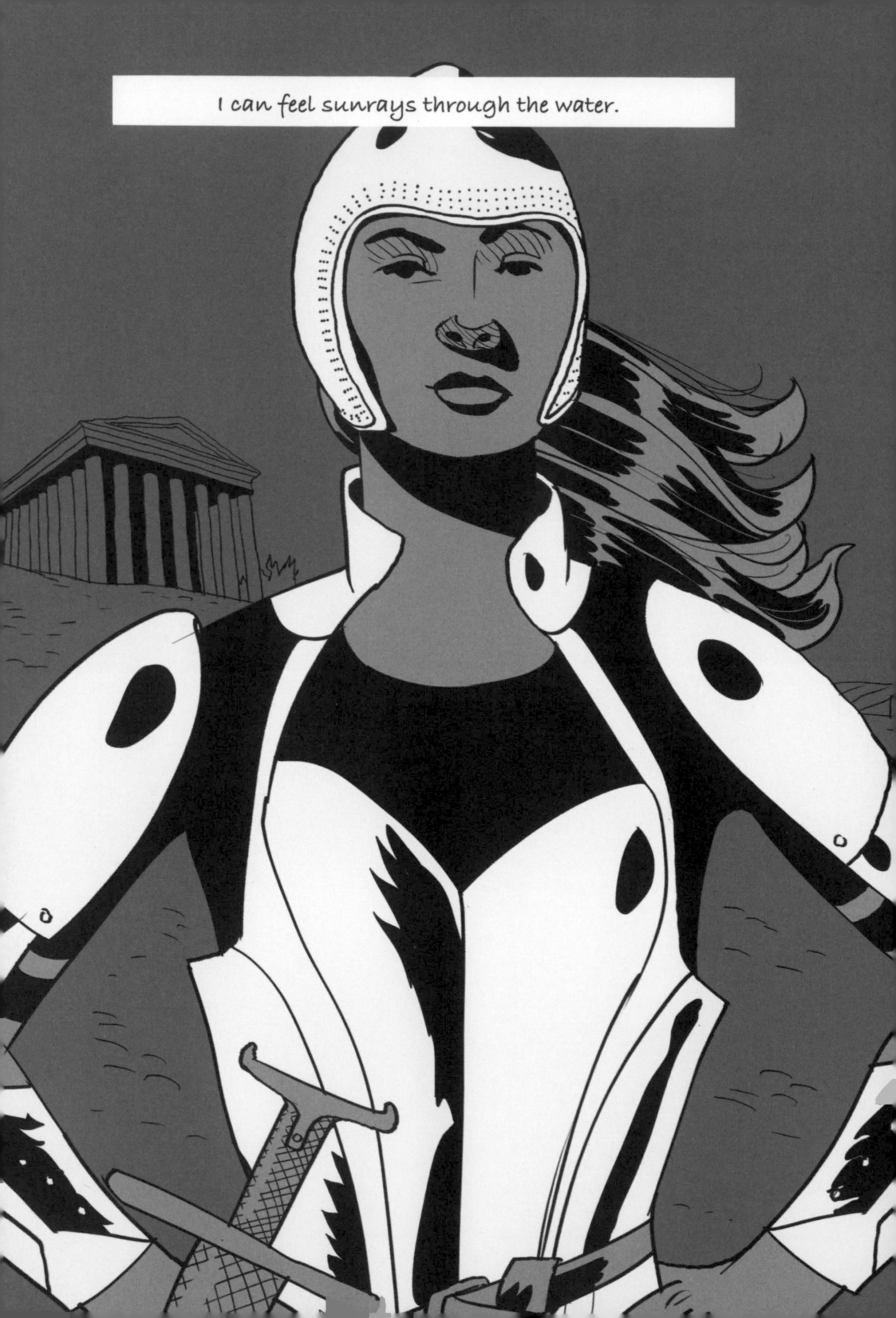
I can feel sunrays through the water.

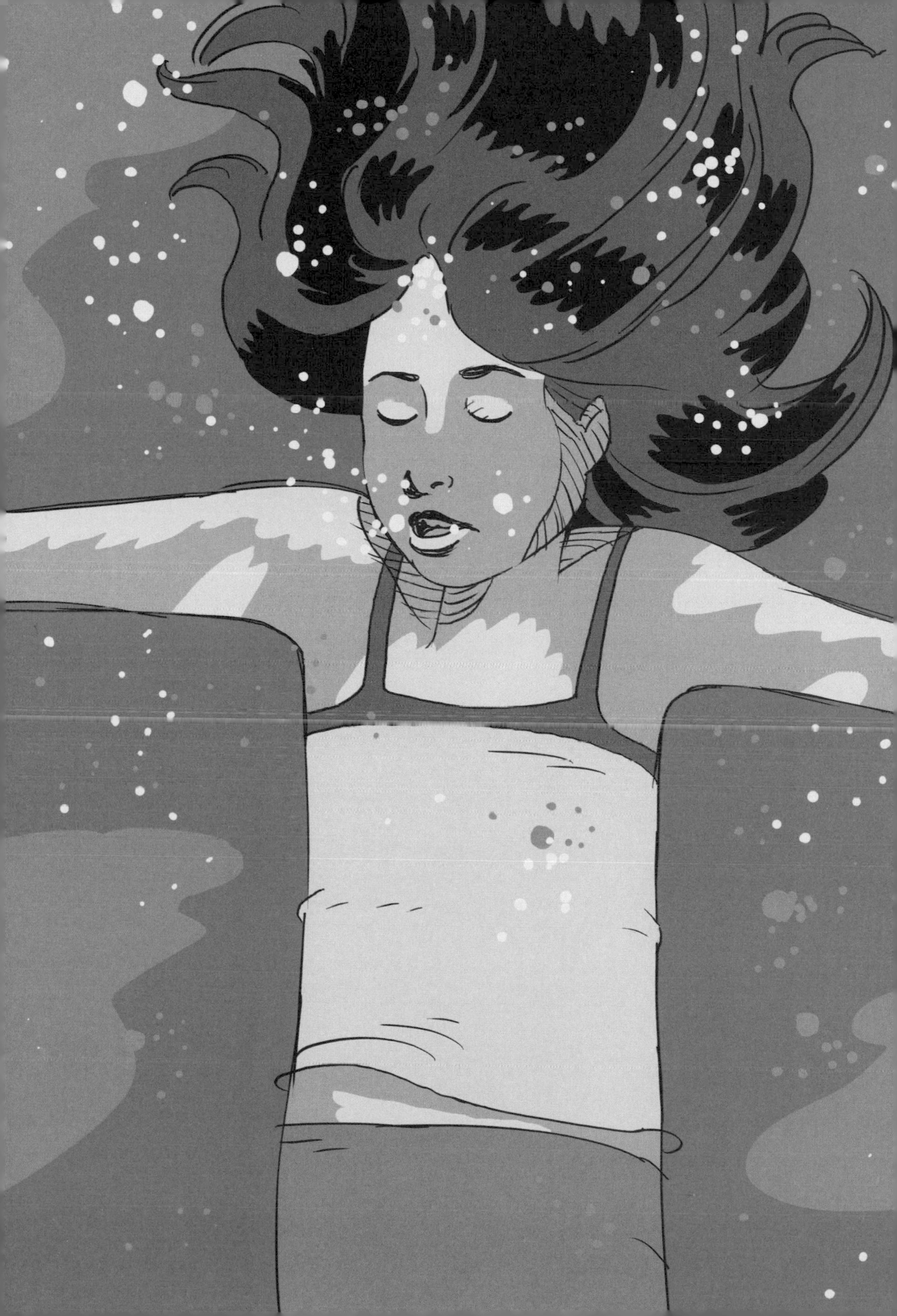

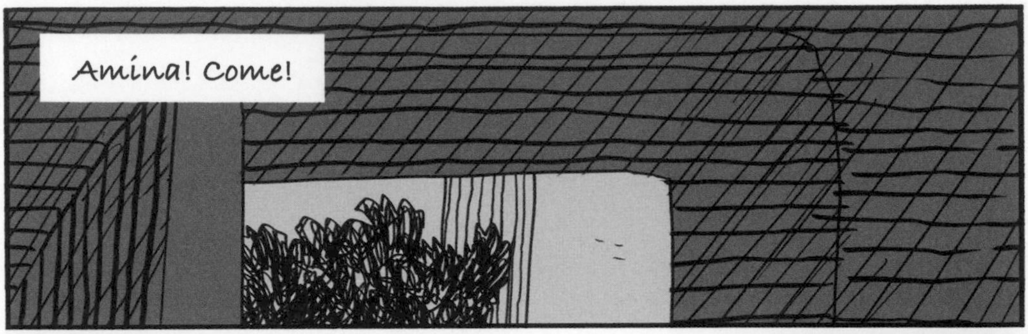
Amina! Come!

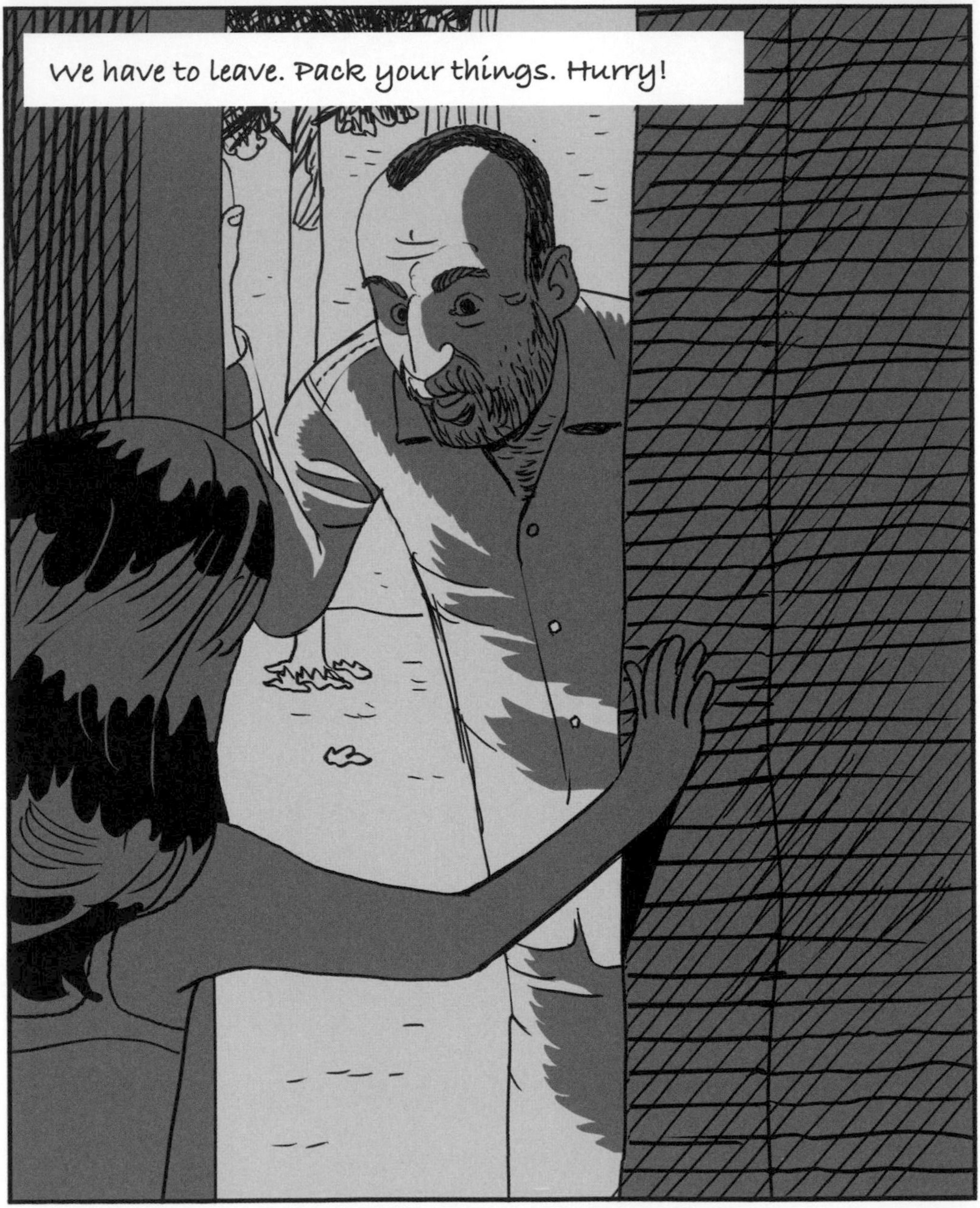
We have to leave. Pack your things. Hurry!

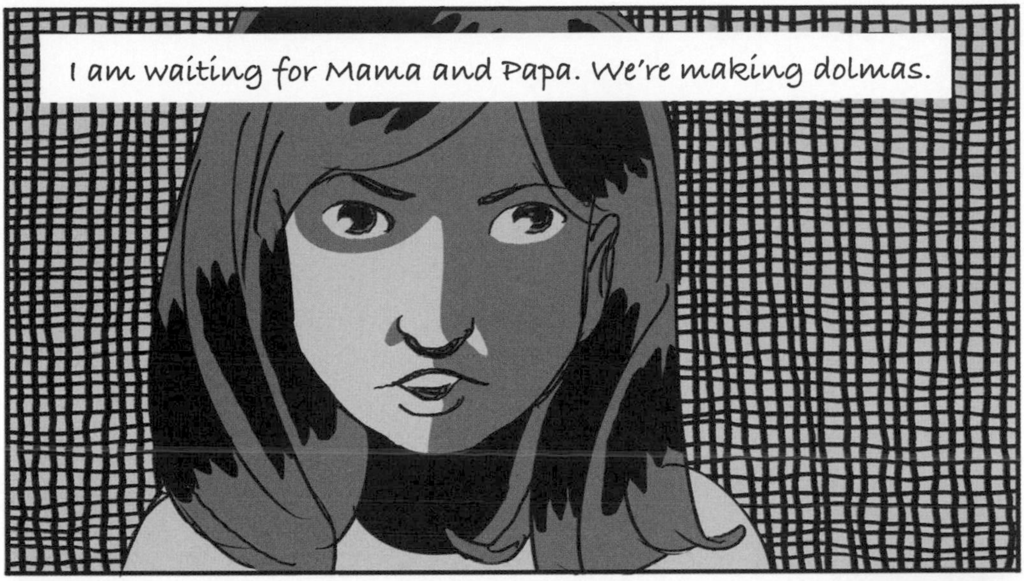
I am waiting for Mama and Papa. We're making dolmas.

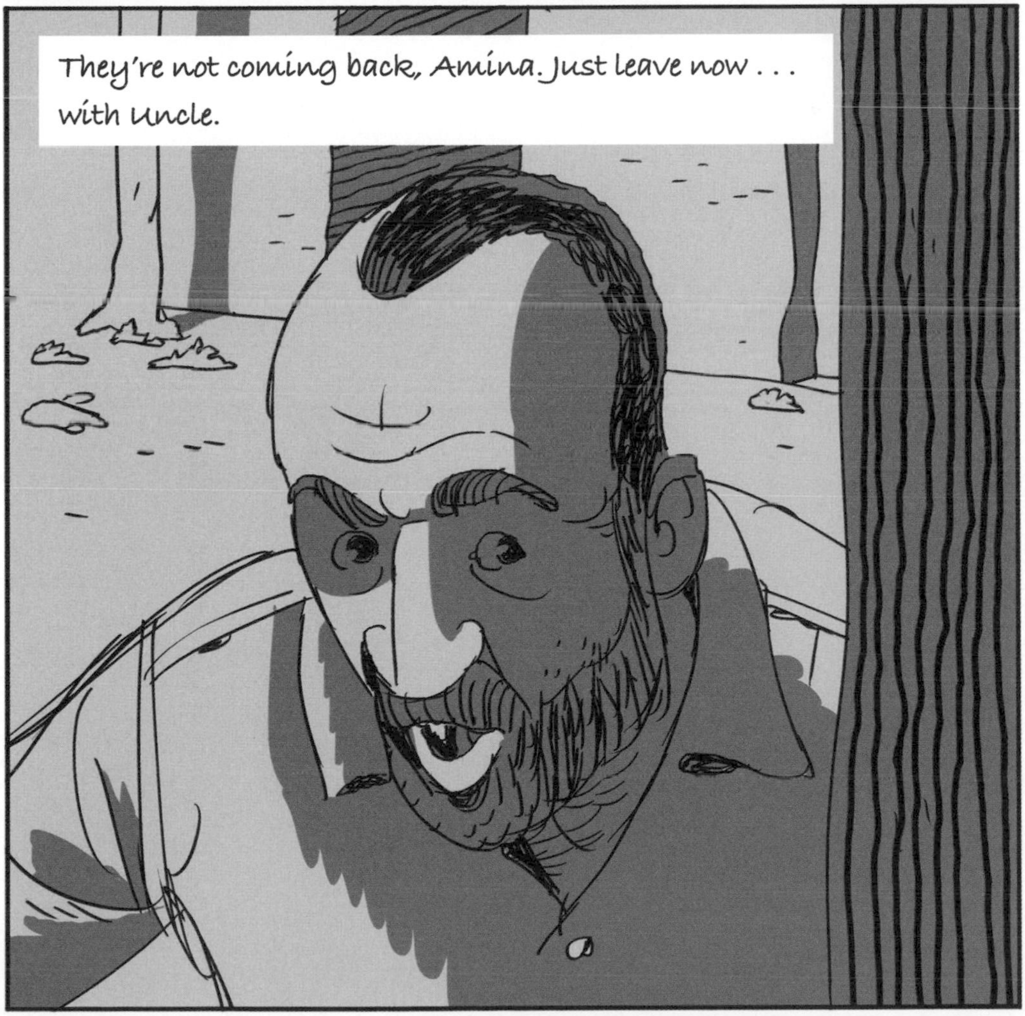
They're not coming back, Amina. Just leave now . . . with Uncle.

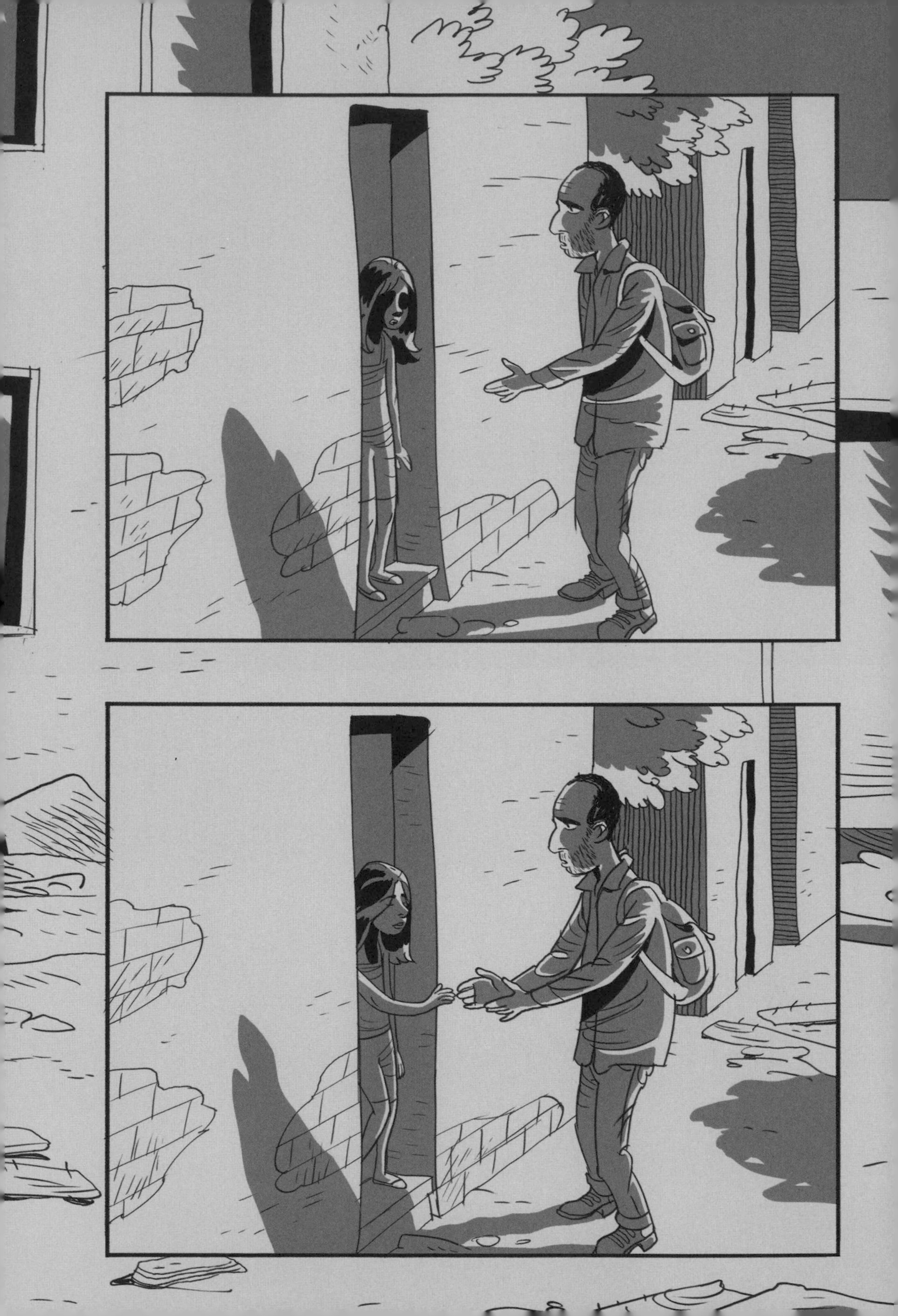

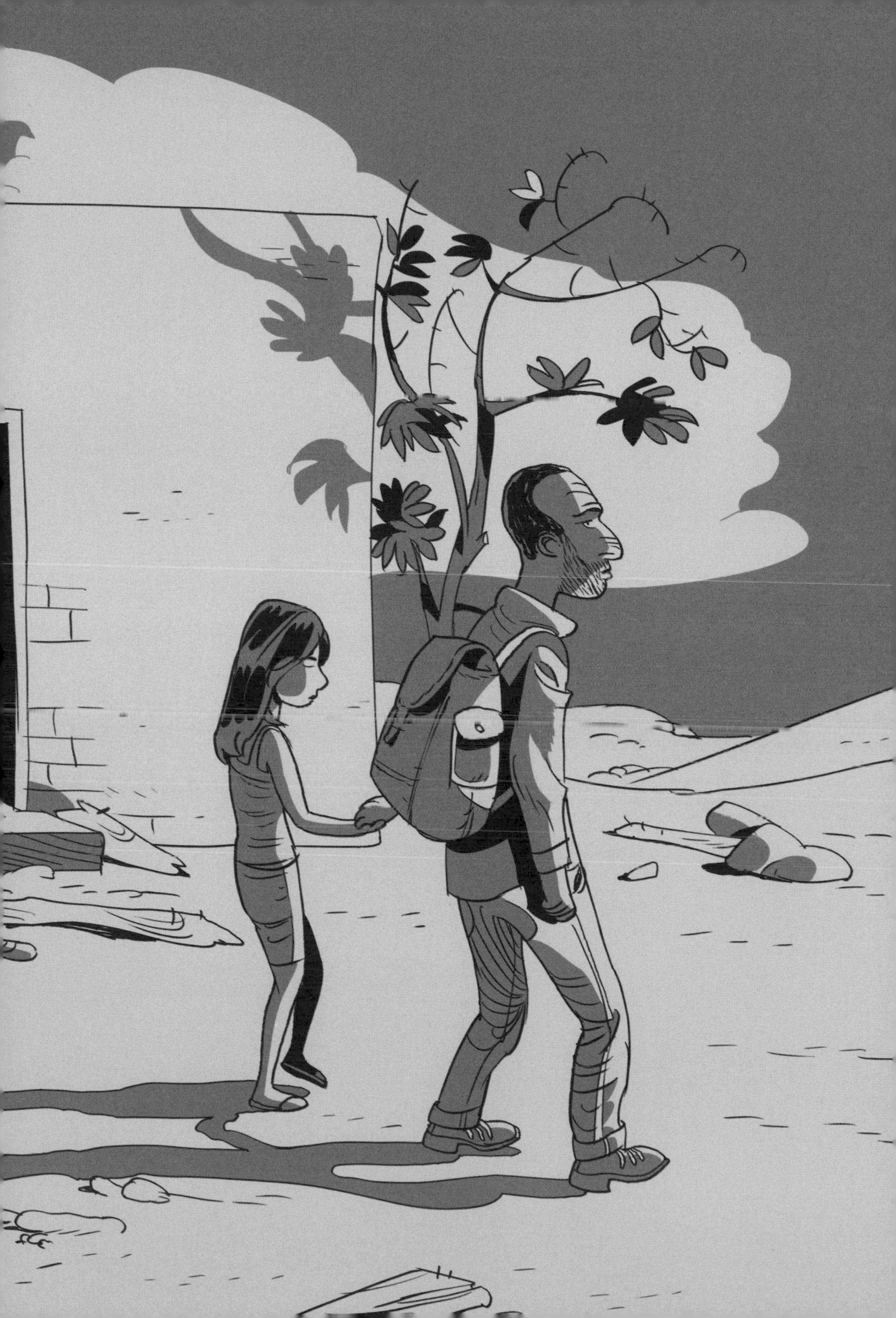

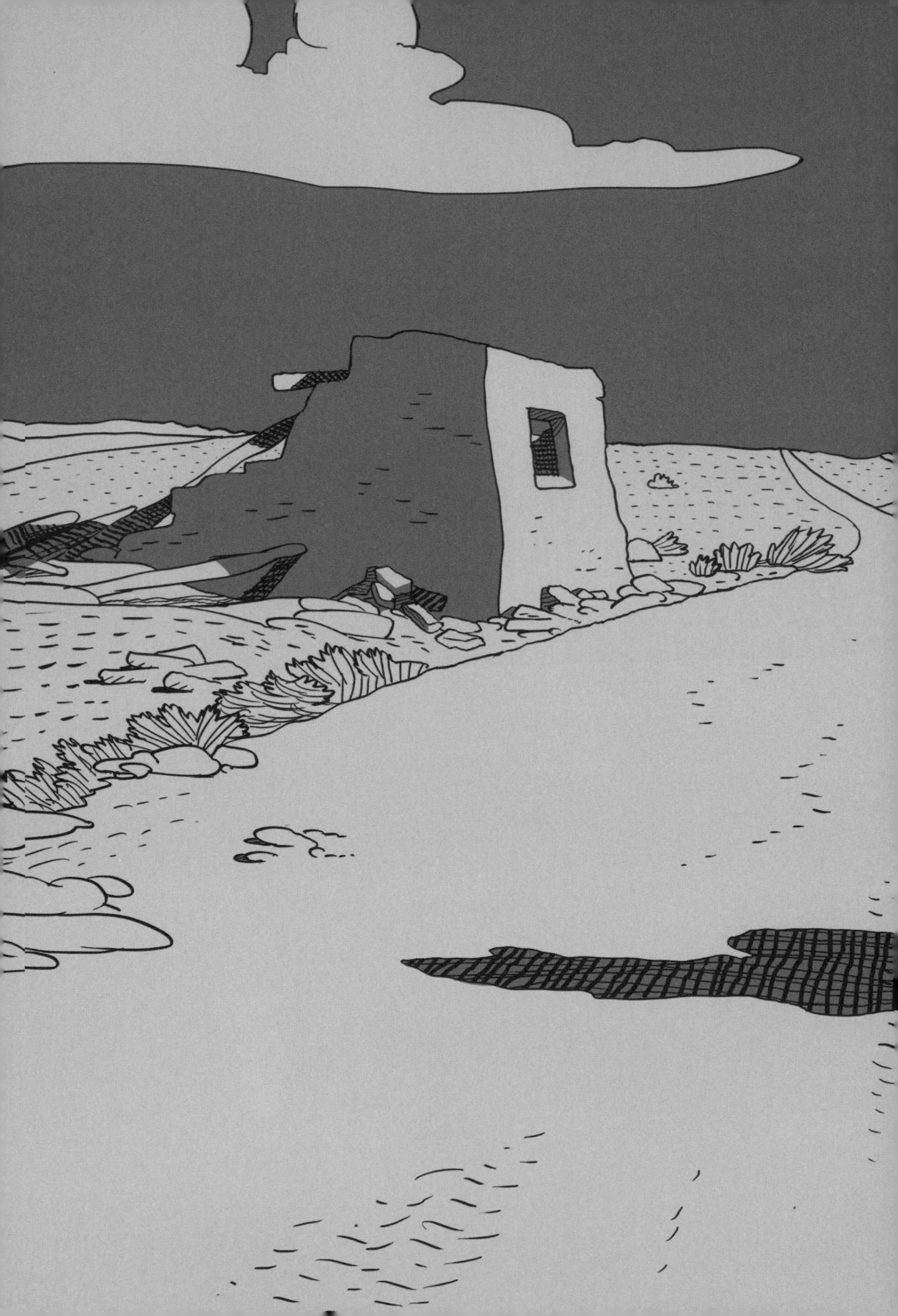

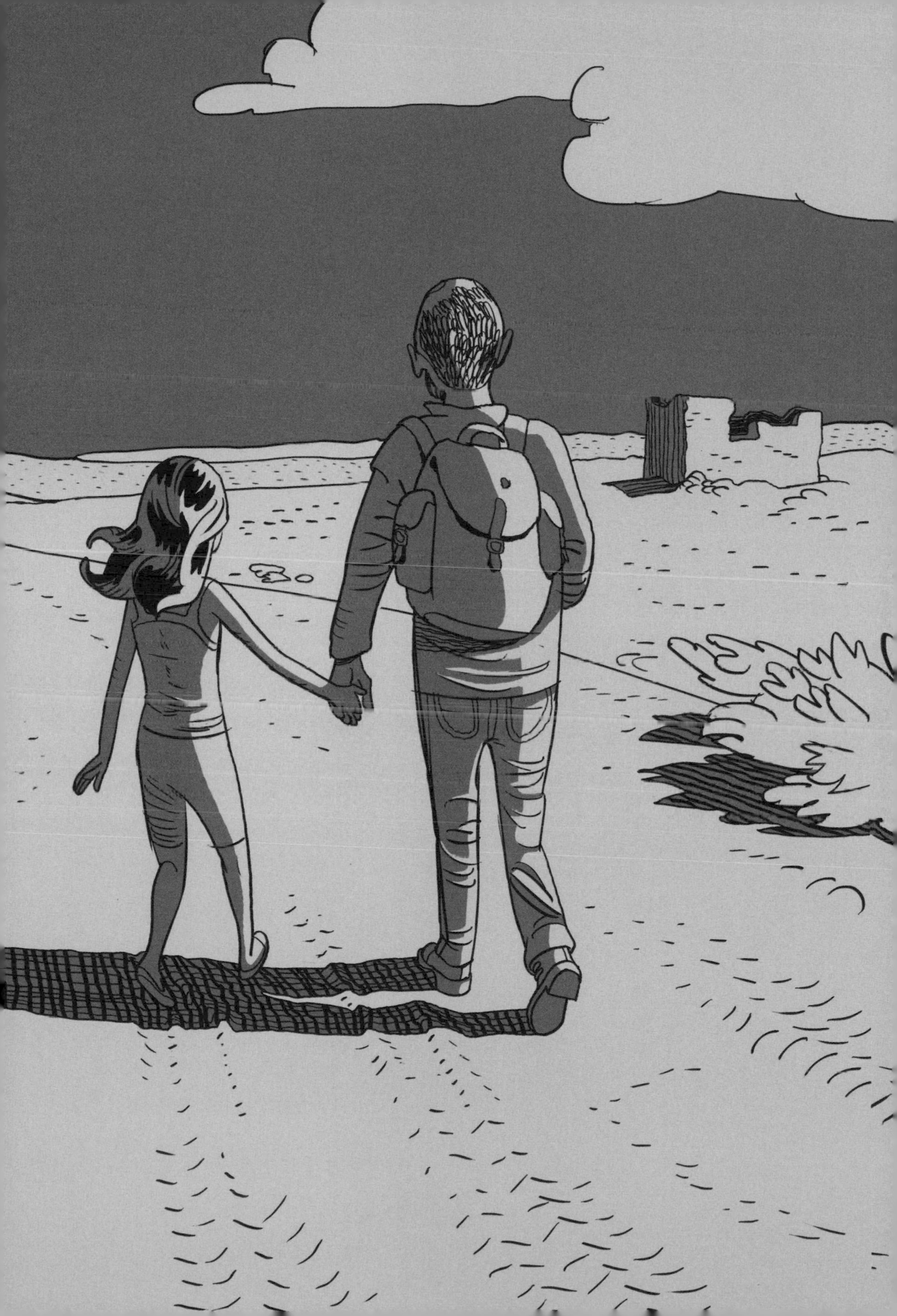

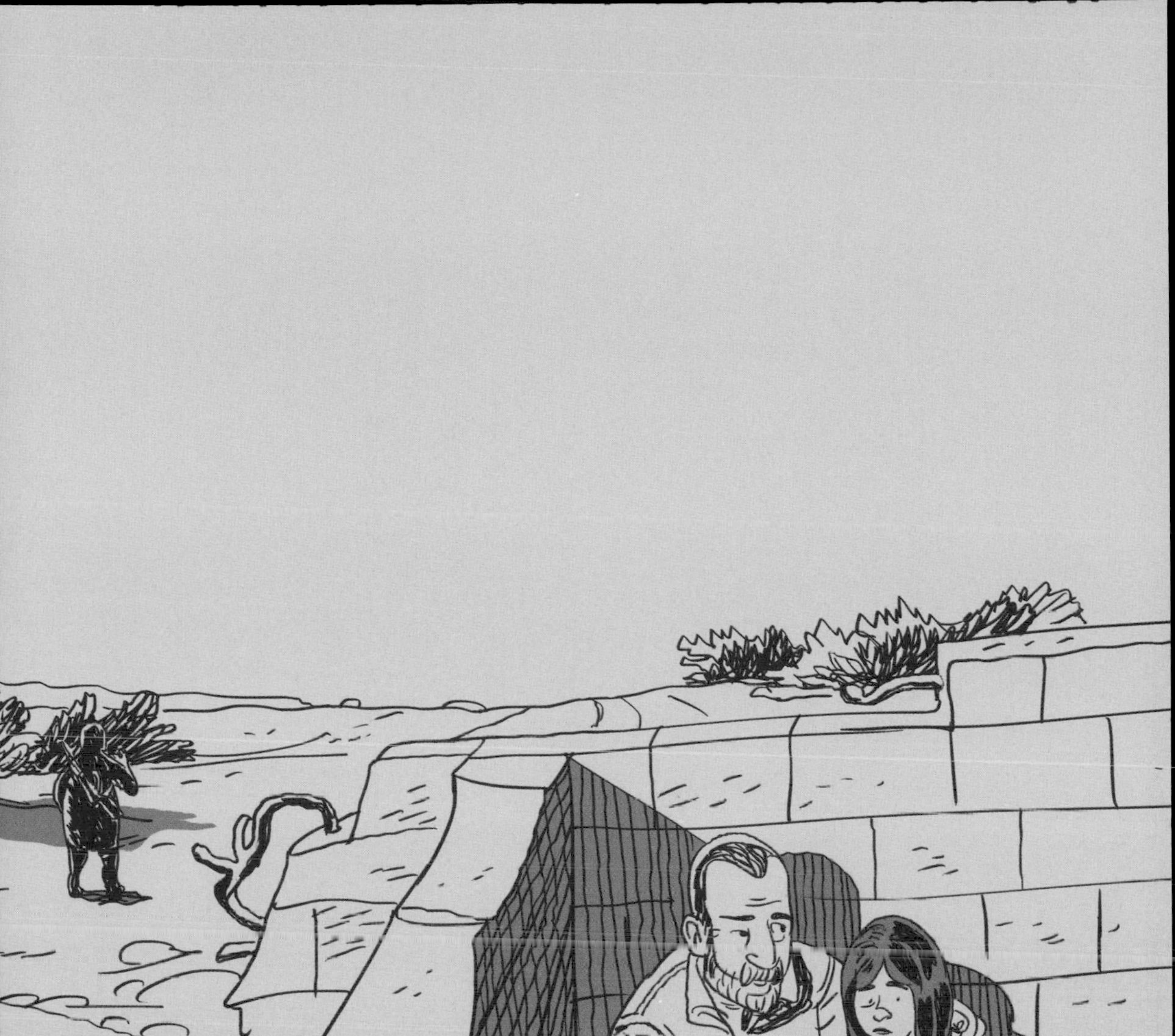

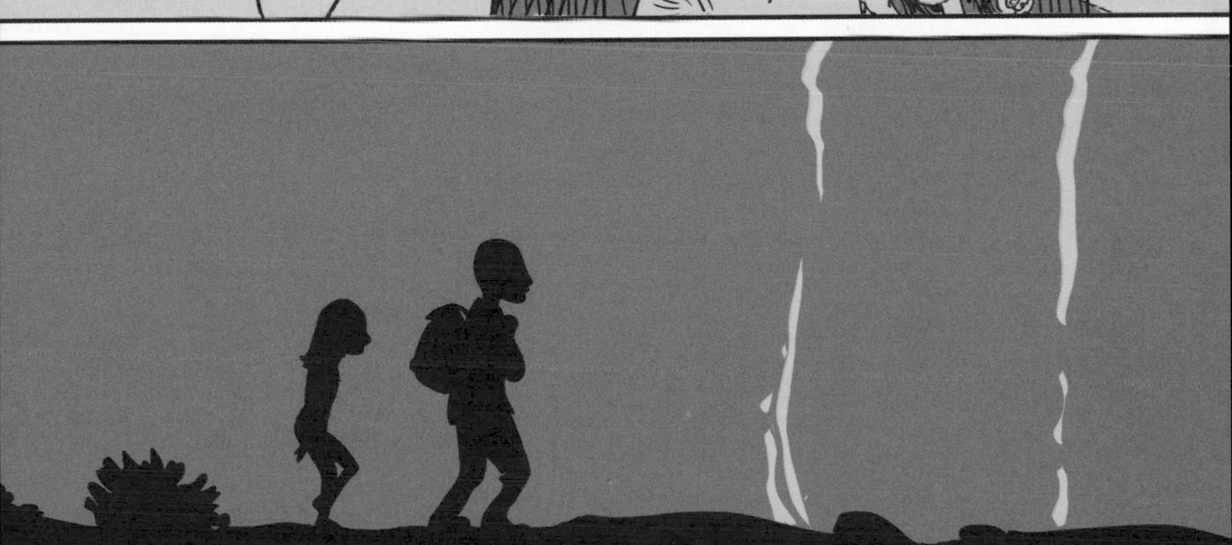

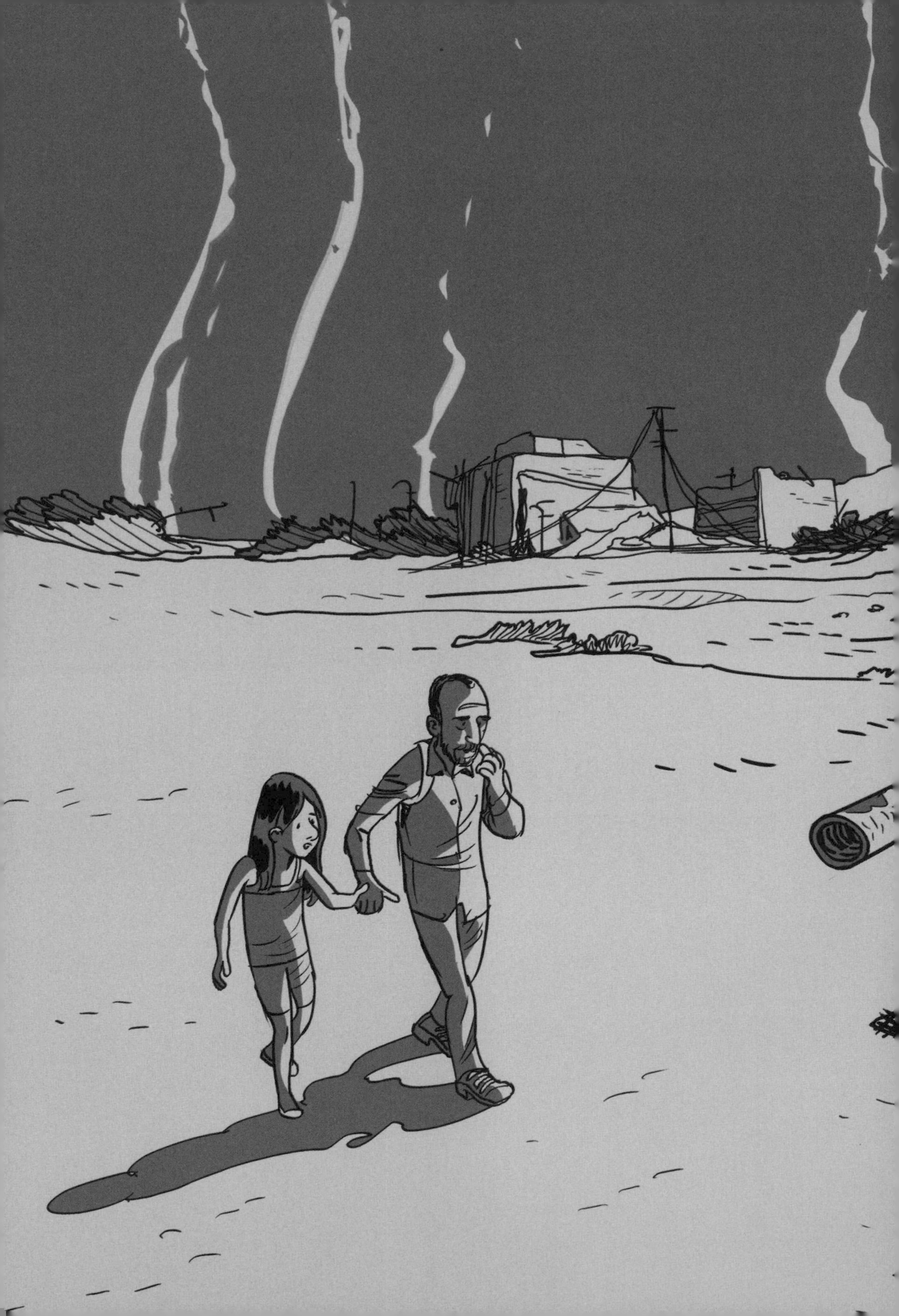

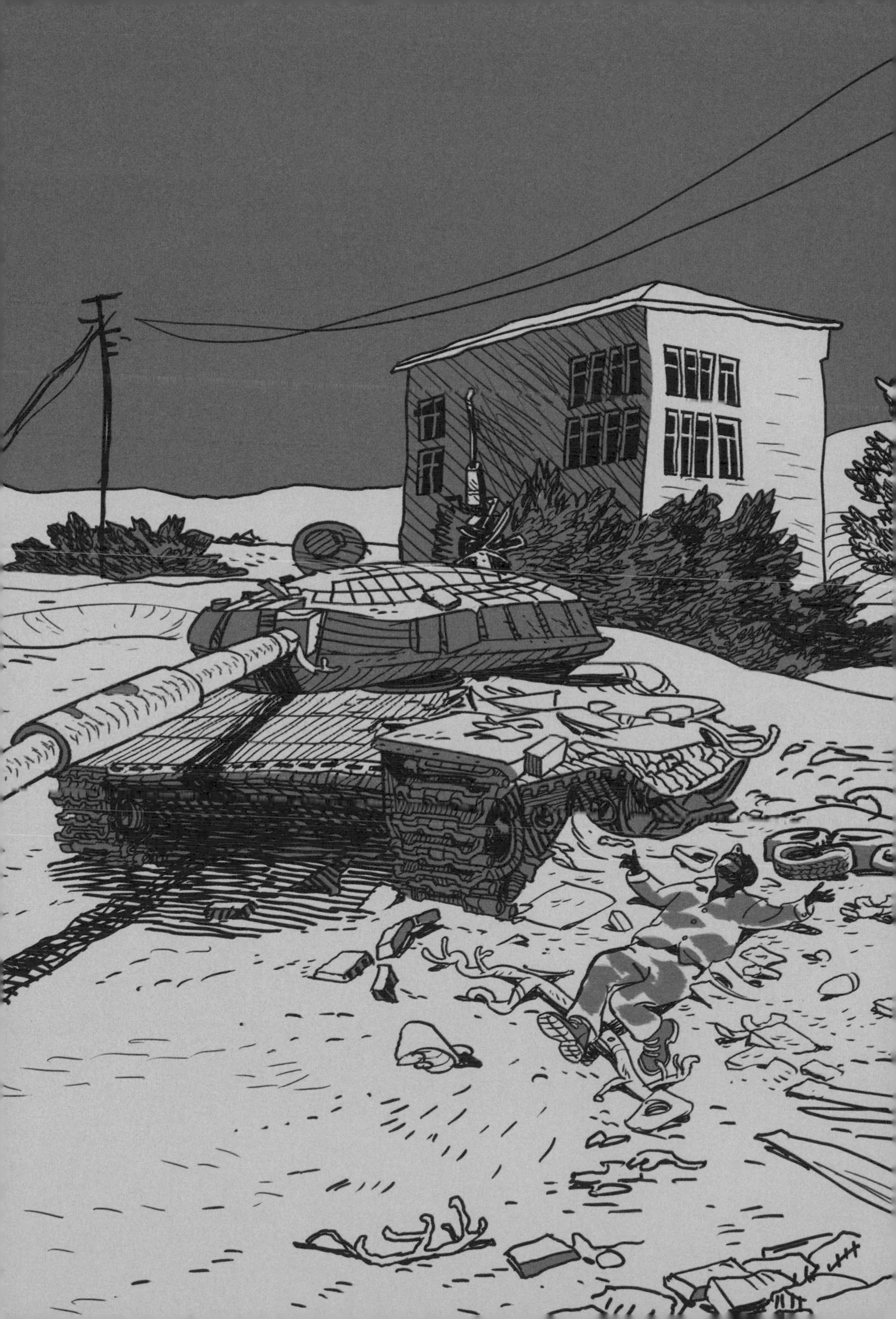

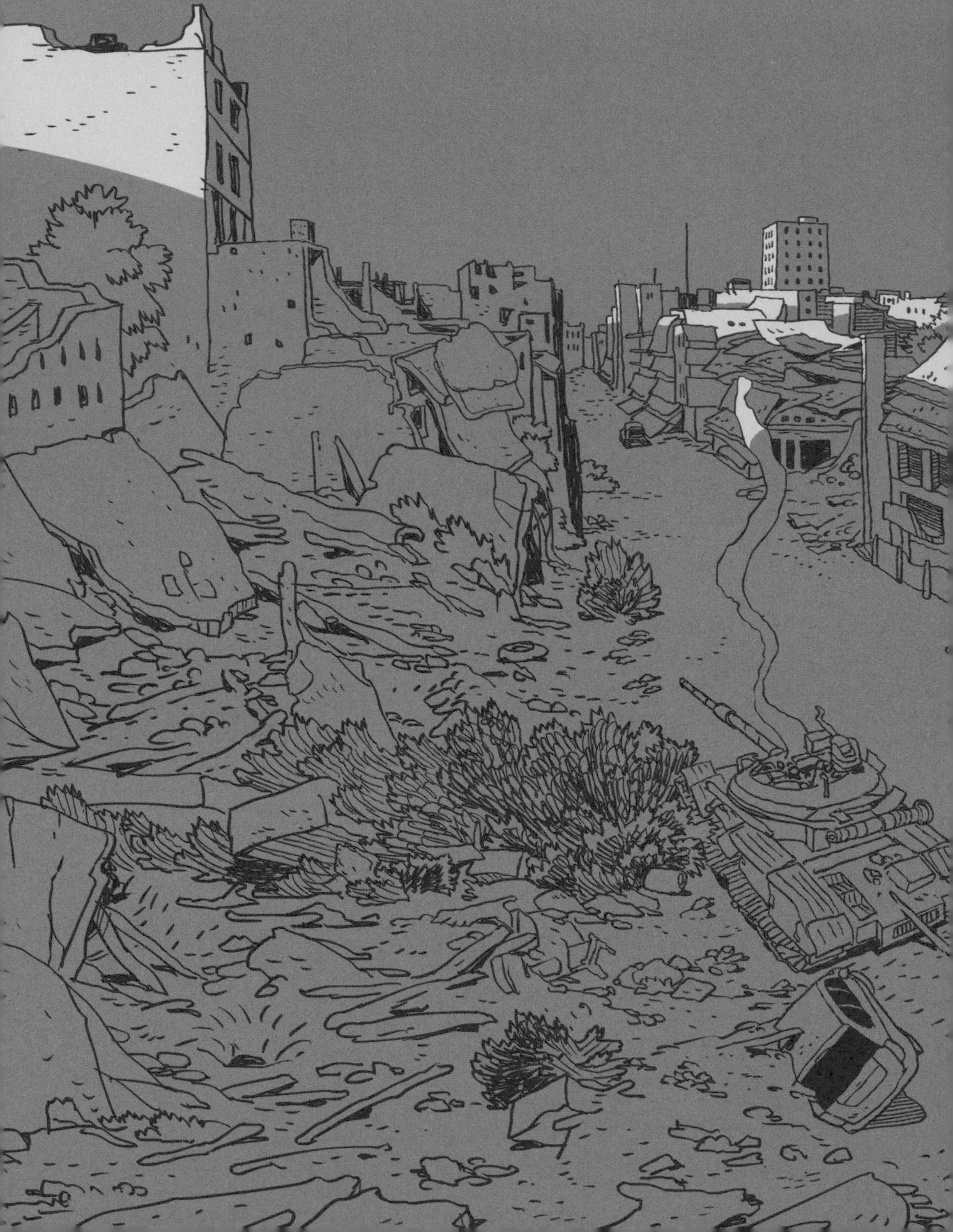

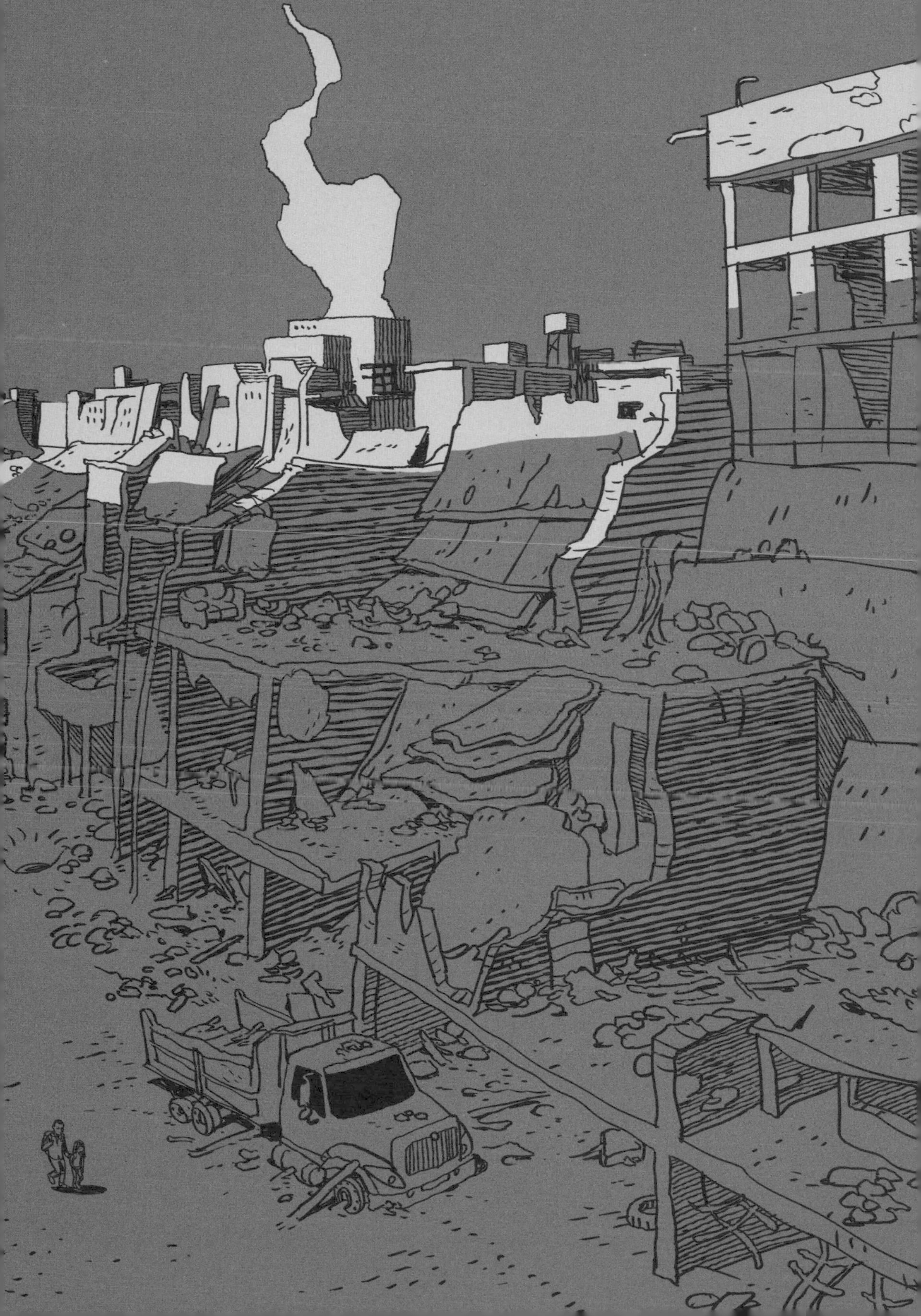

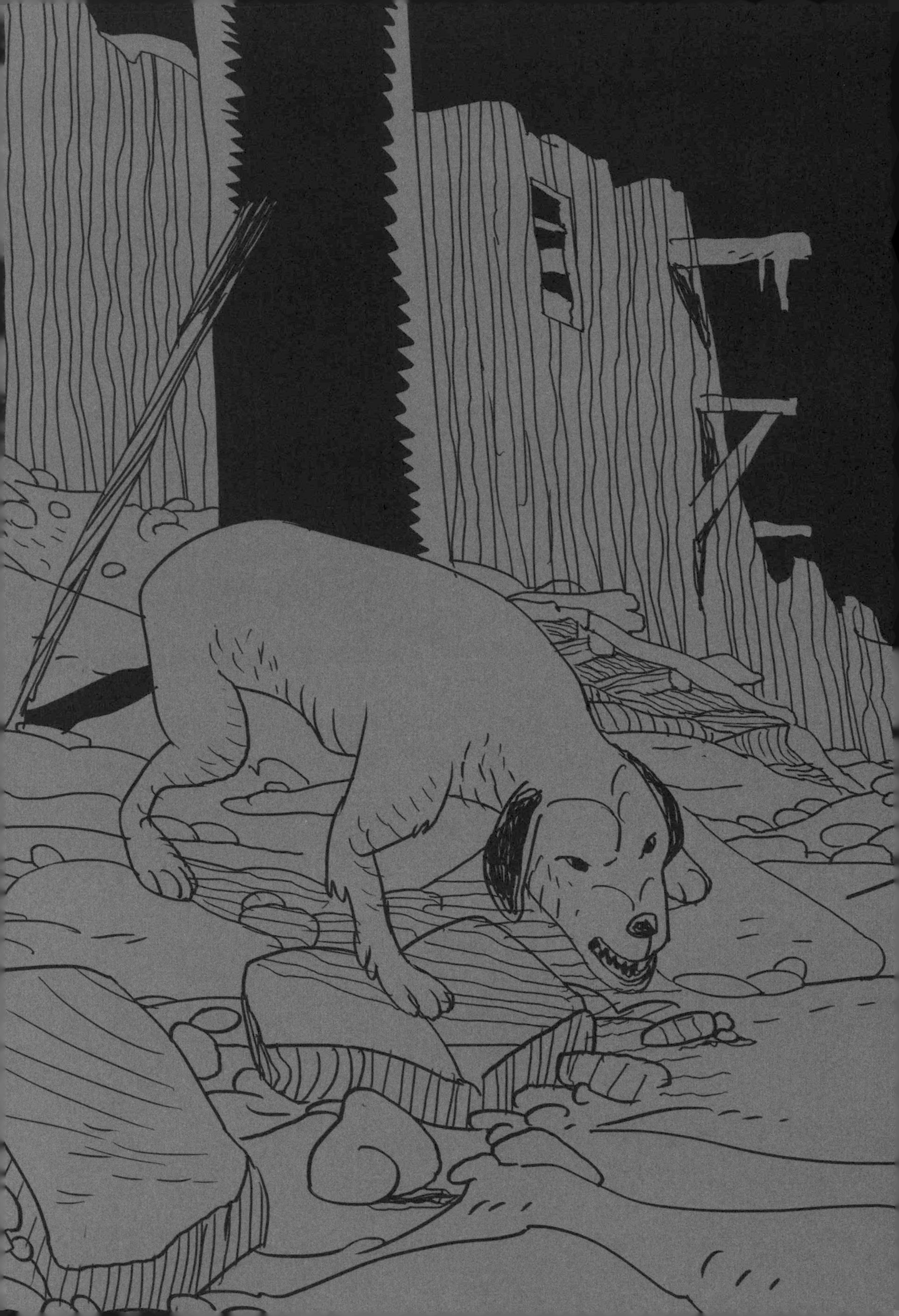

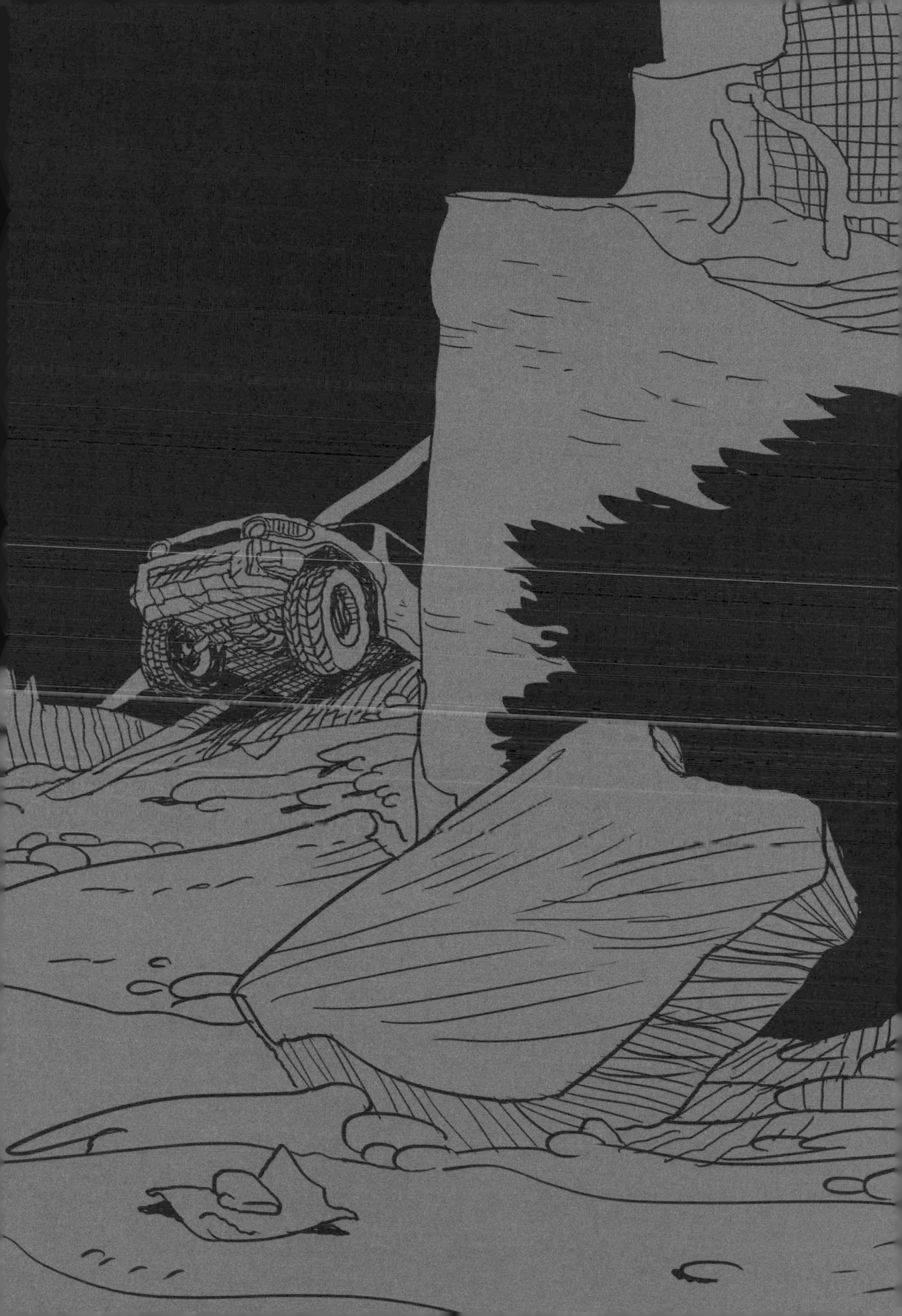

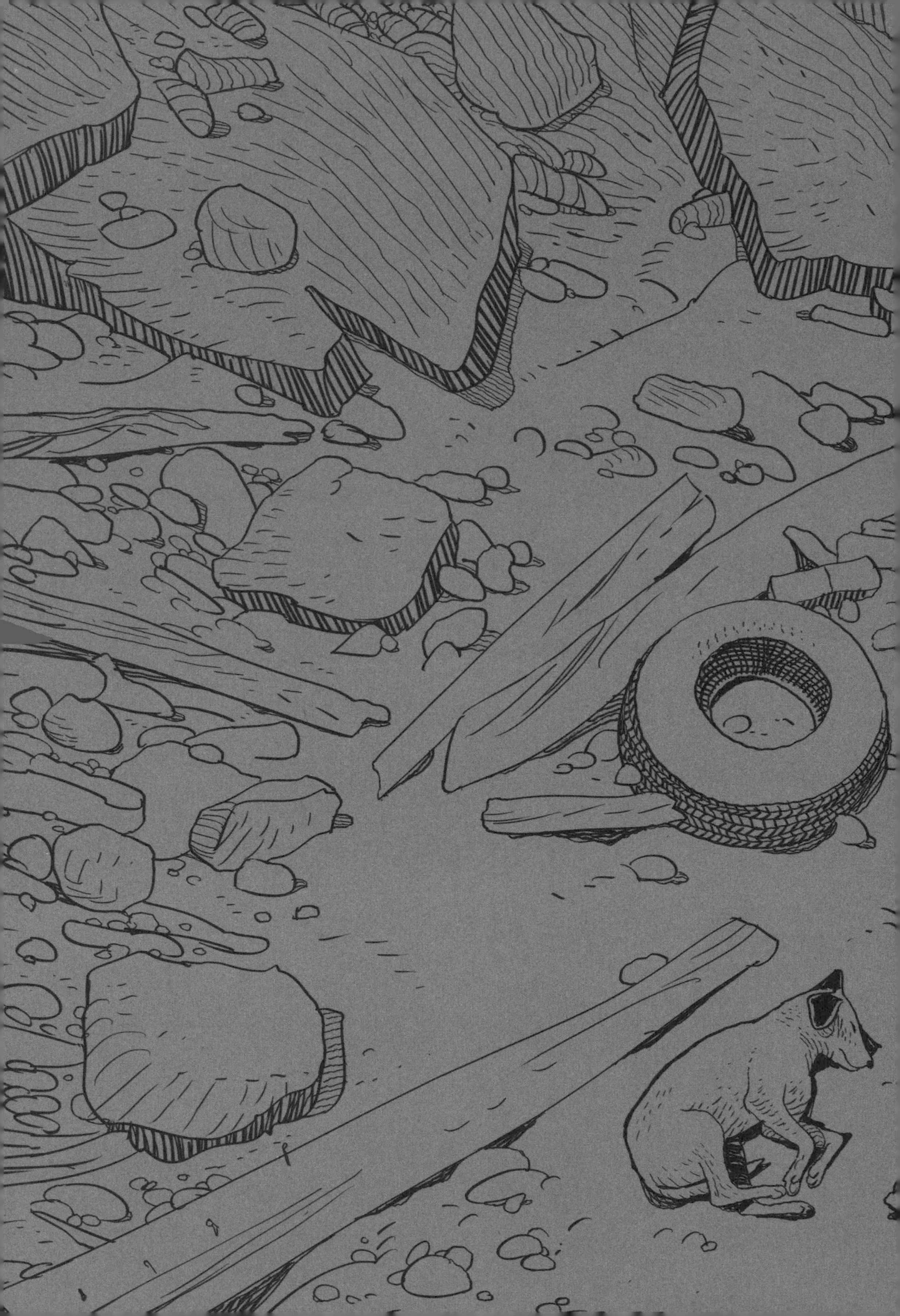

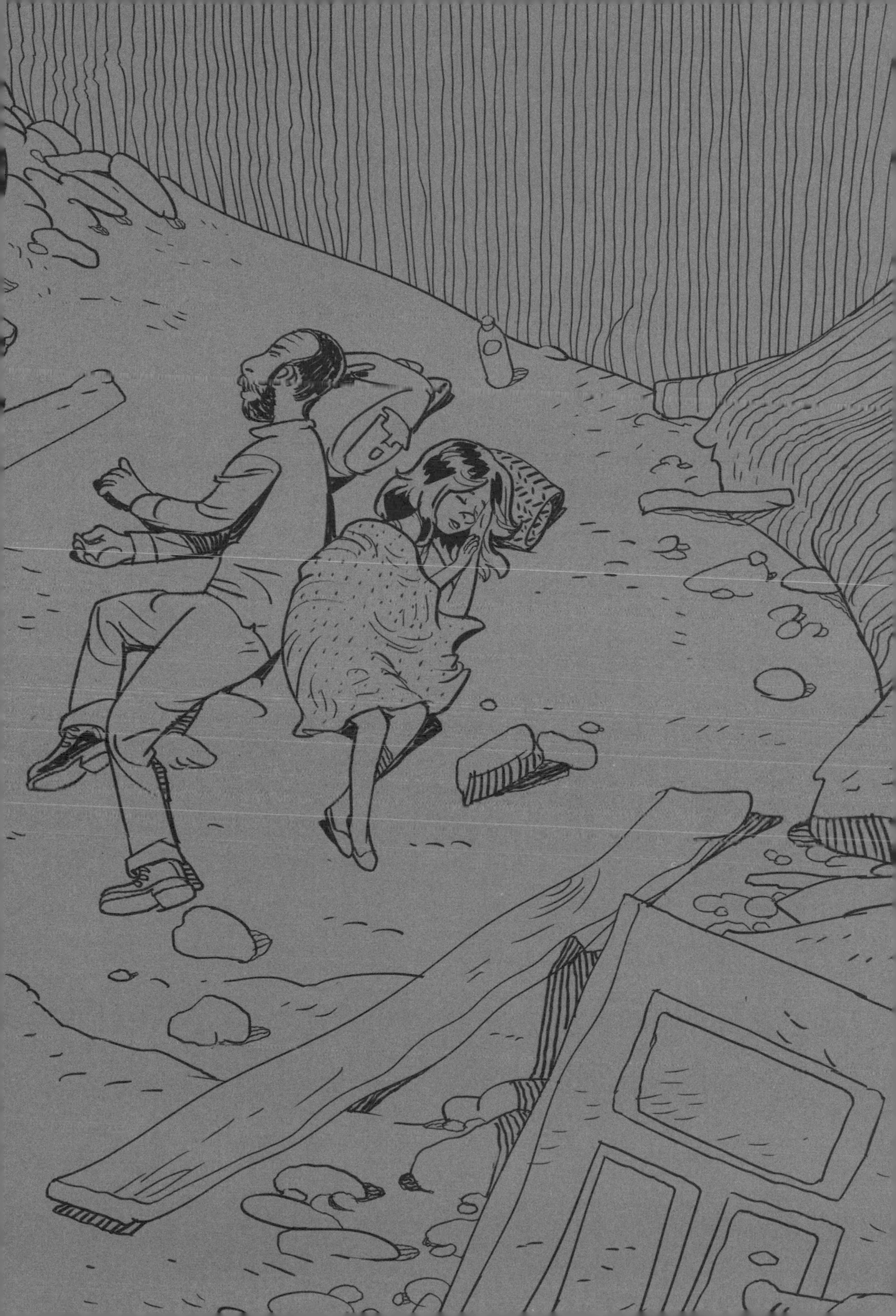

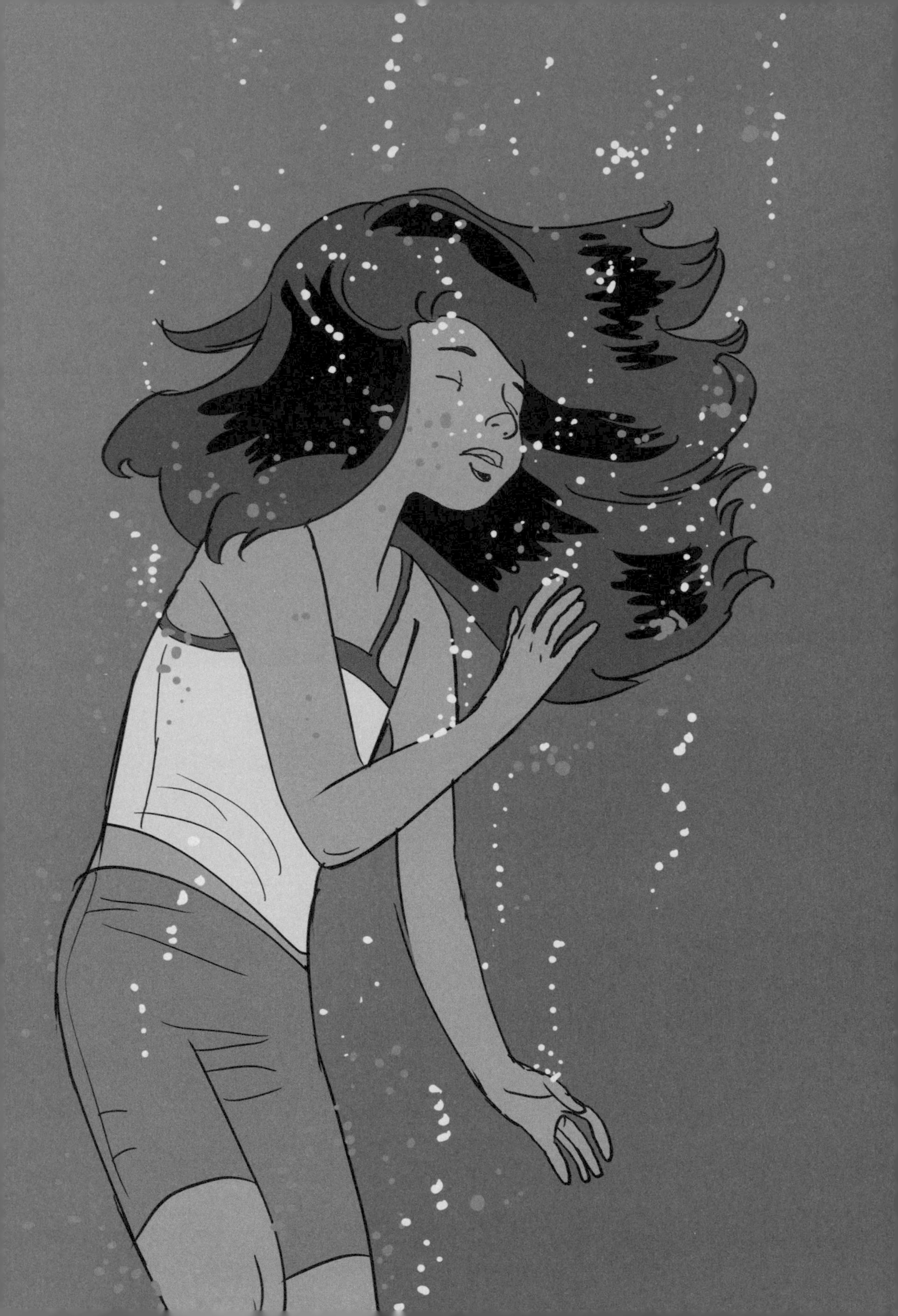

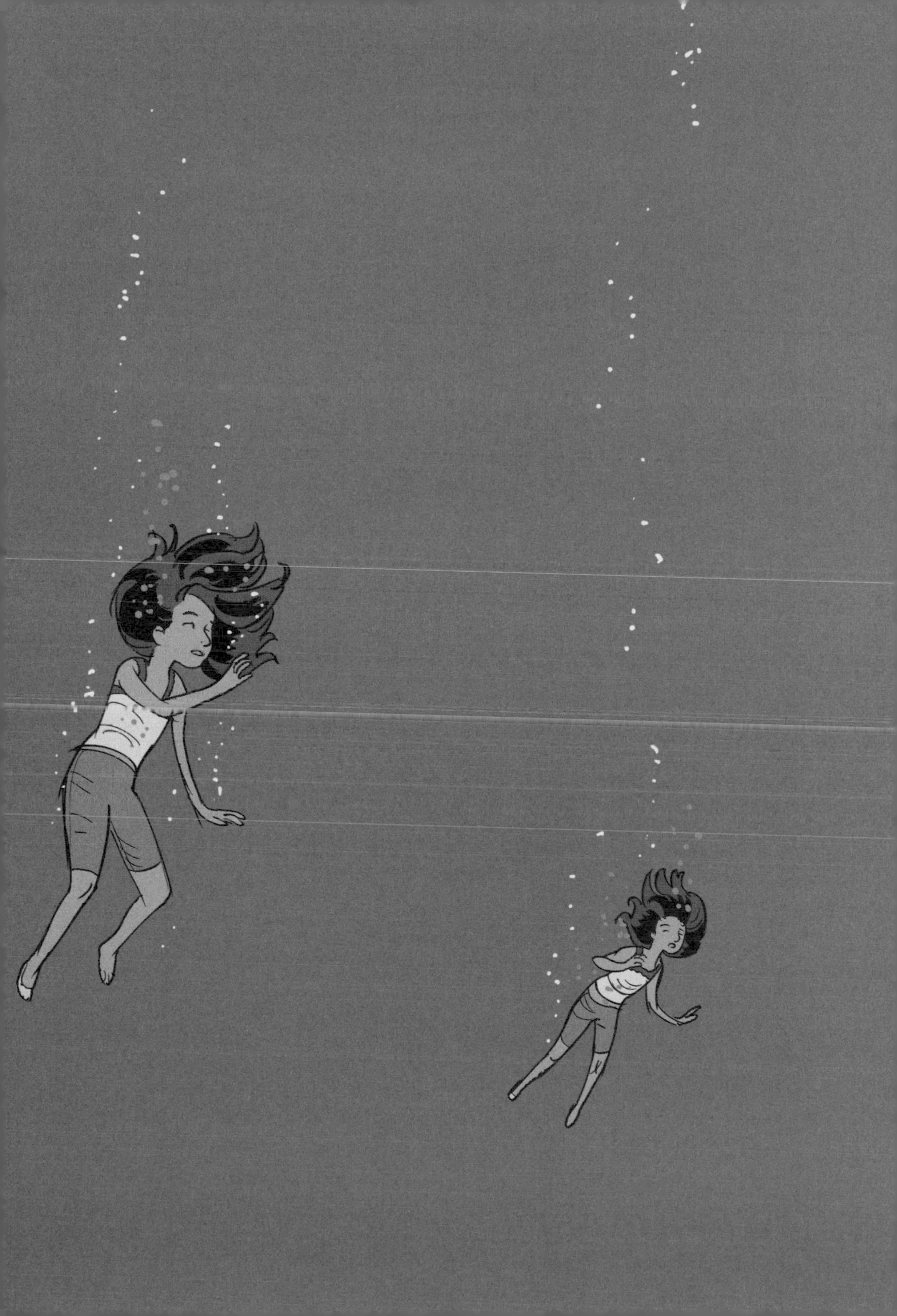

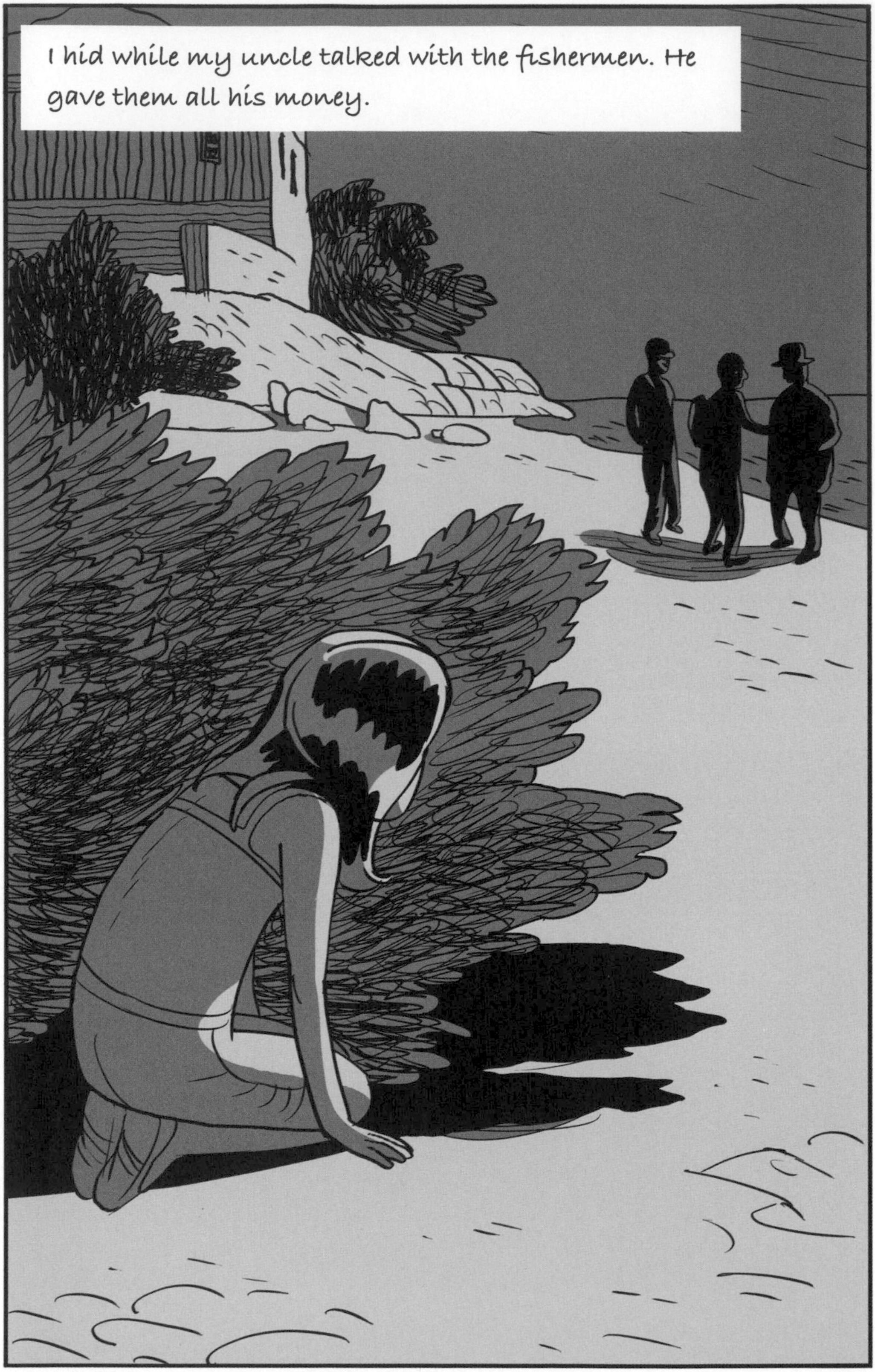
I hid while my uncle talked with the fishermen. He gave them all his money.

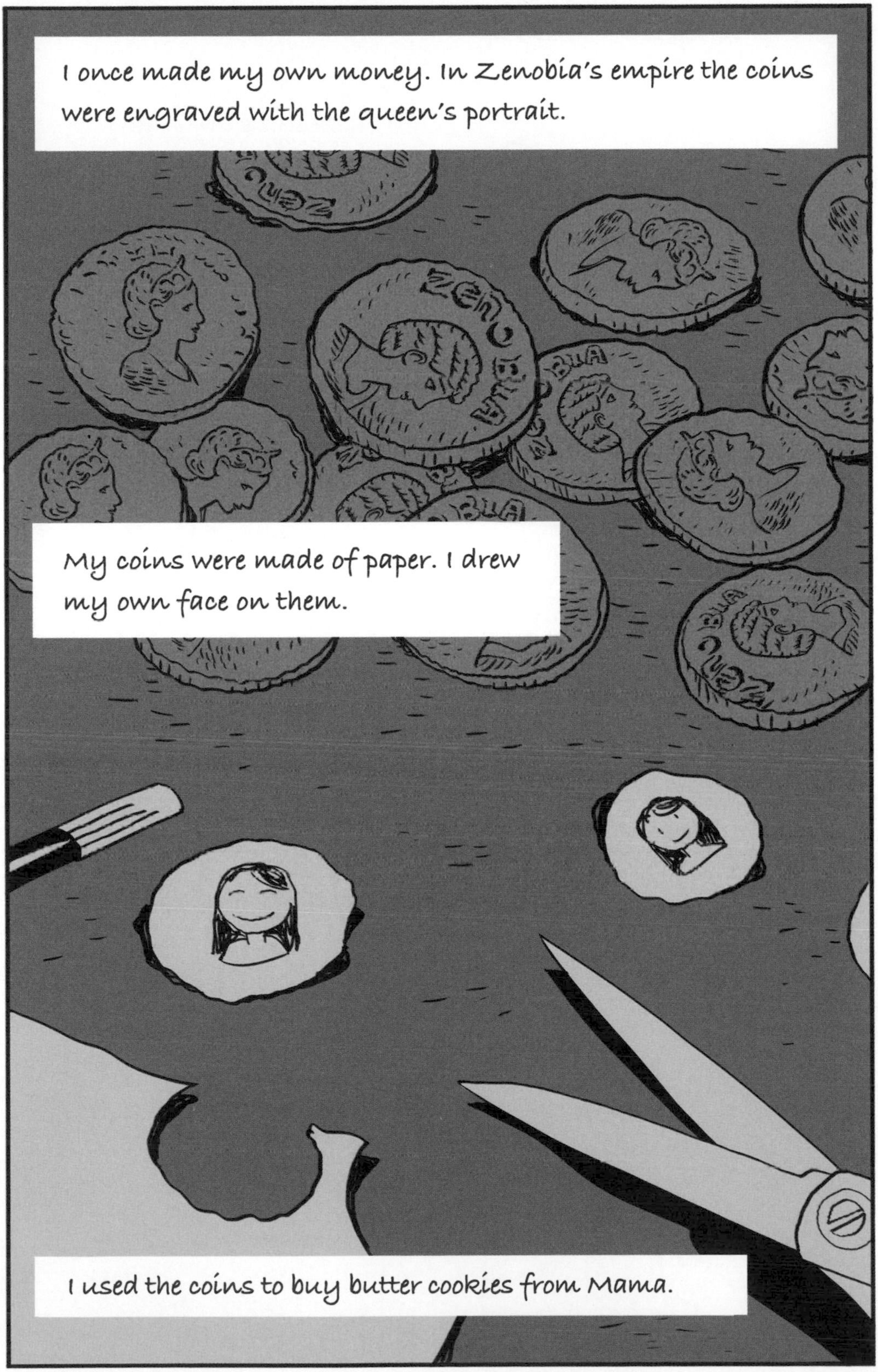
I once made my own money. In Zenobia's empire the coins were engraved with the queen's portrait.
ZENO
ZENOBIA
BIA
My coins were made of paper. I drew my own face on them.
I used the coins to buy butter cookies from Mama.

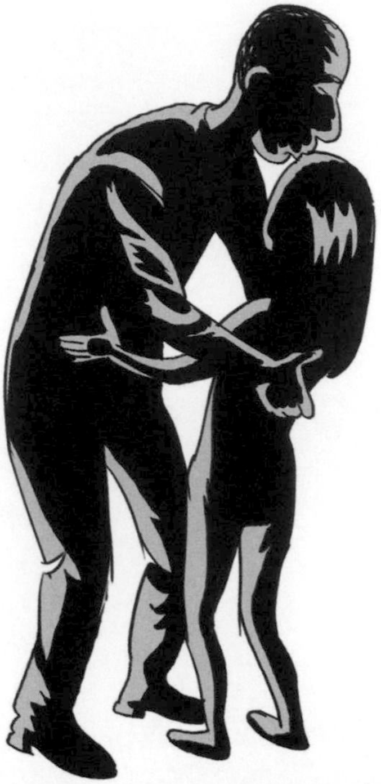

There was not enough money for two people. My Uncle wept when we said goodbye.

I will be all right, Uncle. Remember Zenobia. If she can do it, so can I.
I will be all right, Uncle.

That's what I said.

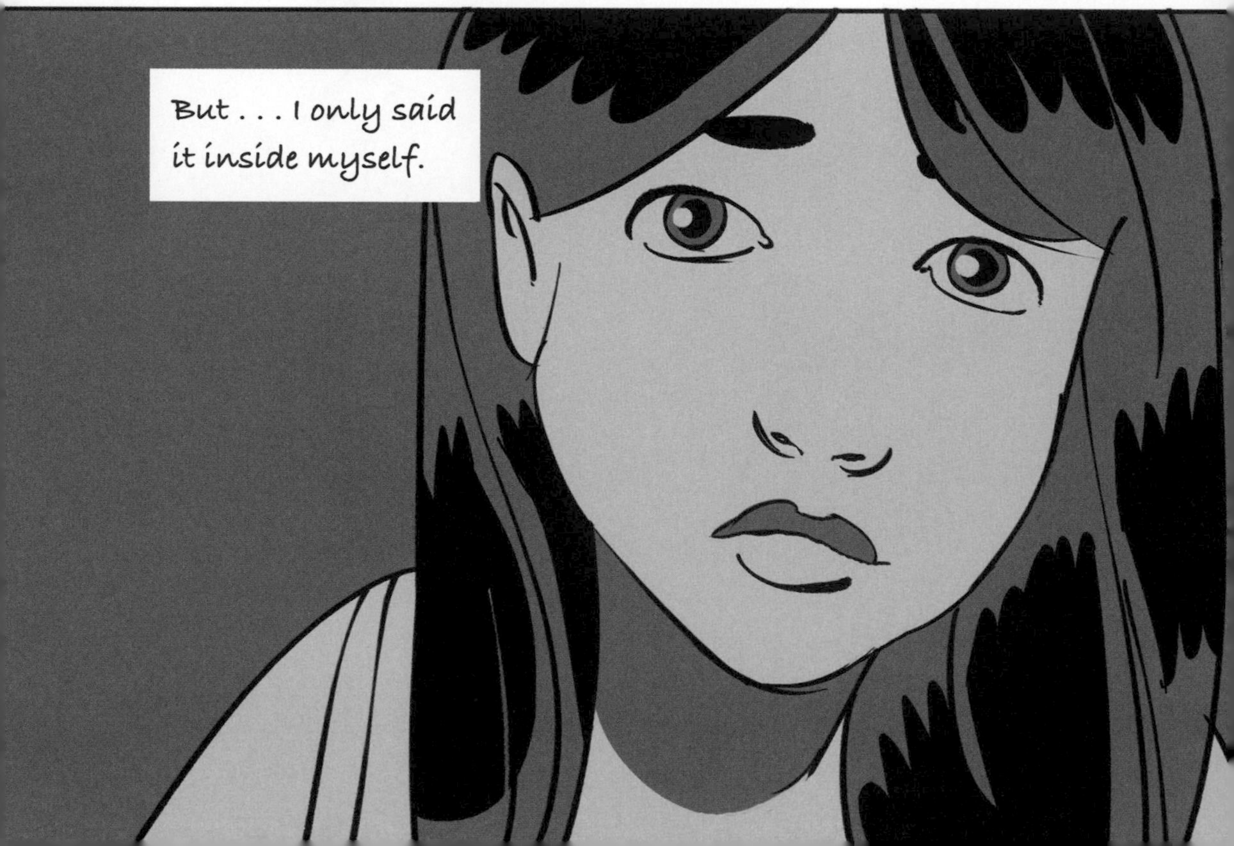
But . . . I only said it inside myself.

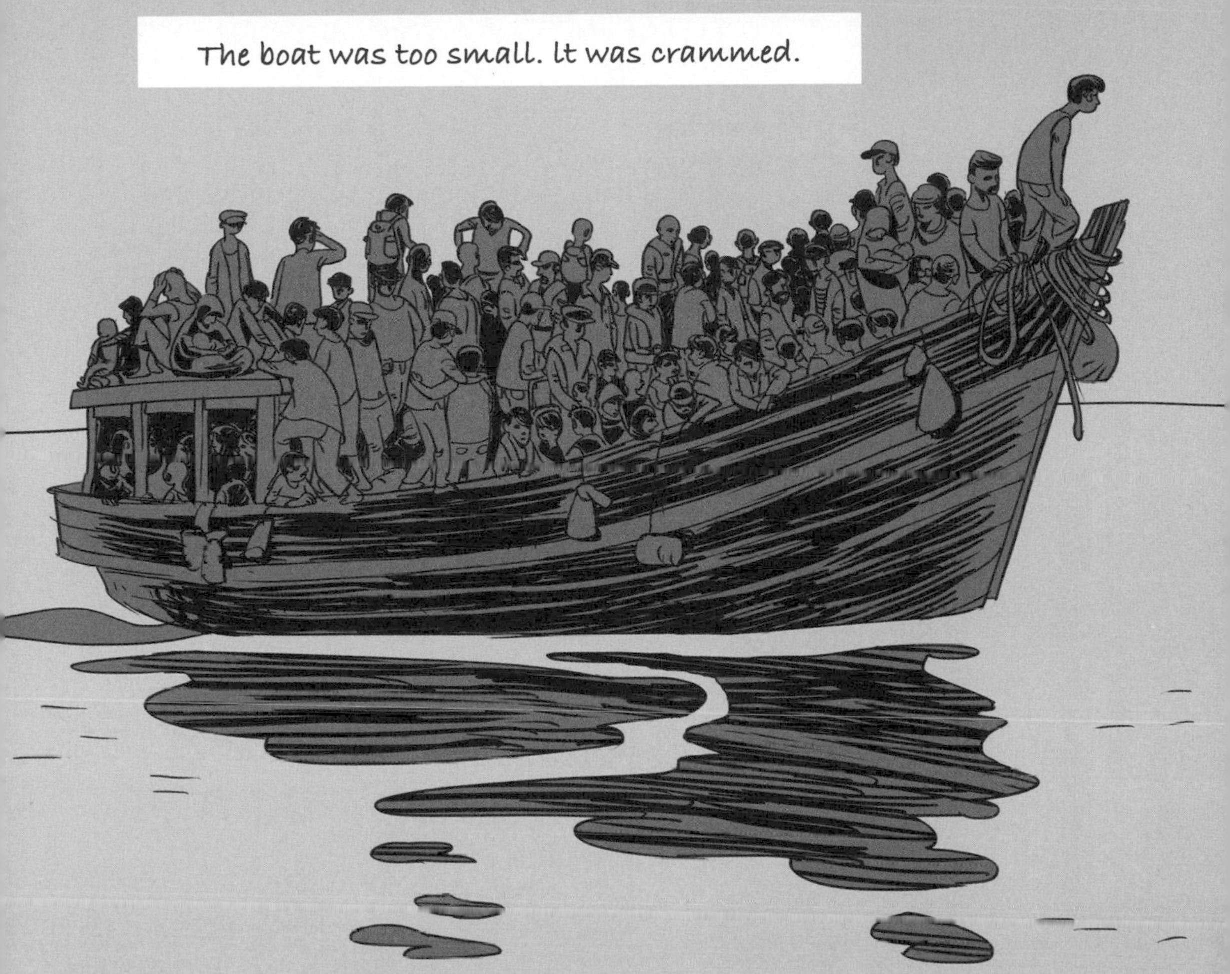
The boat was too small. It was crammed.

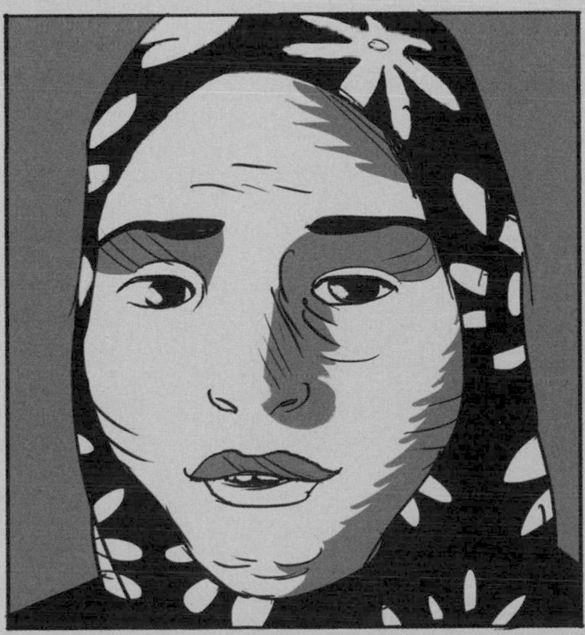

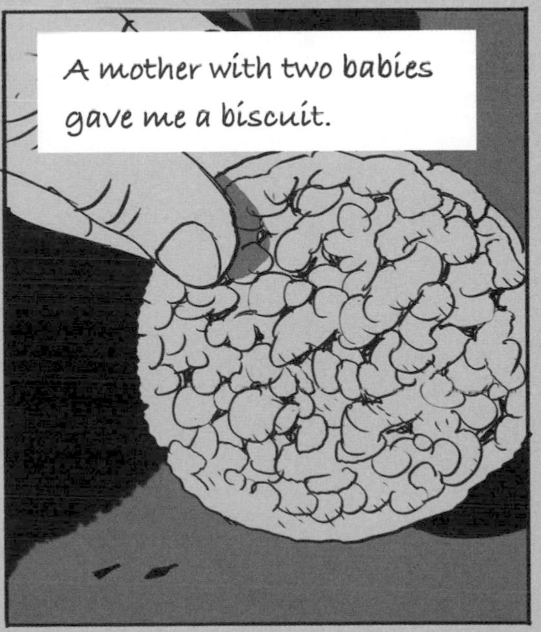
A mother with two babies gave me a biscuit.

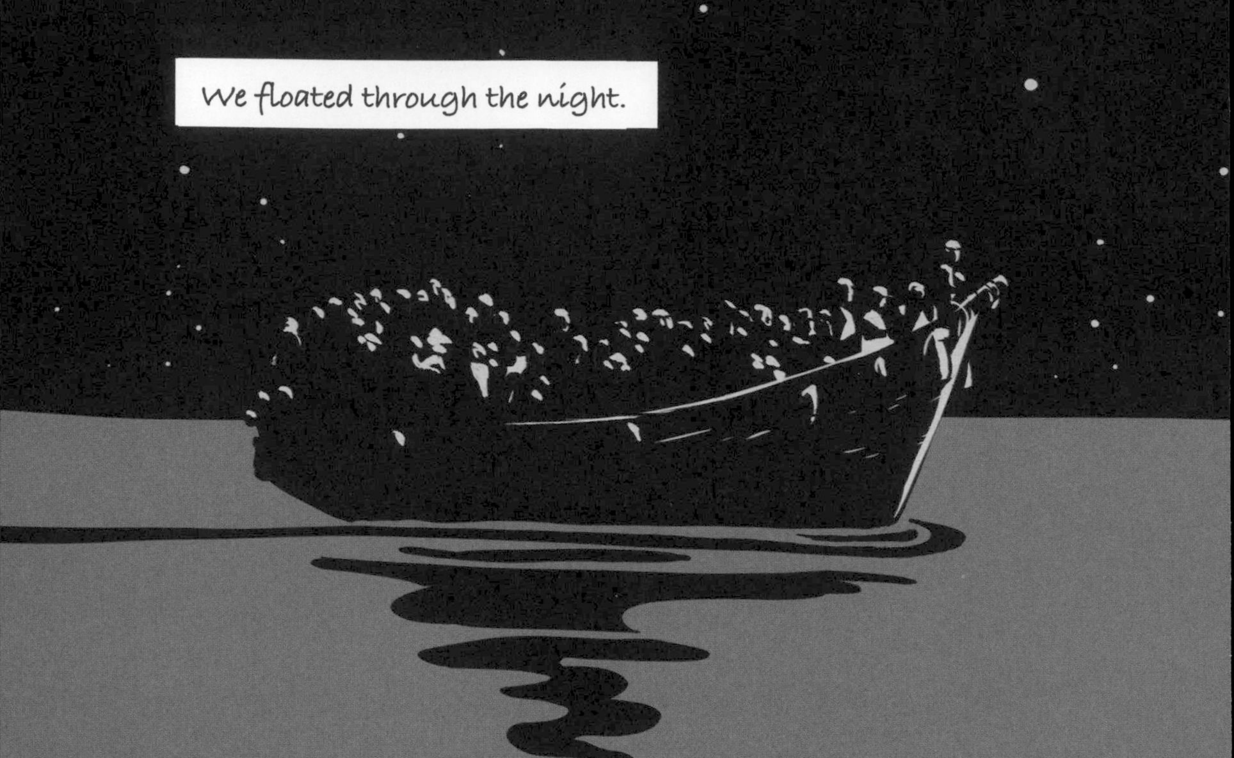
We floated through the night.

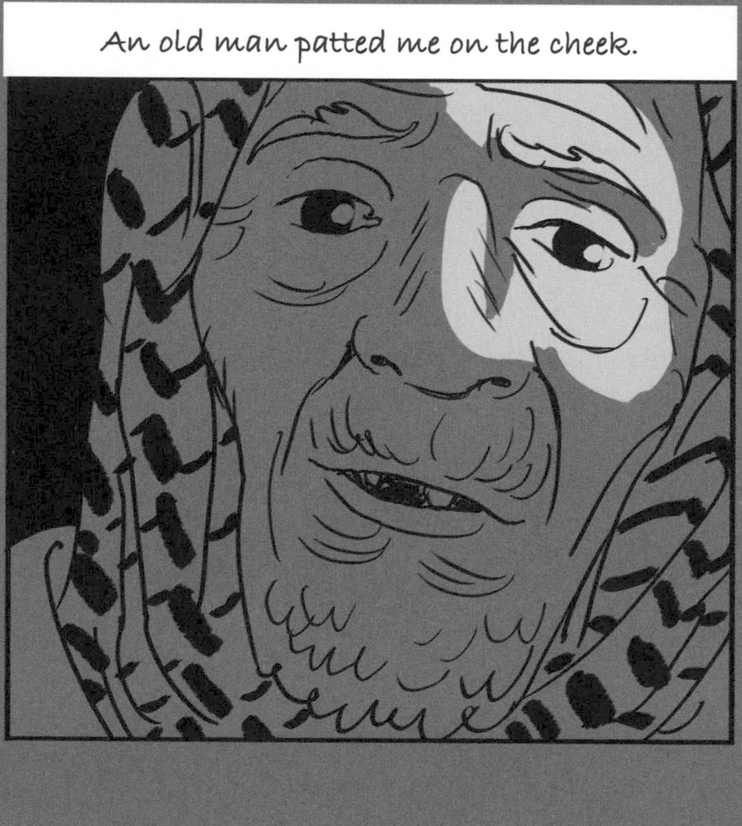
An old man patted me on the cheek.

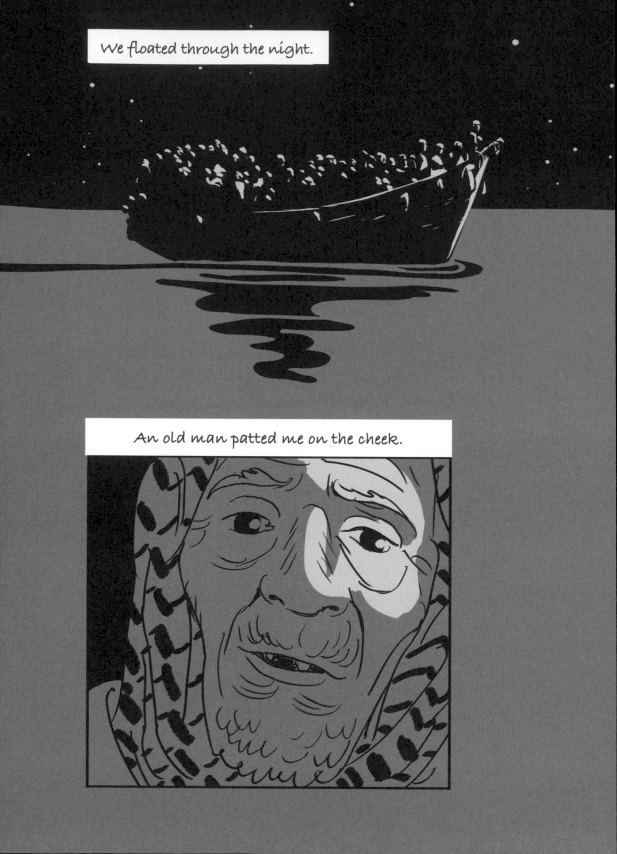

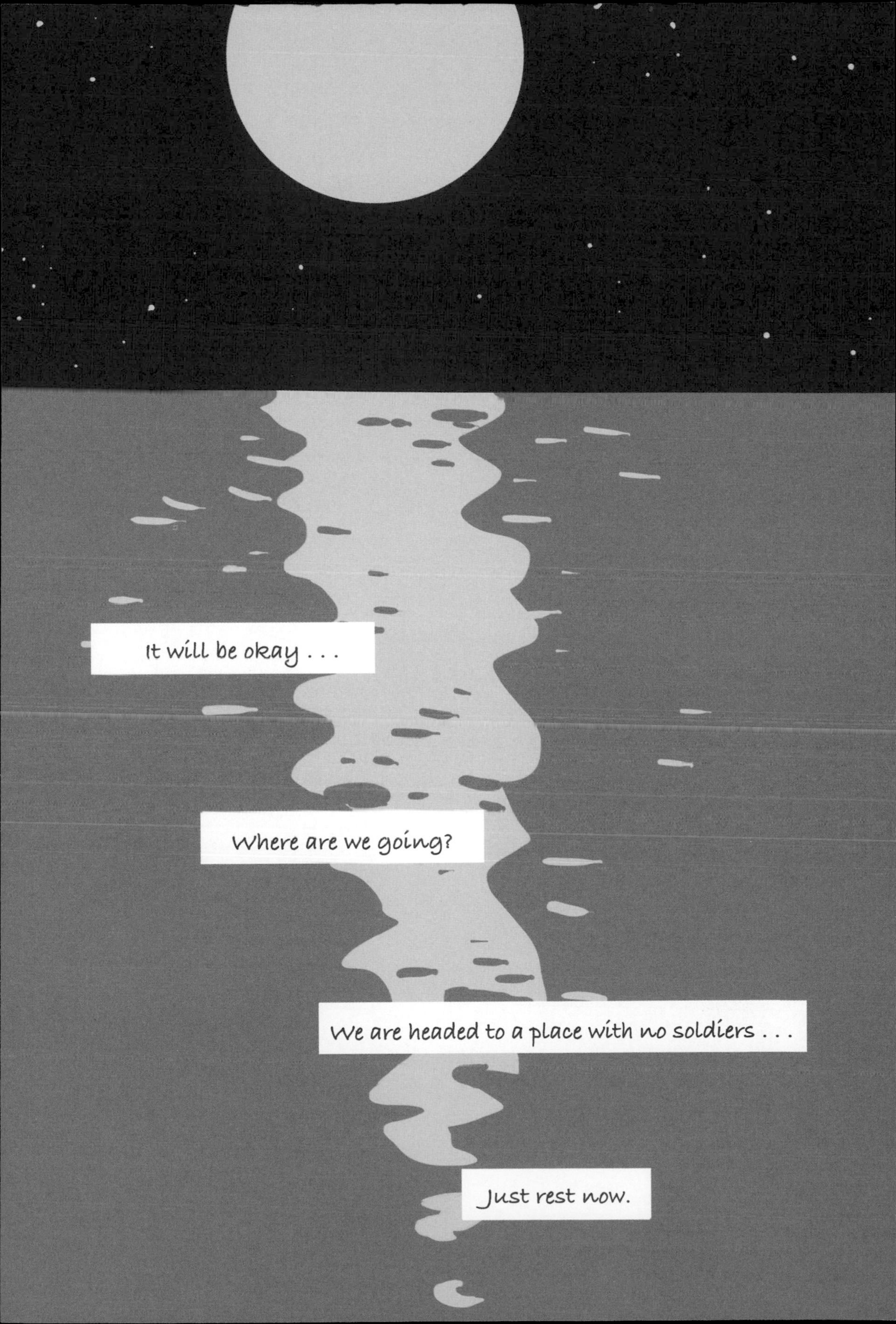
It will be okay . . .
Where are we going?
We are headed to a place with no soldiers . . .
Just rest now.

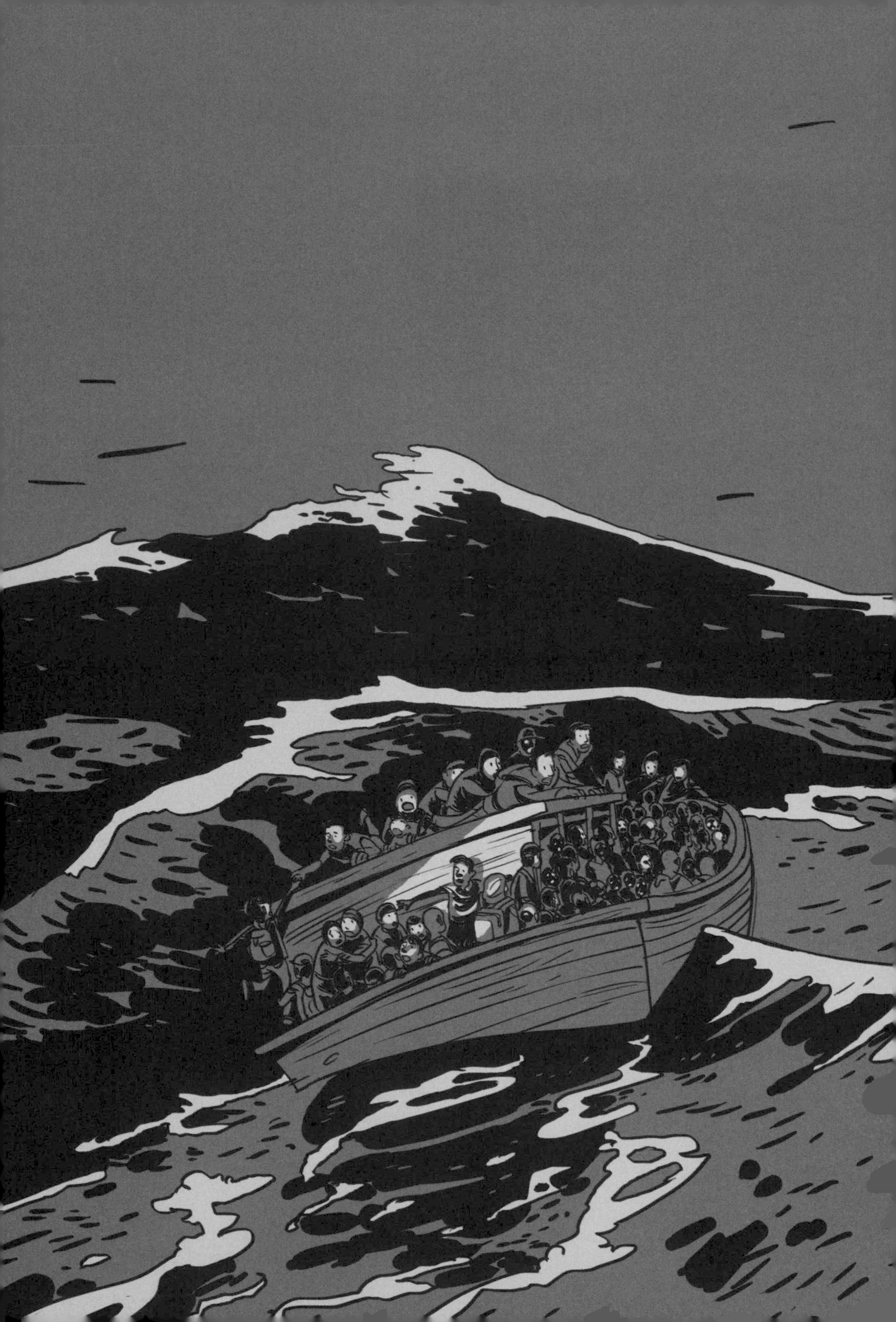

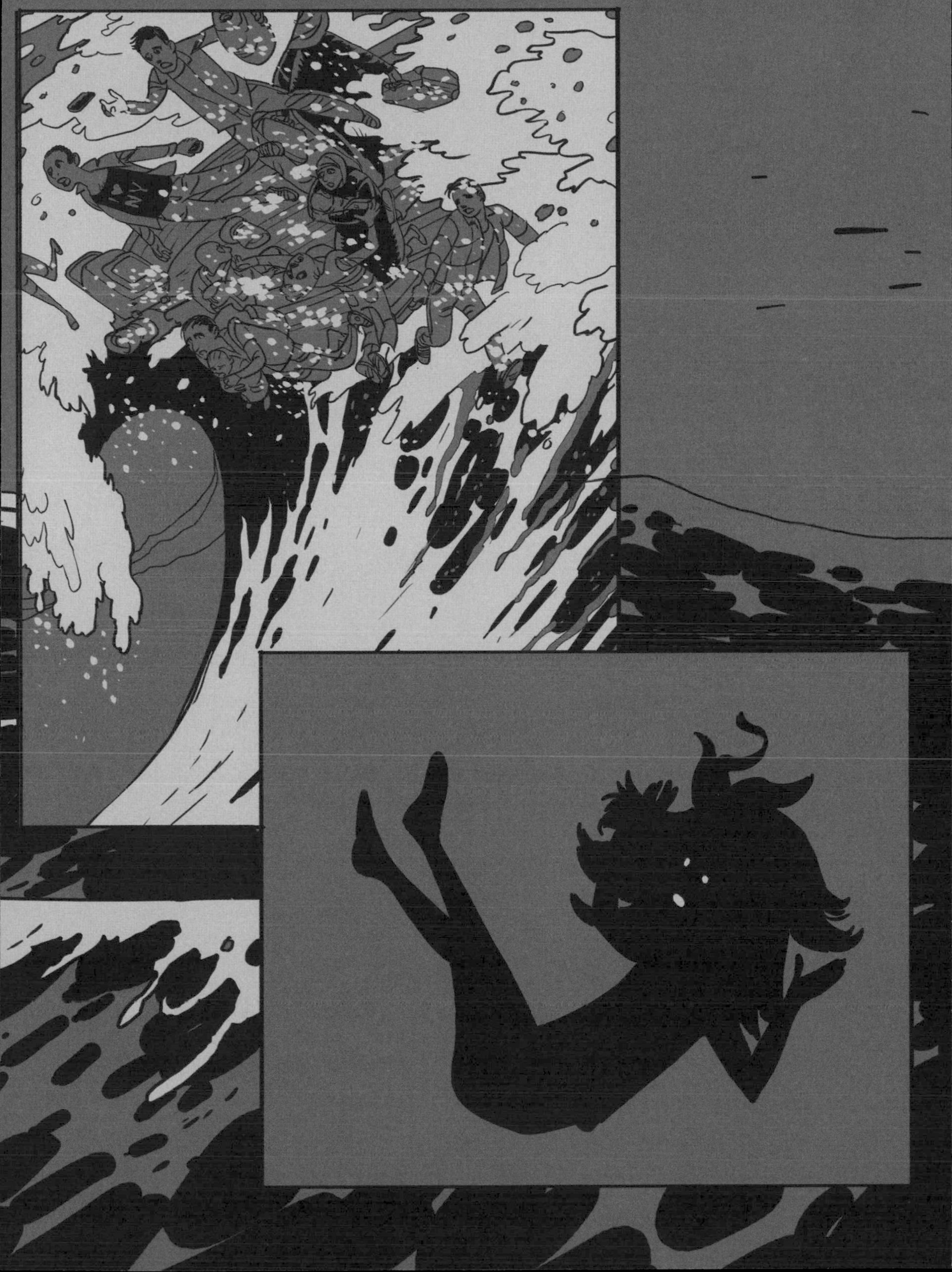
I ♥ NY

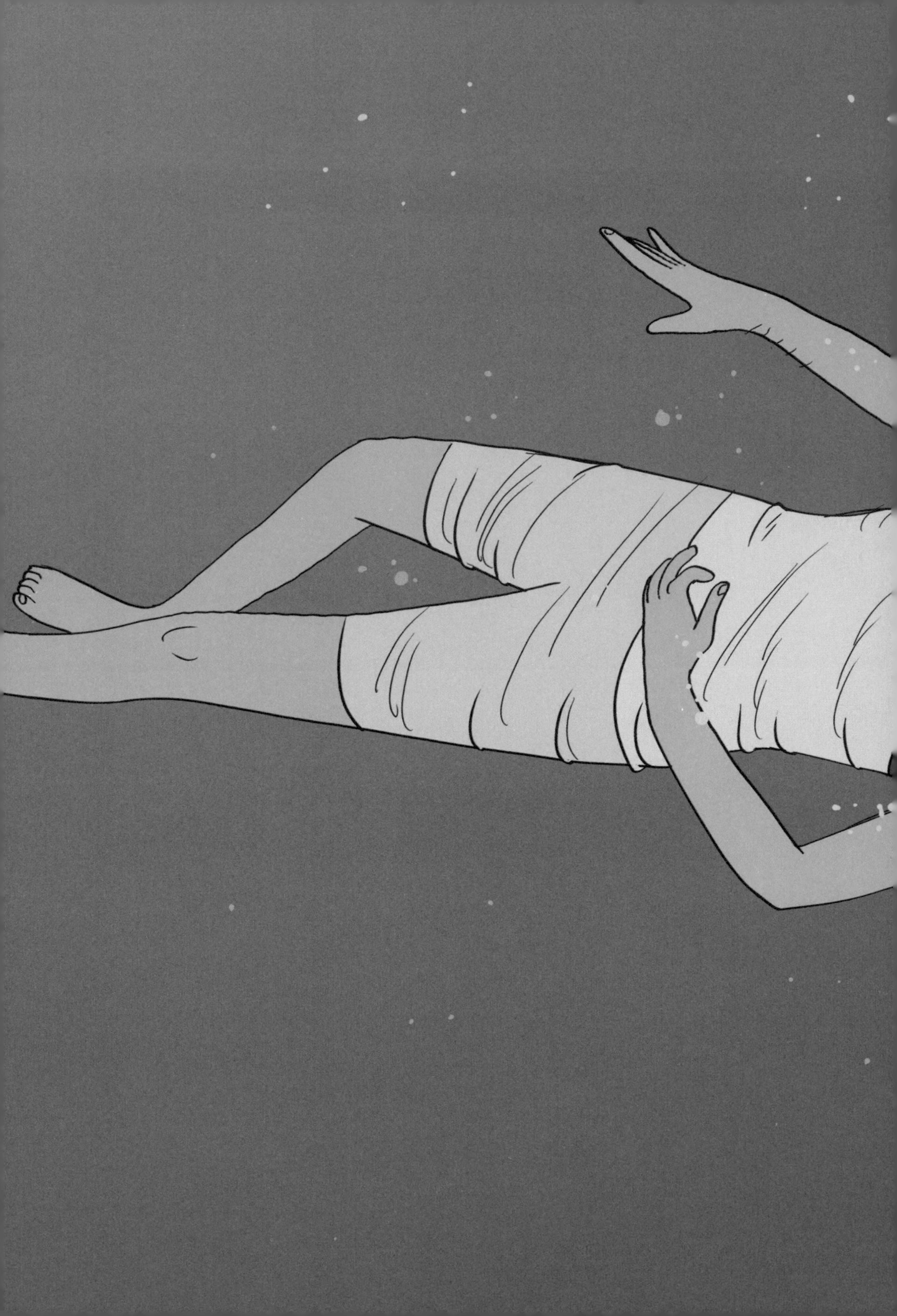

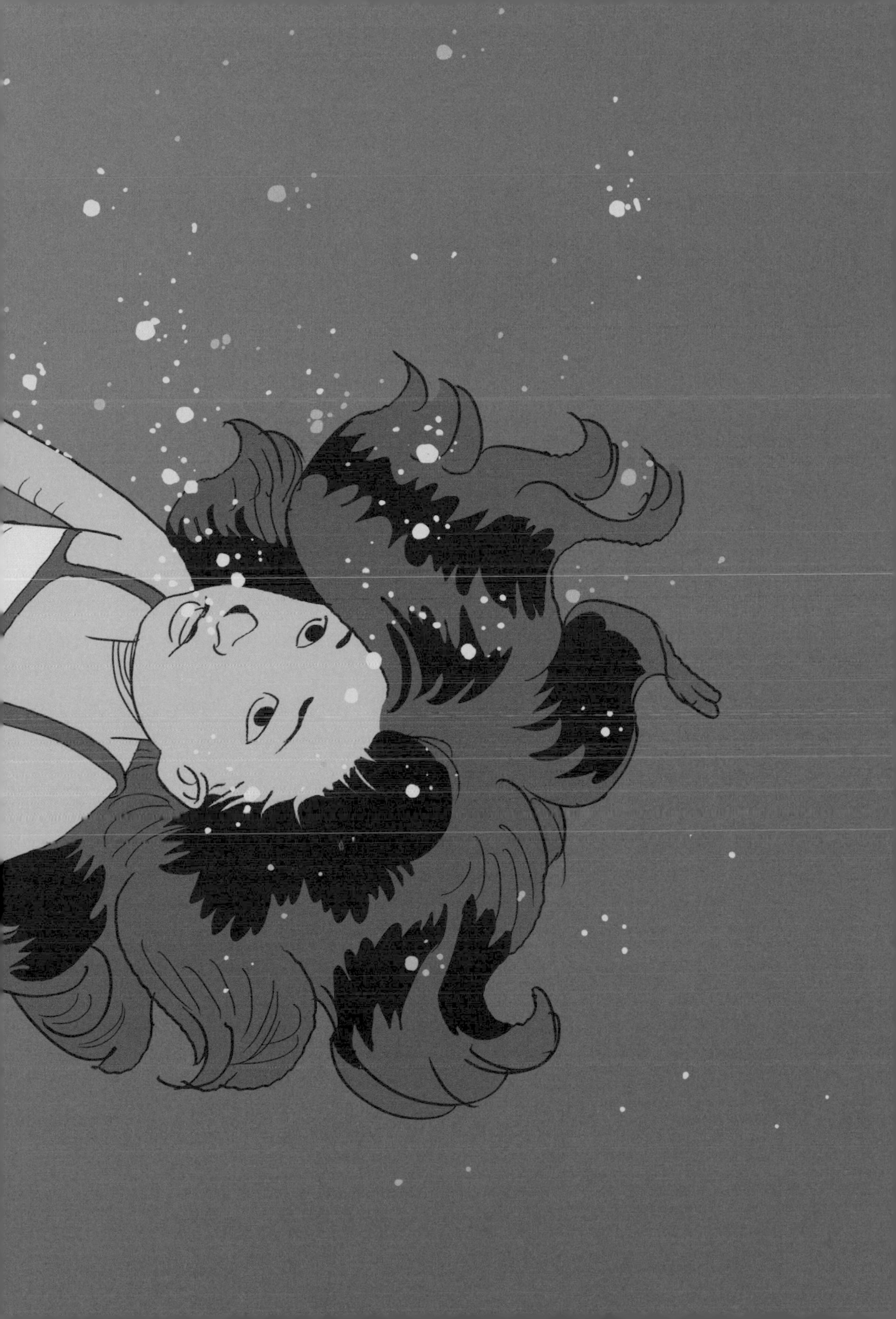

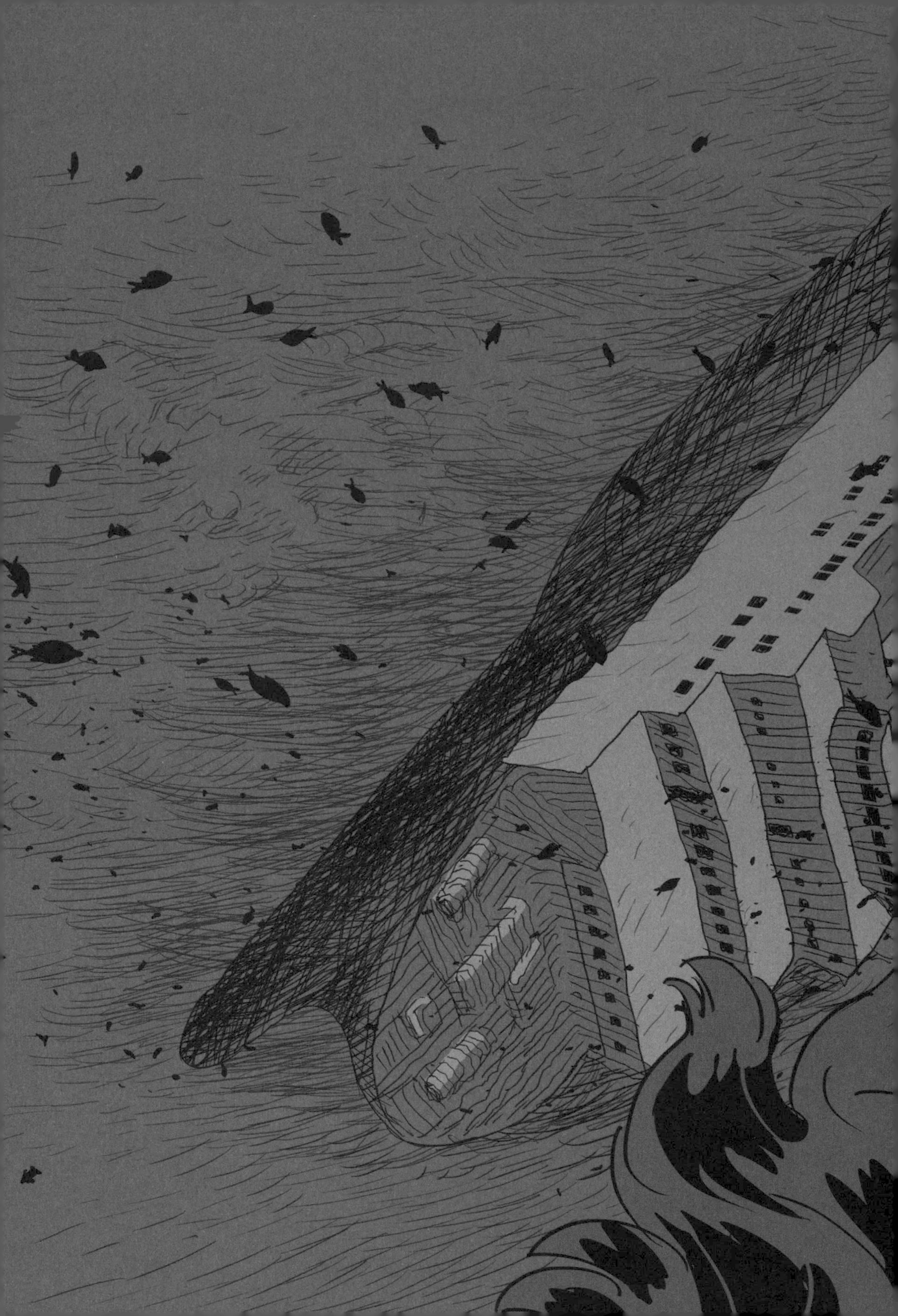

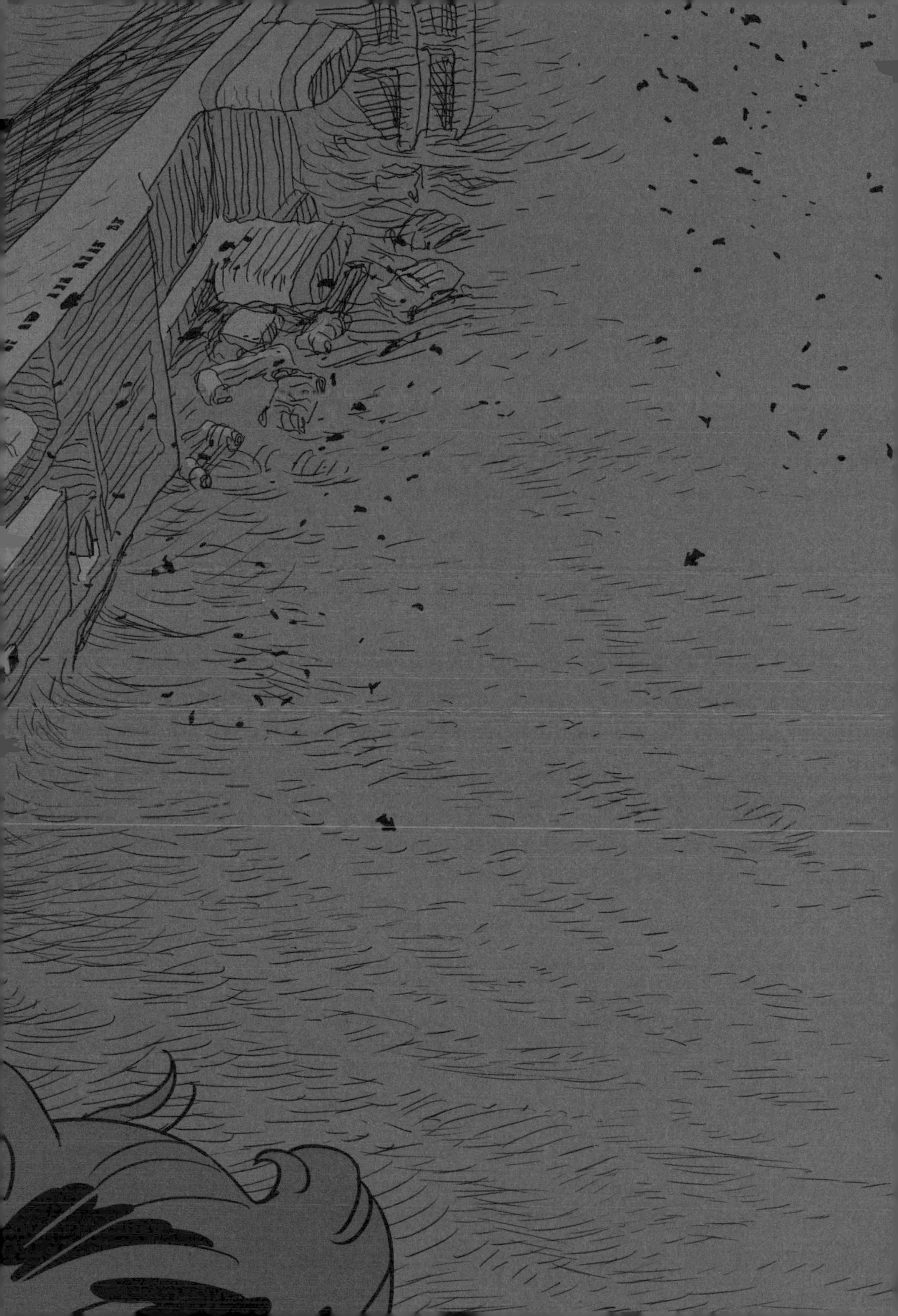

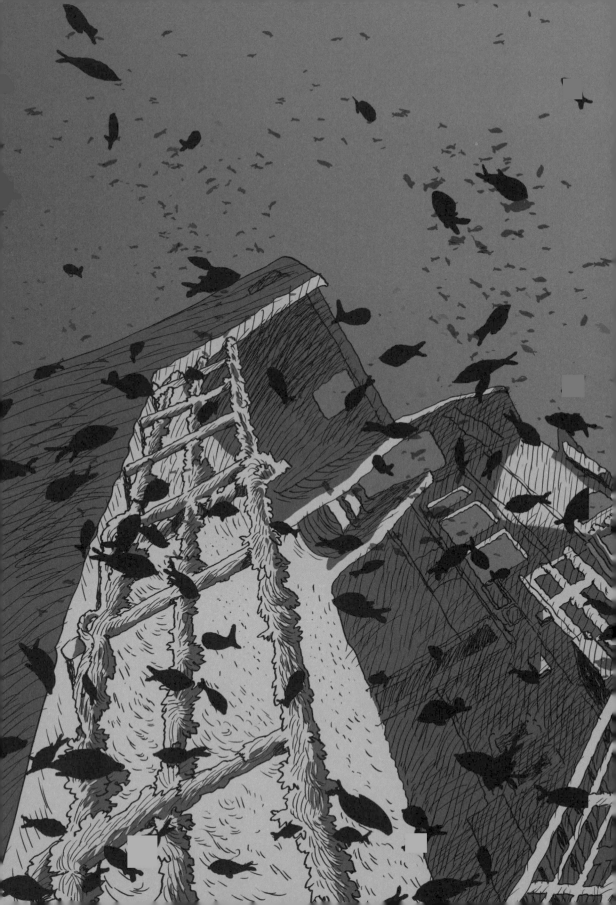

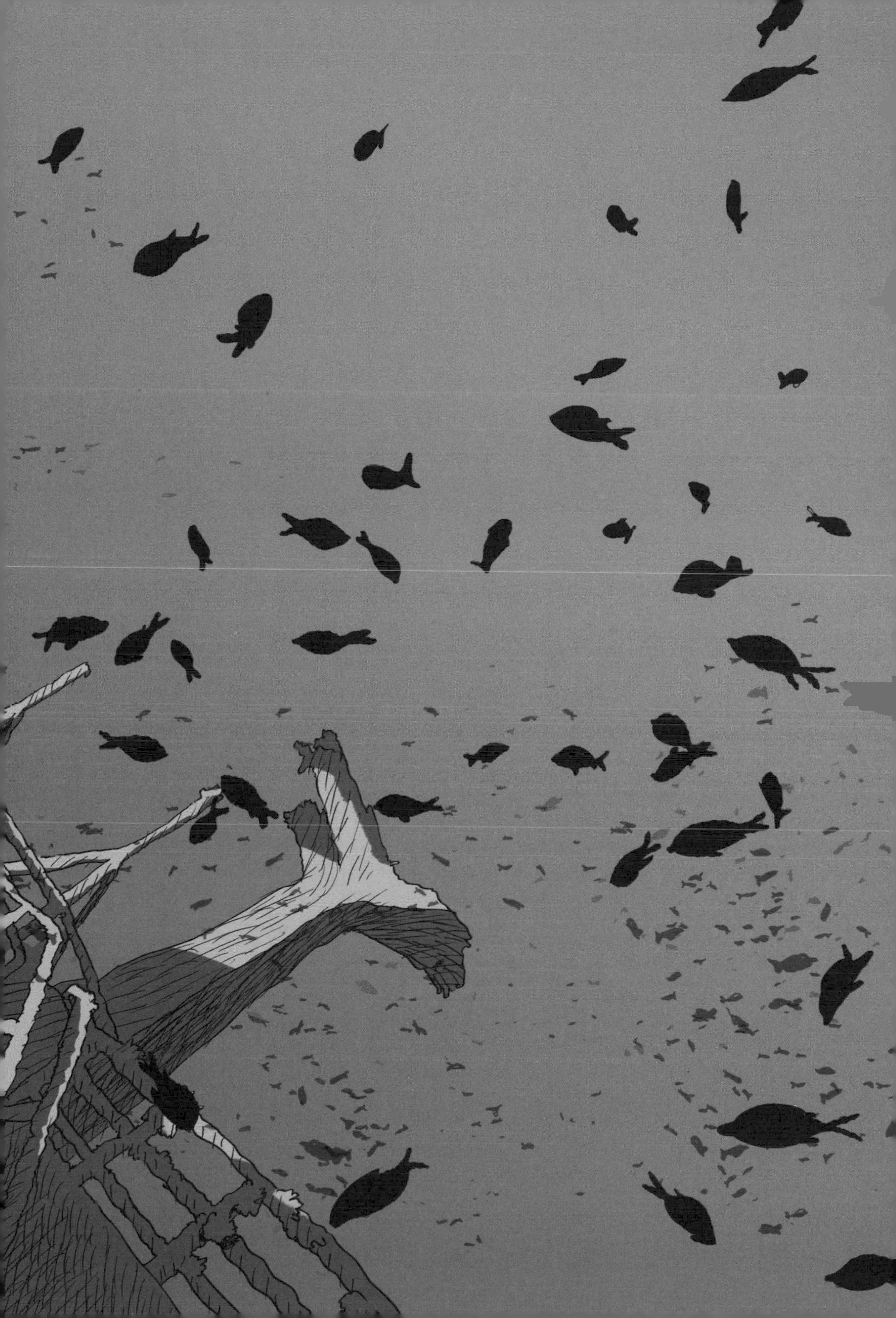

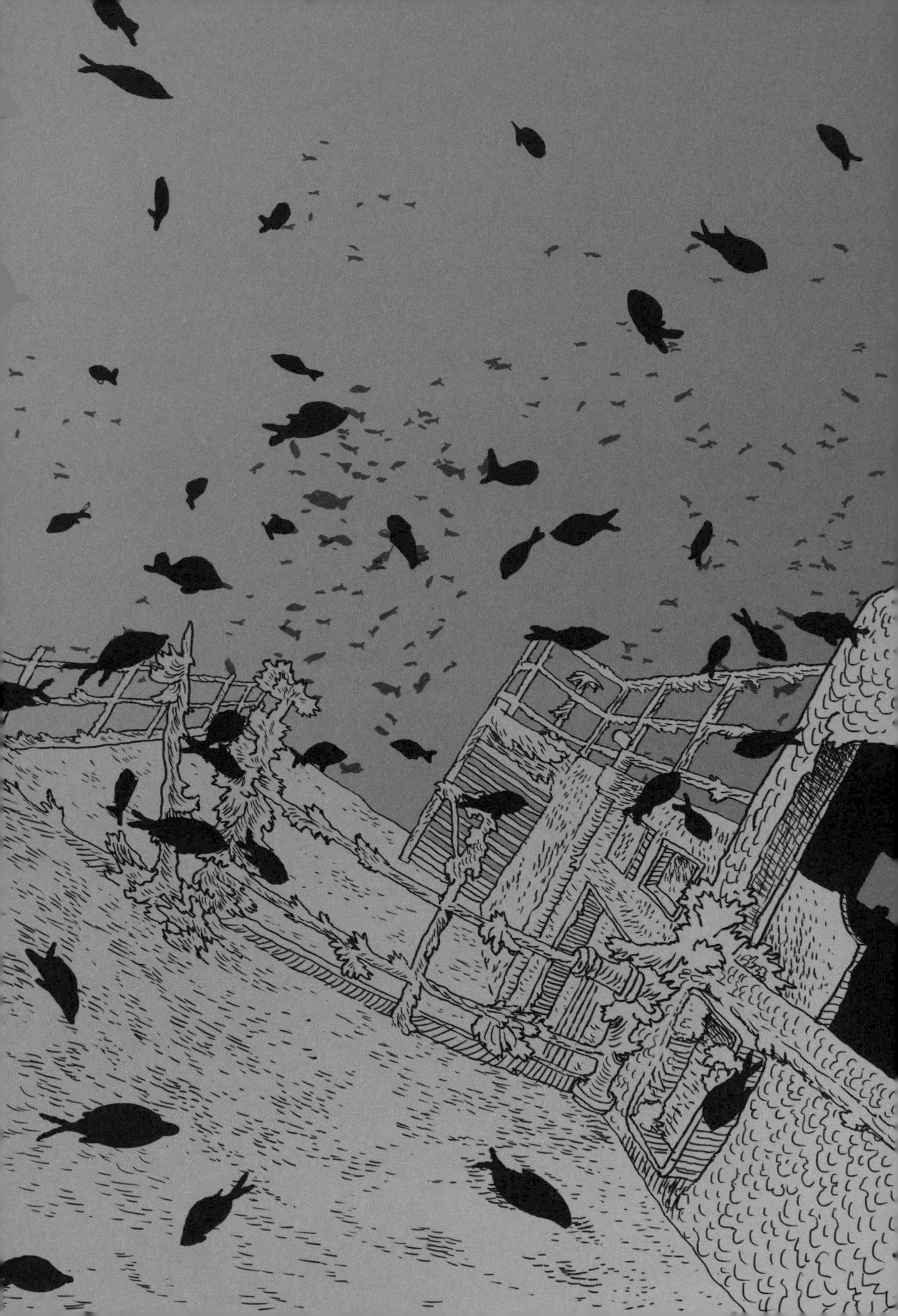

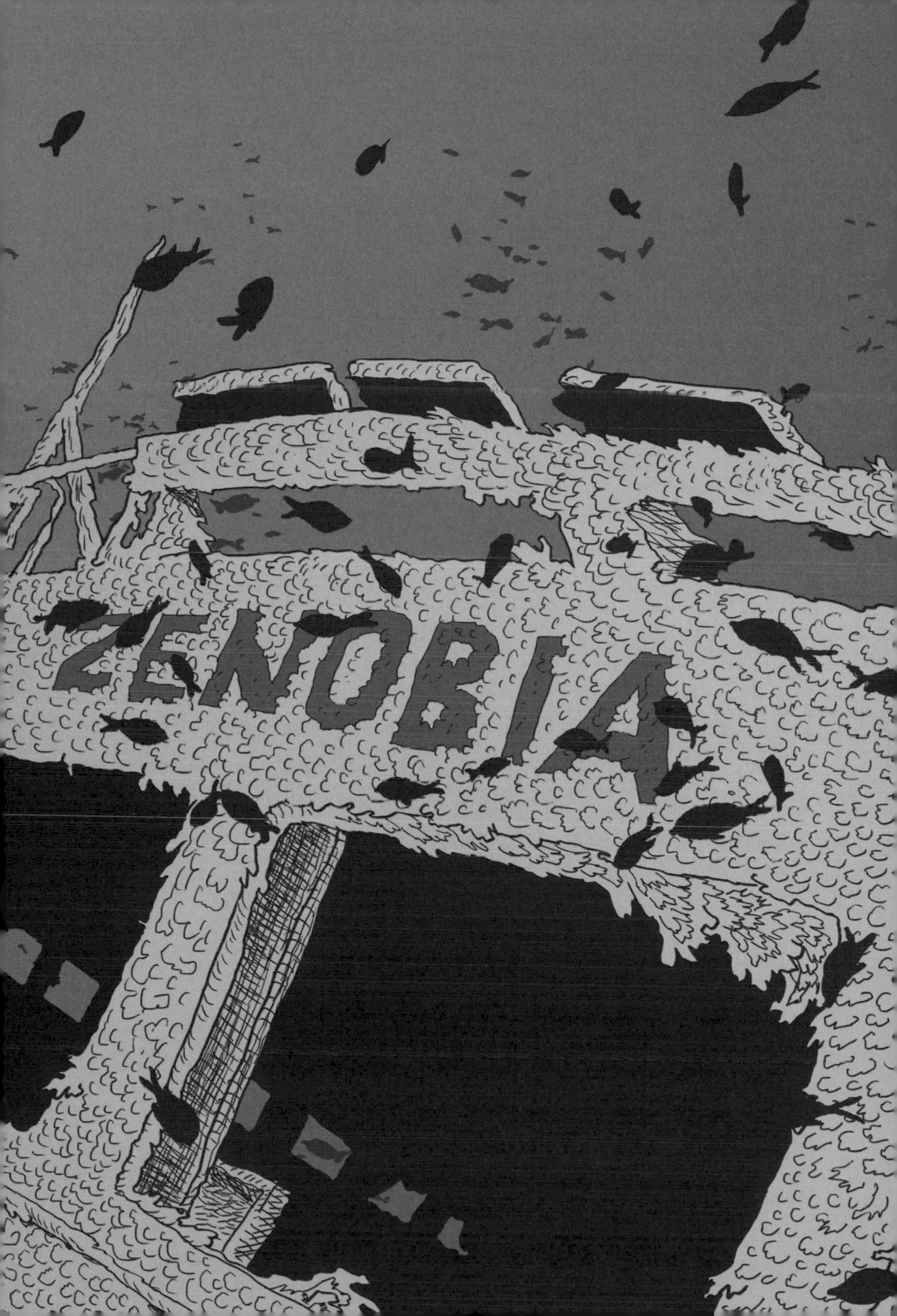
ZENOBIA

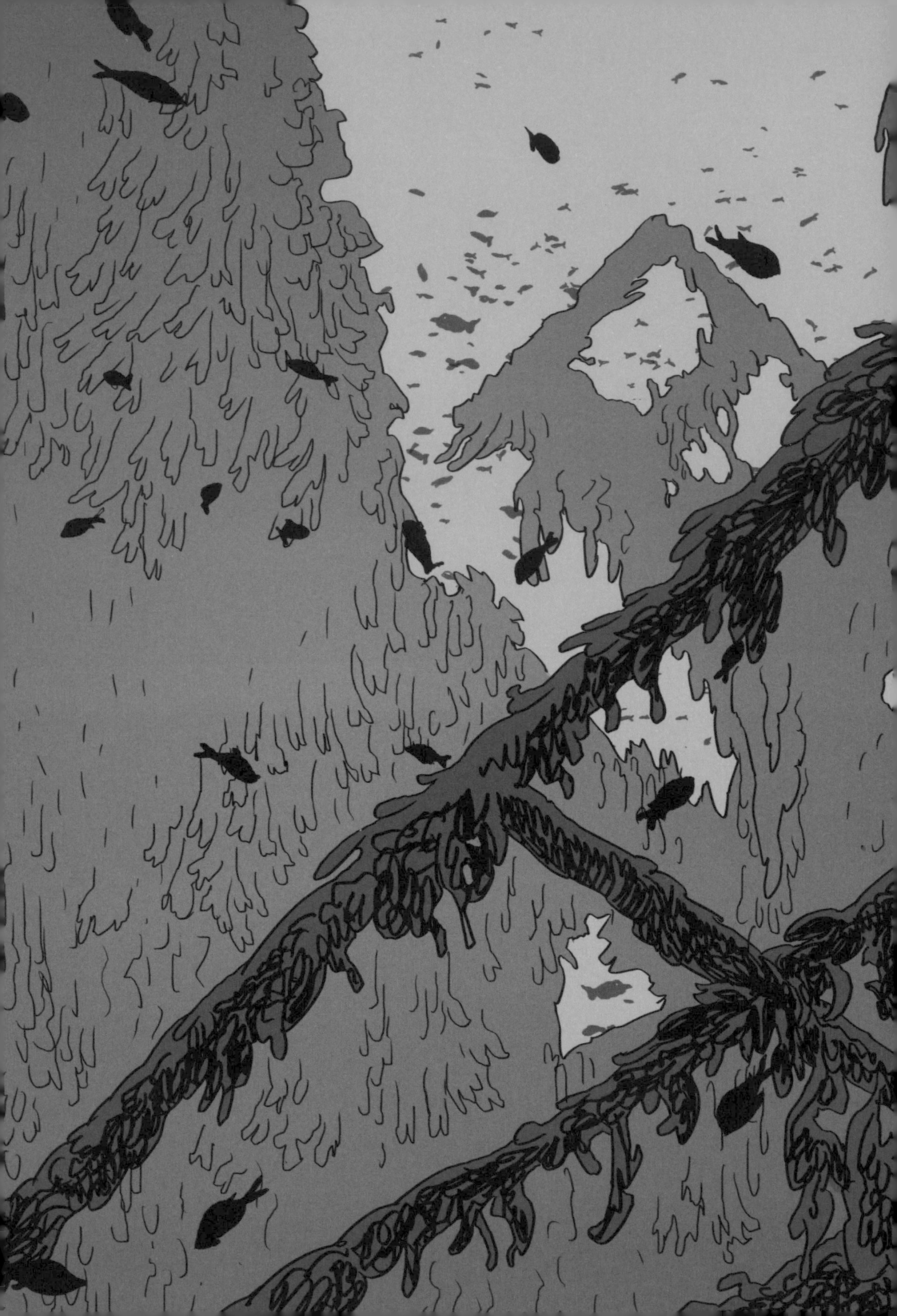

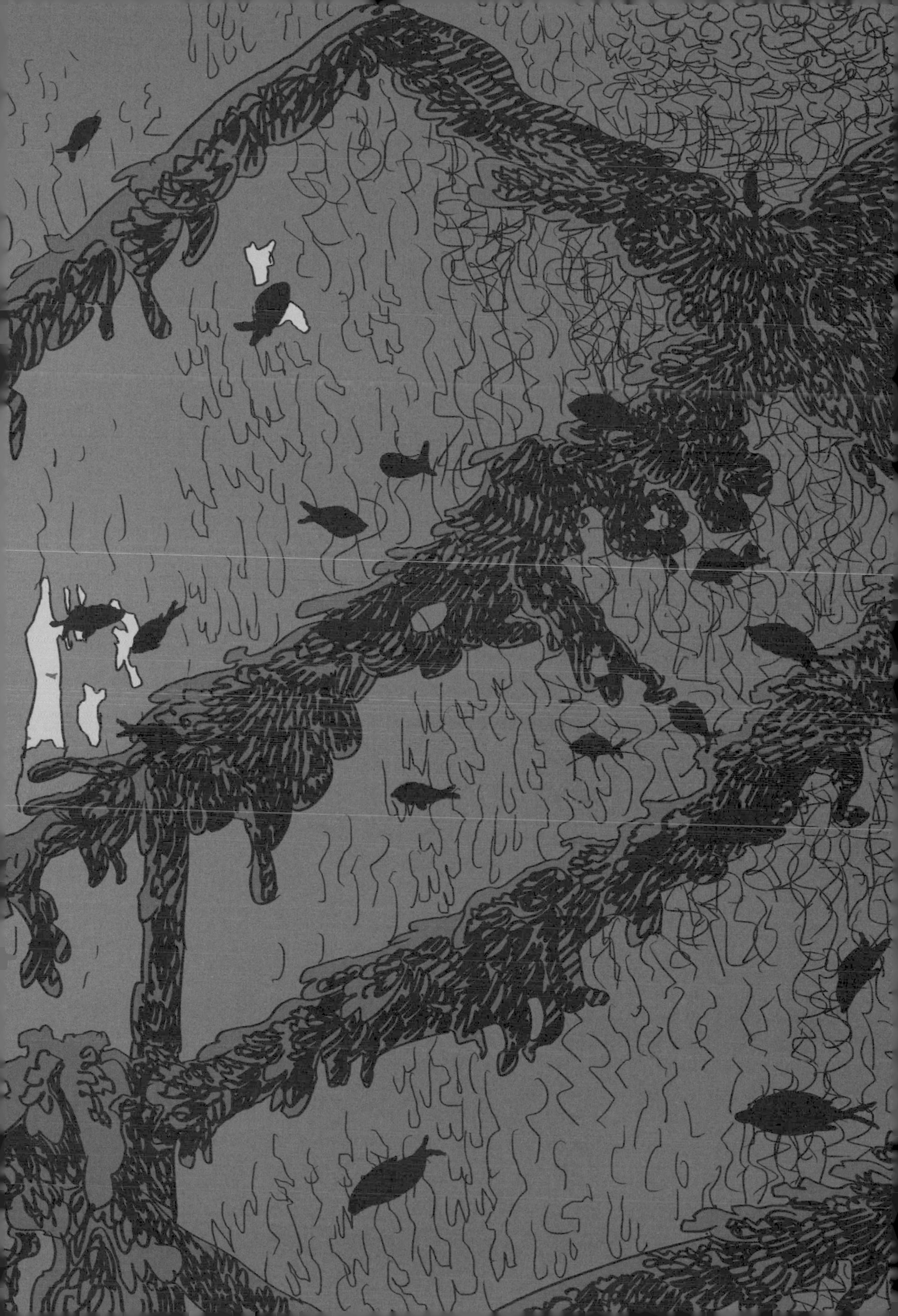

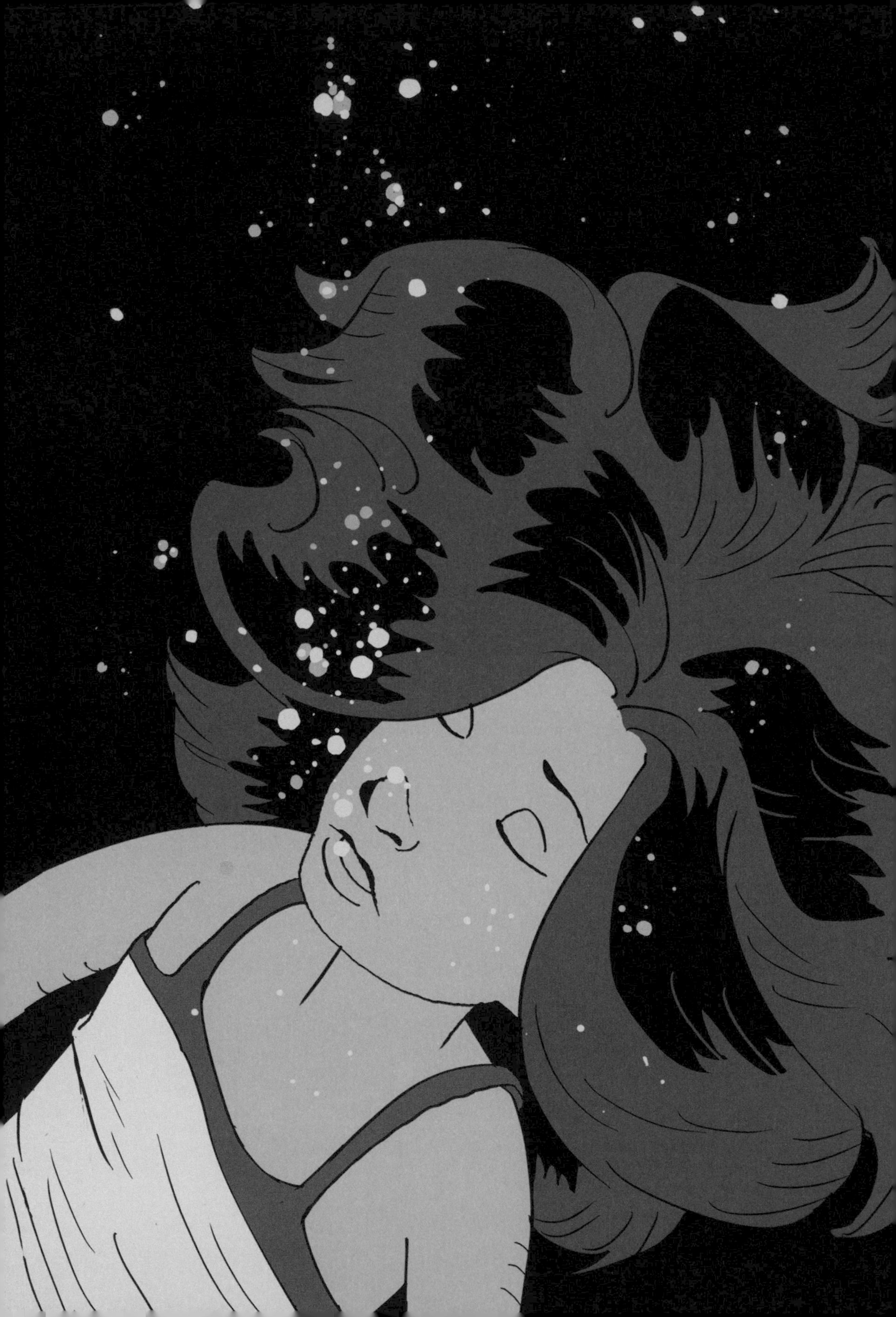

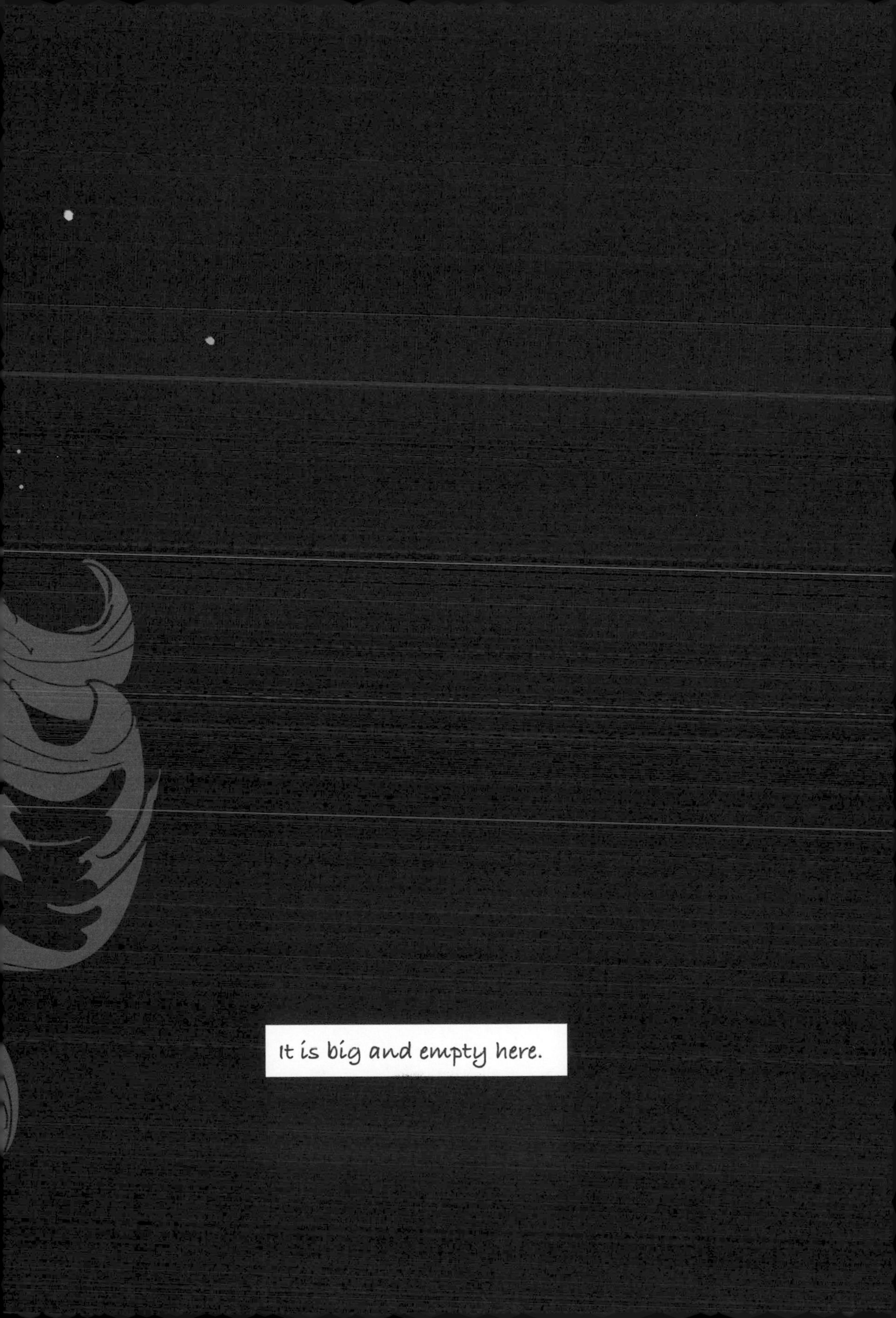
It is big and empty here.

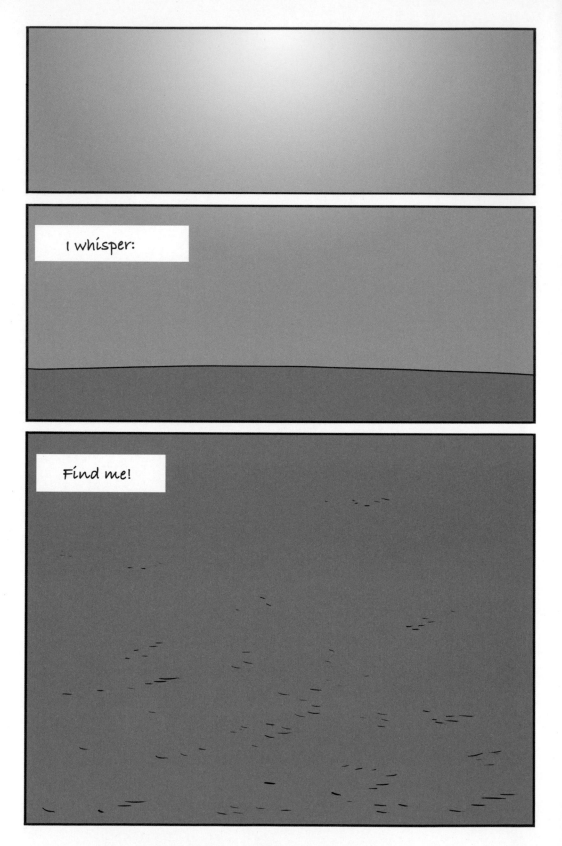

I whisper:

Find me!

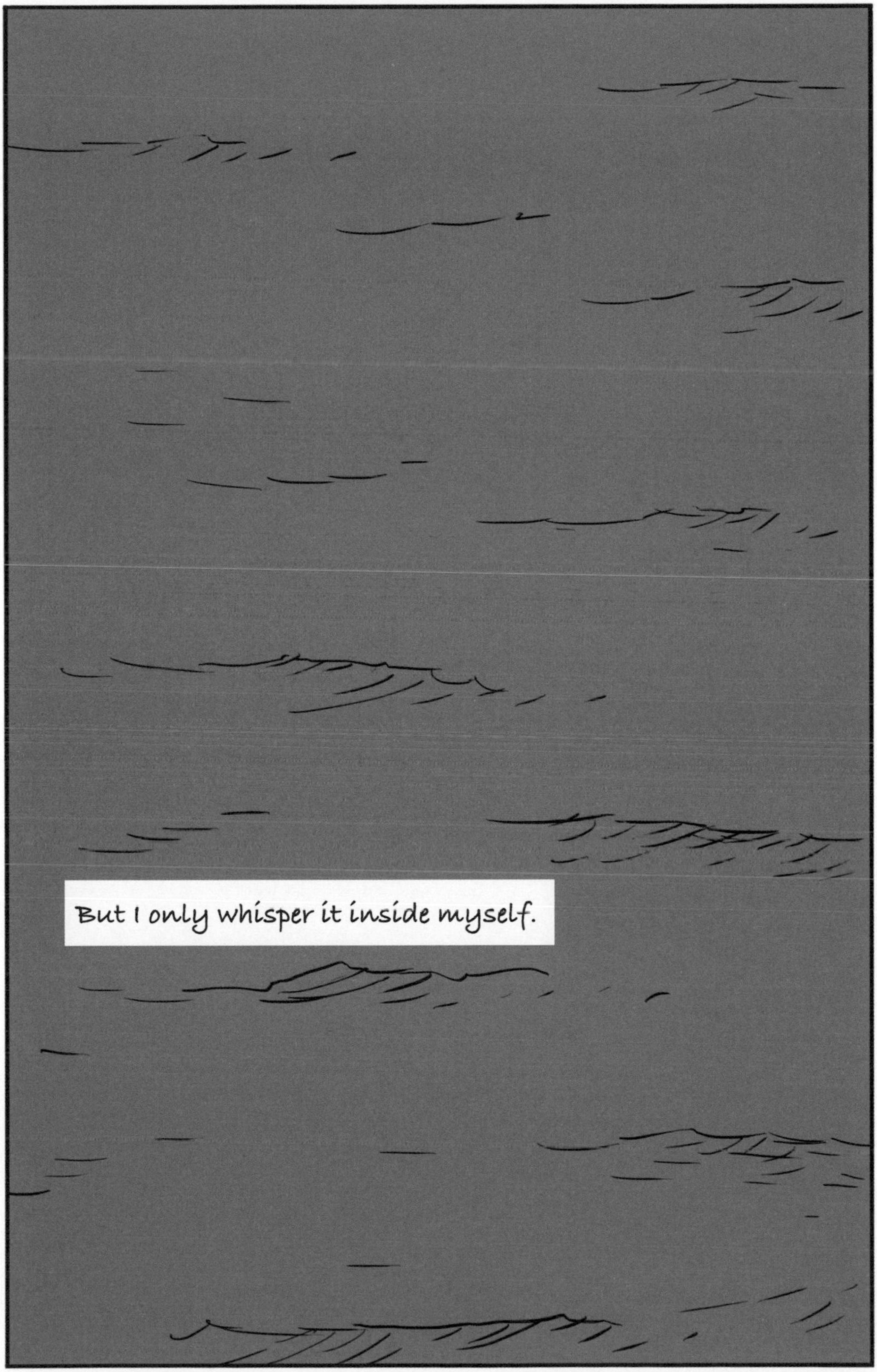
But I only whisper it inside myself.

First English-language edition October 2018

SEVEN STORIES PRESS
140 Watts Street
New York, NY 10013
www.sevenstories.com

College professors and high school and
middle school teachers may order free examination copies of
Seven Stories Press titles. To order, visit www.sevenstories.com
or send a fax on school letterhead to (212) 226-1411.

Library of Congress Cataloging-in-Publication Data
has been applied for.

ISBN 978-1-60980-873-0 (cloth)
ISBN 978-1-60980-874-7 (ebook)

Printed in China

2 4 6 8 9 7 5 3 1

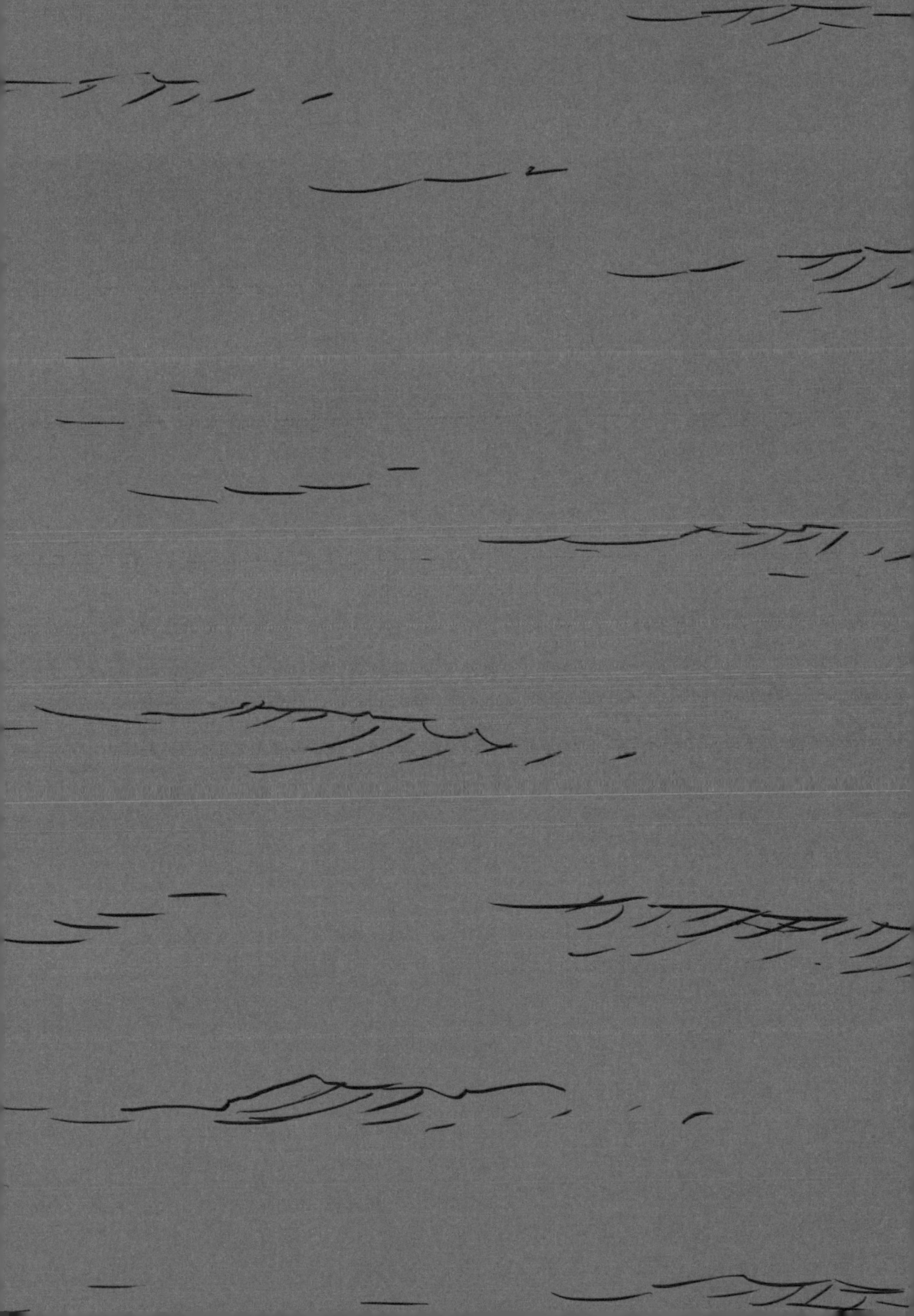

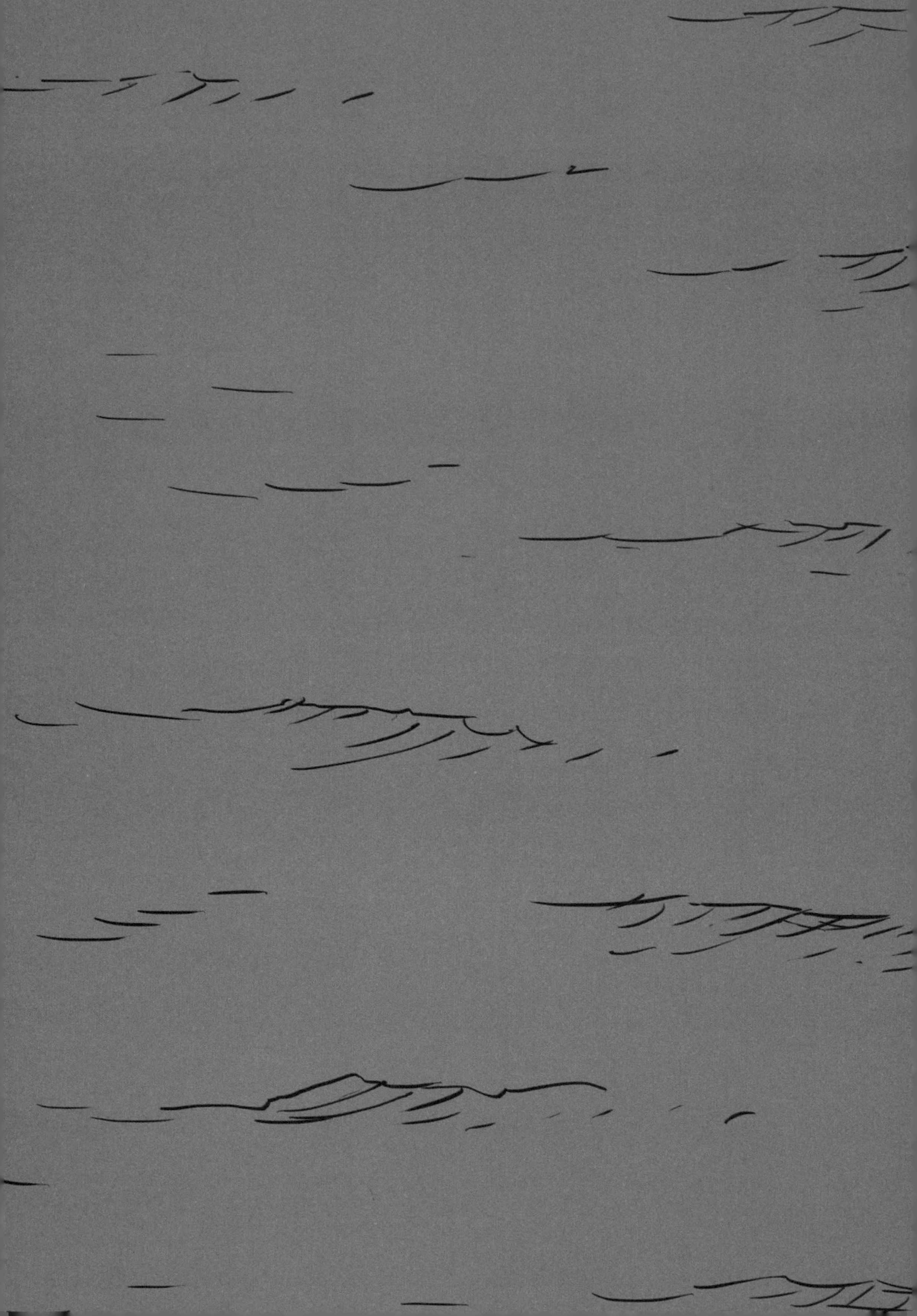

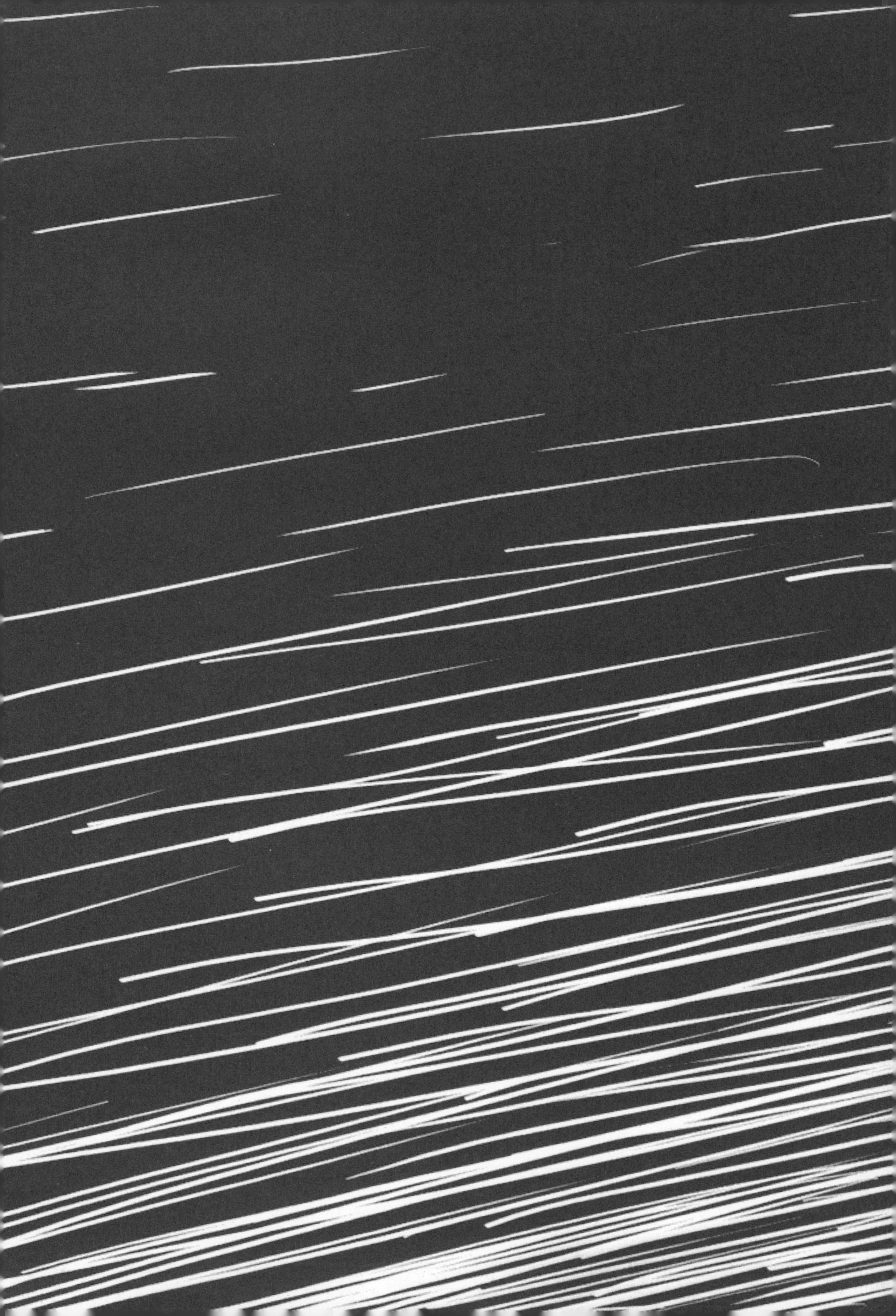